ALEXANDER McCALL SMITH

THE ENIGMA
OF GARLIC

A 44 Scotland Street Novel

Polygon

First published in hardback in Great Britain in 2022 by
Polygon, an imprint of Birlinn Ltd

West Newington House
10 Newington Road
Edinburgh
EH9 1QS

www.polygonbooks.co.uk

9 8 7 6 5 4 3 2 1

ISBN 978 1 84697 590 5

British Library Cataloguing-in-Publication Data
A catalogue record for this book is available on
request from the British Library

Typeset by Studio Monachino
Printed and bound by Clays Ltd, Elcograf S.p.A.

This book is for Anna Marshall

1

Cooking for Men

Domenica Macdonald, anthropologist, resident of Edinburgh, observer of humanity and believer in the old-fashioned and increasingly rare virtue of tolerance, looked out of her window onto the cobbled street below and wondered what to cook for dinner. It was not a question on which she would spend much time – nor was it one with which she engaged emotionally. Domenica was a competent enough cook, but she had never been able to develop much enthusiasm for time-consuming recipes or for the cults surrounding some of the better-known chefs. She was aware of the prominent culinary names of the age, of those described as celebrity chefs, but took no real interest in them or in their doings, other than to be disappointed, in some cases at least, by their rude behaviour. The people who worked in kitchens had not signed up for the Foreign Legion – an organisation in which recruits could hardly complain if they were shouted at; kitchen staff should not have to put up with being sworn at and threatened in their workplace. The fact that you can make a tasty sauce is no ground for thinking you have the right to belittle those who help you make it. There was no excuse for impoliteness, Domenica would like to remind them: politeness cost nothing, did not smell, and there was always enough of it to go round.

Domenica did almost all the cooking in her household. Although her husband, Angus Lordie, a portrait painter of some distinction, did not belong to that generation of men who were completely incapable in the kitchen, his repertoire was nonetheless somewhat limited. In his bachelor days, Angus had relied on a small number of dishes that he prepared for himself and that he was able to make without reference to any recipe book. These included a pasta dish (spaghetti *aglio e olio*); Macsween's haggis, served with mashed potatoes, neeps and peas; and kedgeree made with Arbroath smokies. The ingredients of these concoctions were few in number. Spaghetti *aglio e olio*, as the name suggested, required only spaghetti, garlic and olive oil. You cooked the spaghetti in another readily available ingredient – water – and then you placed it in heated olive oil to which you had added copious quantities of chopped garlic. That was all, and yet the name – *aglio e olio* – was so poetic, so full of Italian promise.

Haggis was perhaps even simpler. You obtained your haggis and you put it in the oven, wrapped in foil. Then you took it out and punctured the skin, having boiled the vegetables in advance. That, again, was all that you had to do, and all this could easily be accomplished, Angus thought, by mere men, possessed of no further culinary skills than those elucidated in a small and well-thumbed book that somebody had once given him entitled *Cooking for Men*.

It was not an unhealthy or unpalatable diet but it was with some relief that, after their marriage, Angus fell into the habit of allowing Domenica to prepare their evening meal. He was aware, though, that there were potential objections to this arrangement, and that the days when men could sit back and rely on being uncomplainingly cooked for by women were over. It was the duty of men to pull their weight domestically, and Angus fully accepted that. It was just that between the recognition of a duty and its fulfilment there was often something of a gap. We all *want* to be good, he told himself; we all *want* to do the right thing; but it's not always easy. St Augustine had had something to say about that, he thought.

"I must get myself organised," he said to Domenica. "I must do more in the kitchen. I really must. I enjoy cooking, you know."

Domenica smiled. One had to encourage men in their inchoate schemes of self-improvement. "Yes," she said. "That's a very good idea, Angus. The kitchen, you may have noticed, is over there."

But somehow Angus had never managed to put this vague intention into practice, and the task of cooking was shouldered by Domenica, just as it is by so many wives whose husbands express an intention to sharpen their culinary skills but somehow never get round to it.

Now, as she looked down on Scotland Street, Domenica decided that they would that evening have tomato soup out of a can, followed by scrambled eggs served on toast. This was plain fare – nursery food, as Angus sometimes called it – but it had the merit of a preparation time of five minutes, at the most. Angus would like it and for her part she had more pressing concerns than those of the kitchen. Domenica was currently working on a scholarly paper, *An ethno-linguistic analysis of a Scottish sub-dialect: conjectures and possibilities*. The paper itself was already written and accepted, in principle, for publication in a reputable scholarly journal. The journal editors, though, had passed on to Domenica various proposals for change made by the peer reviewers to whom the paper had been submitted, and these would need to be attended to.

Reviewers could be irritating; while some of them were helpful and approved publication without change, others seemed to feel it necessary to suggest amendments, even where none were strictly necessary. Domenica was convinced that this sometimes happened simply because reviewers felt that they had to do something to justify their involvement in the whole process. It was a familiar story in so many fields of activity. If you appointed a bureaucrat, for example, then you must expect the bureaucrat to create rules and think of reasons for not doing things. That is what bureaucrats do. If you bought a dog, then you must expect him to bark. That is what dogs do.

It was a matter of regret, Domenica thought, that people felt the need to do things. There were many situations, she felt, where inaction would be a perfectly good policy, where things could be left where they were without any attempt at improvement. The adage that what was not broken should not be fixed was derided as folk wisdom, and yet it was, Domenica thought, profoundly true. There was nothing wrong with inaction, in spite of the widespread belief that everything had constantly to be adjusted and rearranged. Things might be left exactly where they were, unaltered by interference. After all, there was no essential merit in change, in spite of the belief that disaster would follow unless all our arrangements were constantly revisited and reorganised.

Domenica had recently come across a biography of Calvin Coolidge, the American president who served so unobtrusively between 1923 and 1929. It was Coolidge of whom Dorothy Parker, when told of his death, asked, "How can they tell?" Dorothy Parker was extremely witty, but in this case her amusing observation obscured the fact that Coolidge, who was undoubtedly dull, was also a fairly successful president – for the very reason that he did nothing, and said even less. That would not be possible today, of course. People had to do things, and would not rest until they had done them.

Domenica turned round from her window and caught her husband's eye. "I'll cook dinner this evening, Angus," she said. "Nothing fancy."

"Thank you," he said, looking slightly guilty.

2

Dutchitude

The paper on which Domenica had been working, and to which she would return after she and Angus had consumed their dinner of tomato soup and scrambled eggs on toast, represented the first fruits of a significant piece of research. Unlike the fieldwork she had previously done in her anthropological career, which involved travelling to distant and exotic places, Domenica's latest project was one that took her no further than the slopes of the Pentland Hills on Edinburgh's southern boundary. That is not to say that it was without risk: there had been several difficult moments in Fairmilehead and even in Morningside itself, the epicentre of Edinburgh respectability, but by and large there were none of the dangers that she had faced on her earlier forays into Papua New Guinea and the Malacca Straits.

Domenica's career had closely followed the *cursus honorum* of the academic anthropologist. An undergraduate degree had been followed by research for a PhD and that, in due course, led to a postdoctoral fellowship. The PhD was completed under the supervision of the distinguished social anthropologist, Professor Lance Studebaker, an authority on the use of linguistic evidence in support of anthropological conclusions. Studebaker came from a cosmopolitan background. His father had been an American air force colonel who spent some years as air attaché in the American Embassy in Sri Lanka. It was while he was in Colombo that he met Anna-Marie van Vonk, the daughter of a prominent member of the Burgher community. The Burghers were people mostly of Dutch or

Portuguese origin who had lived in Ceylon, as it once was, and Sri Lanka, as it became, for generations. Most of them had intermarried with the Sinhalese and become very much part of the patchwork of peoples who made up Sri Lankan society. The van Vonks were tea merchants and had their own small tea garden not far from Galle. Anna-Marie, the eldest of three daughters, was a bird painter whose works had attracted an international following; her delicate watercolours of the island's birds were displayed in museums all over the world and had been published, too, in a handsome, privately printed book. Lance was born in Colombo, but was taken back to the United States at the age of four. He was educated at Phillips Exeter Academy and then at Princeton, where his interest in anthropology was first aroused. Because of his family connection with the country, it is perhaps not surprising that he should have chosen to do postgraduate research into an aspect of his mother's country, concentrating on the sense of Dutch identity experienced by the Burgher community. To this concept he gave a name – *Dutchitude* – a nod in the direction of Léopold Sédar Senghor's influential work on identity.

The notion of *Dutchitude* attracted considerable attention, and rapidly became widely used in several cognate disciplines, including sociology and social philosophy. Asked what exactly it meant, Studebaker explained: "*Dutchitide* is what the Dutch feel *in their essence*. It is not a state of being that will exclude those who are not of Dutch extraction, but it is admittedly difficult to feel Dutch if you are something else – Belgian, for example. *Belgitude* is a different thing altogether. True *Dutchitude* is a matter of identification with a totally *positioned* personal provenance."

Although he did not make much of his own Burgher antecedents, it was clear to those who knew him that Lance's sense of identity was influenced by his Dutch heritage, even though the family had long since detached itself from the country and become absorbed into the Colonel's wider family in the American Midwest. That was where Lance first took employment as an associate professor of anthropology – at Oberlin College – but by the time he was thirty-five he had moved to Britain, and to a post at King's College London, to be followed, after a few years there by his first chair in the subject, which was in Glasgow. Studebaker was an inspiration to Domenica in her postgraduate years and continued to be so throughout his career.

Her postdoctoral fellowship had allowed Domenica to travel to that promised land of anthropology – a remote region of New Guinea where, on the Sepik River, the Great Crocodile Spirit is worshipped by local people. Domenica's paper, *Two months with the crocodile people of the Sepik River*, had attracted widespread attention and had brought anthropologists to the area from scores of major European and North American universities. Such was this influx that the tribe in question, hospitable by instinct, had created a special lodge to accommodate their academic visitors. This building, described in Melanesian pidgin as *haus bilong anthropology-fella*, had such creature comforts as were available that far up the Sepik, including an ingenious river-cooled fridge for the storage of beer. The lodge itself was later to be the subject of anthropological study by a team from the University of Frankfurt in that classic of anthropological self-reference, *Reinforcement of otherness in the self-view of anthropologists amongst the Crocodile People of the Sepik* by Professor Dr Wolfgang Zimmermann.

A subsequent project had taken Domenica to the Malacca Straits, where she undertook ground-breaking research on the domestic lives of contemporary pirates. That had involved living for several months in a pirate village, tucked away in a mangrove swamp from which the male pirates issued each day in high-speed motorboats. While they were out, their wives remained at home, home-schooling the pirate children and preparing meals of *nasi lemak* for their menfolk on their return from their day's labours. Domenica found that the pirate wives were bored; their men were absorbed in their own concerns, spent a great deal of time discussing the Singaporean football league, and gave them little intellectual stimulation. Against this background, it did not take her long to set up a thriving book group and a *nasi lemak* recipe circle. The pirates' wives responded enthusiastically, and when Domenica returned to Scotland they remained in touch for several years. "We miss you so much," they wrote. "Each day we think of you and remember how it was when you were among us."

"Anthropology," Domenica once said to a friend, "may be all about the study of human bonds, but its practice nonetheless requires one to break them regularly. Friendships are made, but must then be broken. We say goodbye to those amongst whom we have lived. They say goodbye to us. That is our condition. That is the source of our private and individual grief; that is the source of *la tristesse eternelle de l'anthropologiste.*" And added, "So to speak."

3

Domenica Thinks About Time

They sat down to their meal of tomato soup and scrambled eggs on toast. *Here,* thought Domenica, *are two people sitting down to a meal of tomato soup and scrambled eggs . . .* She looked across the table at Angus, and he looked back at her. There is a strange quality to the glances that any couple give one another. There is no curiosity in them, because they are not looks that are intended to find anything out: all is known by people who have been together for more than a few months. *From whom no secrets are hid . . .* The words were familiar to Angus, with his Episcopalian background – words pronounced in the chapel at Glenalmond, all those years ago, ignored by most of those present, because most would be thinking of something else altogether (sex, probably, for that was the film that played in the teenage mind much of the time) but remembered by him. He remembered them because he found that he could remember poetry, and there was enough poetry in that Cranmerian prose to stay with one through life, if one listened. *Through thought, word and deed . . . we are heartily sorry . . . the memory of them is grievous unto us . . . whose property is always to have mercy . . .*

Now the looks they exchanged had reassurance rather than enquiry at their heart. Are you happy with the way things are? Are you enjoying this – this moment, right now – or would you rather be doing something else? Are you expecting me to say something significant, when all that I am thinking about at present is tomato soup? And what can anybody say about tomato soup when it comes down to it?

Domenica, though, was thinking about time, because her mind was elsewhere – on an article she had been reading in an anthropological journal. She knew that Angus liked to hear about those – or so he assured her – because he found the topics they raised rather interesting. Of course, he did not have to wade through the data and the endless discussions of methodology; he was interested only in the kernel of what was being discussed – the conclusions that tended to be encapsulated in a short paragraph at the end.

Now she said to Angus, "What are we waiting for, Angus?"

He looked up from his tomato soup. "Scrambled eggs on toast?"

Domenica smiled. "In the immediate sense, I suppose that's true."

"Well, it is what you said we were having," said Angus, glancing at the top of the stove.

"It is, yes, but my question was broader, really. I meant waiting in the sense of waiting in general, so to speak. Not waiting for something that's going to happen in the next few minutes, but for what's going to happen in the more distant future. Next year. The year after that. Five years from now. When we're all a bit older."

Angus put down his spoon. It was difficult to eat tomato soup at the same time as one discussed the concept of waiting. Some people might be able to do that, he thought, but not me, nor the late President Ford, poor chap.

"I don't mean to interrupt your meal," said Domenica. "Please carry on with your soup."

Angus picked up his spoon again. "All right, waiting. What about it?"

"It's a whole field of anthropological inquiry," Domenica said. "The anthropology of time. How people feel about the future and what the future means for them."

Angus wiped at his mouth with his table napkin. He noticed

that it left a red stain on the gingham cloth of the napkin. He had read somewhere that napkin rings were a bourgeois invention – that grand houses, or grand tables, perhaps, did not have them because the idea of using a napkin more than once was foreign to people accustomed to fresh table linen every time. Well, he thought, that will have to change, and people like that would have to get used to living life more modestly.

Mind you, there would be limits: one would not expect to go into a restaurant and discover that somebody had used the napkin before you. It would be distinctly off-putting to find the imprints of others' lips on the linen . . . In the same way as you might be forgiven for feeling uncomfortable on finding lipstick on your glass in a restaurant when you didn't wear lipstick yourself . . . Or to stay in a hotel and discover a toenail in the bathroom, as had happened to one of his Scottish Arts Club friends when he went down to London and stayed in a cheap hotel near King's Cross Station. Of course, that was hardly the hotel's fault: the cleaning staff might have done their very best and still missed the toenail.

Domenica continued with the theme of waiting. "People wait for things," she said. "If you ask them: *are you waiting for something?* most people will say yes. They're waiting for their holiday, or their next promotion, or for the time when they'll have saved a deposit for a flat. There's always something."

She paused. Her soup was getting cold, and she took a few further spoonfuls. She made a face. "This tomato soup's awful. Sorry, Angus."

He shook his head. "There's nothing wrong with it. Nothing."

"That's what comes from just opening a can," said Domenica. "You get what you deserve if you open a can."

"What about waiting? What about it?"

She put down her spoon and pushed her plate away from her. "I can't finish it."

"Let me." He took her plate from her and finished the last of the soup. "There. All gone – as they say."

She looked at him thankfully. "I could make something different."

"No, let's go on to the scrambled eggs. You can't go wrong with scrambled eggs."

Domenica looked doubtful. "But you can, you know. Most people make their scrambled eggs far too quickly. You have to cook them really slowly if you want them to taste nice and creamy. And you shouldn't use milk."

"In other words," said Angus, "you have to be prepared to wait."

Domenica smiled. "Which most people aren't willing to do. Although waiting is ubiquitous." She paused. "Look at people out there in the street."

"In Scotland Street?"

"Yes, and beyond. In virtually any street in Scotland. Everybody is waiting for something. Half the population is waiting for constitutional change. The other half is waiting for those who want constitutional change to give up waiting for it. The result is a strange state of uncertainty. And that pattern, you know, is repeated in all sorts of societies all over the world. People are waiting for something, and when what they're waiting for doesn't come, they can become apathetic, discouraged – really unhappy. Depressed, even."

"Oh."

"And waiting slows down time. It moves you into a strange zone in which the passage of time is somehow suspended."

"Oh."

"Yes."

Angus glanced at the pan on the stove. "Will the scrambled eggs be ready?"

"I should have been stirring them," said Domenica, "instead of talking about the anthropology of time and waiting."

"Grub first, then ethics," said Angus, and added, "Not that I'm reproaching you." He smiled. "Grub first, then anthropology, should I say? I'm sure Brecht wouldn't mind my taking liberties with his words."

"No coiner of an *aperçu* minds that sort of thing," said Domenica.

4.

Stuart Is Unactivated

As Domenica and Angus began their meal of tomato soup and scrambled eggs, in the flat below theirs at 44 Scotland Street, Nicola Pollock was preparing dinner for her son, Stuart Pollock, having slightly earlier on that evening made egg and potato pie for her two grandsons, Bertie and his younger brother, Ulysses. Bertie loved egg and potato pie and would willingly have eaten it for breakfast, lunch and dinner, were it to be offered for him. Such an offer, though, was never made: breakfast was invariably a plate of muesli and a boiled egg, and lunch, which he normally had at school, was vegan fish fingers or soya mash, or something of that sort, served shortly before midday eurythmics. Only at dinner could egg and potato pie become a possibility, and not every day at that.

The preparation of meals in the Pollock household was very much a shared responsibility, with Stuart and his mother taking it in turns, day and day about, to cook dinner for the two sittings – early, for the children, and late for the adults – to supervise the evening bath, and then to read the bedtime story. The last of these was far from simple, as the expectations of the two boys were so radically different. Ulysses would listen only to stories about dogs – of which there was, of course, a finite supply – while Bertie, who was a keen reader on his own account, had a taste in literature far beyond what would be expected of the average seven-year-old. He had recently completed Walter Scott's *Waverley* and had now embarked on the first volume of Proust's *À la recherche du temps perdu* in the Scott Moncrieff translation. Now, in the session with

Stuart, he was currently engrossed in *The Odyssey*, which Stuart was reading out to him, five pages at a time, before lights out. When it was Nicola's turn to read to the boys, Bertie preferred the Katie Morag books, which he considered to be only slightly Proustian, but most enjoyable nonetheless.

On that particular evening, with the boys off to sleep, Nicola was preparing a simple dish of grilled salmon and mustard potatoes for the two of them. As she flipped the salmon from the skillet onto a serving plate, she mentally rehearsed what she intended to say to Stuart. She had a potentially awkward subject to discuss with him: that of his emotional life. That had, in her view at least, stalled. She had her ideas about this, and had been meaning to discuss these with him, but had been putting off the matter because she was concerned that it could turn into a fraught conversation and possibly even a confrontation.

Now, as she passed Stuart his plate of salmon and potatoes, she made her opening gambit. "I've been thinking," she began.

Stuart looked at his plate. "This is a very nice bit of salmon," he said.

"Good," said Nicola. "I've been—"

He did not let her finish. "Farmed, of course. I don't suppose it's possible to get wild salmon these days."

"Possibly not," said Nicola. "I've been thinking . . ."

Stuart put his fork into the salmon steak. "I'm not sure where I stand on the issue," he went on. "I know that we're going to have to farm fish – if we want to carry on eating it. Wild fish supplies will soon be exhausted, I imagine. Flag-hopping is the problem."

Nicola abandoned her attempt to direct the conversation. "Flag-hopping?" she asked.

"Using flags of convenience to get round international controls. Large fishing vessels are registered under a flag of convenience – Liberia, the Bahamas and so on – and then they go off and overfish in the territorial waters of others. They don't report their catch and the coastal states may be too weak or disorganised to police their bit of sea. Result: fish are disappearing. We're hunting them to extinction – just as we hunted so much else out of existence in the past."

Nicola shook her head. "We never learn, do we?" She paused. "Who's doing this?"

"China," said Stuart. "Russia. Spain. Their great factory ships have been sweeping the oceans of life."

Nicola sighed. The world was a lawless place, it seemed, and becoming increasingly so. What had Hobbes said about this? Without the social contract, life would become nasty, brutish and short. Well, it already was.

"We delude ourselves," Stuart continued, taking a mouthful of salmon, "if we think that people will stick to the rules. They won't. There are some countries that will never co-operate with others to preserve something for the future. They just won't. And we fondly imagine that they will act with concern for others – well, they won't. That's not in the DNA. It just isn't. It's *sauve qui peut.*" He paused. "There are plenty of places that would eat others for breakfast, you know, and indeed are doing so right now."

Nicola sighed again. "Of course, we aren't perfect ourselves, are we? Look how we expropriated the assets of others during the high days of empire."

"True," said Angus. "But we aren't doing it now, are we? Or not so brazenly."

Nicola tried again. "Stuart," she began, "I'm your mother—"

He interrupted her with a laugh. "I've long suspected that. You know, the way you've encouraged me to change my socks . . ."

"Don't laugh at motherhood," Nicola said. "Or apple pie for that matter."

Stuart looked apologetic. "I'm not laughing, Mother. Far from it."

"Good. And what I was going to say is that, as your mother, I'm worried about you."

Stuart waited.

"How long is it since Irene went up to Aberdeen?"

"A year?"

"Yes, a year. At least."

He watched her. Nicola had no time for Irene; he had always known that.

"And what have you done about replacing her?"

Stuart struggled to conceal his astonishment. "Replacing her? You make her sound like a household appliance that's gone wrong."

"You know what I mean, Stuart."

He shook his head. "I don't know if I do."

"You need to find somebody. Now, I know that you had that brief dalliance with that young woman – the one who was interested in poetry. But that didn't last, did it? And in my view – it's just one view, of course – you should have tried again. You can't expect these things just to happen."

Stuart bit his lip. He wanted to tell his mother to keep out of his affairs – or, lack of them, perhaps. But you did not say that to your mother. So, instead, he said, "Well, Mother, what do you suggest?"

"I've put you online."

He stared at her. "*You've* . . . put *me* online?

Stuart stared at his mother. She returned his stare.

"I'm only trying to be helpful," she said.

Stuart struggled. What did you say to your mother when, without permission, she puts you online – like an unwanted item for which a buyer is sought?

She sought to reassure him. "I haven't *activated* you yet," she said. "I'd obviously get your consent for that."

5

Stereotypes, Bullfighting, Danger

"Mother," said Stuart. "I appreciate what you're trying to do. I wouldn't want you to think that I didn't."

Nicola inclined her head. "I know that. I know you do, Stuart."

"But there are factors that make my position a bit complicated."

Nicola frowned. "I know that Irene isn't the easiest of people," she said. *An understatement,* she thought. *Irene is unspeakable . . . A termagant without equal . . .* She searched for the right Scots epithet: Irene was *argle-barglous* – that expressed it so well: she was an *alagrugous, ackwart, pictarnie.* The finding of just the right words made Nicola feel much better: linguistic revenge had its points.

"It's not that," said Stuart. "Well, she enters into the equation, I suppose, but not in such a way as to make much difference to anything. No, it's not her, Mother."

"Is it financial? You don't have to worry too much in that regard, Stuart. As you are aware, I have my resources."

He knew that. Nicola had been well provided for in her divorce from her Portuguese wine-producer husband. In addition to that, she had her interest in Inclusive Pies (formerly Pies for Protestants), the pie factory in Glasgow that she had inherited. Stuart had his salary as a statistician, which was reasonable enough, and even with the payments that he made to Irene, he got by. The cushion made by Nicola's contribution to the household was welcome, but hardly necessary.

"It's nothing to do with money, Mother." He cast a glance

towards the door that led off the kitchen, where they were sitting, to the bedrooms beyond, where Bertie and Ulysses were sleeping. Nicola followed his gaze.

"Of course," she said. "Of course."

"Yes," said Stuart. "I'm not exactly unencumbered."

Nicola lowered her voice. "Plenty of people have children – plenty of people who make a go of it for a second time, that is."

Stuart sighed. "I know that. But very often, it's the woman who has the children. The new man comes along and agrees to take them on, so to speak. It's easier for a man than for a woman."

Nicola shook her head. "Where on earth did you hear that?"

"Everybody knows it," said Stuart.

Nicola made a dismissive gesture. "What nonsense, Stuart."

"It's not," he said. "Women don't want to take on other people's children. They know the risks."

"The risks?" Nicola challenged.

"They know that the children may reject them. Children don't want somebody to replace their natural mother. They resent it, and it leads to all sorts of problems."

Nicola held up a hand. "Hold on, Stuart, let's look at this dispassionately. Are you saying that you don't want to meet somebody because you think the boys won't accept her?"

Stuart hesitated. "Yes, I suppose I am. I've been reading about it."

Nicola shook her head. "You're complicating matters unnecessarily, you know." She paused. "What have you been reading?"

"*Cinderella*," Stuart replied.

She stared at him blankly. "*Cinderella*? As in the pantomime story?"

"The pantomime gets the gist of it," said Stuart. "It's a bit more sophisticated than that, but the elements are all there."

She sat back as he continued.

"Cinderella is kept at home, in the kitchen."

"I know that bit."

"And she has a stepmother, a wicked stepmother, of course."

"Not all stepmothers are wicked," said Nicola. "Let's not get bogged down with stereotypes."

"The point about stereotypes," Stuart said, "is that they're there for a reason. Stereotypes exist because in so many cases they reflect reality."

"I'm surprised at you, Stuart," Nicola scolded. "You're meant to be a professional statistician. You believe in evidence, not prejudice. And here you are defending stereotypes."

"Not completely," said Stuart. "When people say today that you shouldn't pay attention to stereotypes, they're the ones who are rejecting the evidence. If there's a common stereotype, it's because there are a fair number of instances of whatever the stereotypical feature is. The trouble with people who reject stereotypes is that they want to ignore that evidence."

Nicola was robust. "With good reason, I would have thought. Stereotypes are unfair. They preclude judgement on the basis of what actually *is*. You know that, Stuart."

Stuart shrugged. "So, we pretend that there are no such things as national characteristics? So there's no difference between Scotland and England?"

Nicola looked uncomfortable. "I wouldn't say that."

"Or Spain and Sweden?"

"Spain and Sweden? There are cultural differences – of course there are."

"Bullfighting is less popular in Sweden?"

Nicola hesitated. "Marginally," she said, and smiled at the familiarity of the scene: they were back to when he was a teenage boy – he used to argue just like this.

"Well, there you are," said Stuart. "Aren't you proposing a stereotype – or two, in fact? The cool, rational non-violent Swede, and the fiery Spaniard who enjoys nothing better than getting into a tight-fitting uniform – with lots of glitter – and tormenting a poor bull in front of a roaring crowd?"

Nicola sighed. "Not all Spaniards enjoy bullfighting. Don't defame them all." She paused. "I detest bullfighting. The mere thought of it."

Stuart agreed. "I don't see how they can do it. How can they sit there and watch a terrified fellow creature being put to death? And then there is that ridiculous race through the streets where they run in front of bulls."

Nicola shook her head. "What drives people to do things like that?"

"The quest for excitement. It would all be too tame if there were no danger."

"So, it's not just that they enjoy the bulls' suffering?" asked Nicola.

"No, it's more complex than that," said Stuart. "People love danger, especially if all risk is removed from life – or as much risk as possible. The absence of risk makes life boring – for some people. Why do you think they watch Formula One racing? It's noisy and smelly and consumes vast resources. It's the danger, I think, that people love. We know that some of the cars are going to spin out of control. The crowd loves a good smash. Loves it. If it were entirely safe, it would be far less fun for everybody."

Nicola knew nothing about Formula One. She thought it was a shampoo, and she was still thinking of Spain. "Do you remember Kenneth Clark's *Civilisation* programmes?" she asked. "Did you ever see them?"

"Some," said Stuart.

"I always remember how it more or less ignored Spanish art," said Nicola. "Clark didn't have much time for it."

Stuart raised an eyebrow. "That's extreme. He had his critics, of course."

"Don't we all?" said Nicola, and added, "Except you, of course." She paused. "I'm proud, you know, Stuart. I'm proud that I'm the mother of a son who treats others well."

He looked away. He was embarrassed. "I'm no better than the next person."

"No," said Nicola. "You're considerably better. The next person, as a general rule, is deeply flawed." She thought about it a bit more. "And those who say they are no better than the next person, are almost always the very best of us. Fact. Well-known."

6

A Strawberry-blonde Experience

Bruce Anderson, surveyor and former narcissist, was waiting
in his flat in Abercrombie Place for the arrival of his old
school-friend, Borthy Borthwick. Bruce had known Borthy
– whose real, never-used name was Arnold – from the age
of five, when they had first eyed one another with suspicion
on their first day of school in Crieff. The friendships of very
early childhood are notorious for their fickleness, although a
few survive those early years in which all others are, at best,
potential rivals for attention. Bruce and Borthy continued
to be friends as they went through school and through life.
Both finding themselves in Edinburgh in their early twenties,
they joined the same rugby club, shared common friends, and
had even both been briefly arrested by the Polish police on a
rowdy stag party in Kraków and found themselves sharing a
cell for a few hours.

Borthy had always stood in awe of Bruce, whose style and
general insouciance he admired but could never quite match.
In his eyes, Bruce had that almost indefinable quality of
coolness that, although difficult to explain, was immediately
recognisable when one encountered it. It was not just a
question of outward presentation, important though that
might be; more significant was the projected sense of self-
assurance, the unruffled confidence, that led people to believe
that everything that Bruce did was planned and nothing was
a response to the exigencies of the moment. While most of
us have to accept the world as it presented itself to us, and
do so with a varying degree of resignation, Bruce gave the

impression of being in perfect command of the circumstances in which he found himself. It was this apparent mastery that so impressed Borthy and for which he would have given a great deal to possess himself.

At Morrison's Academy in Crieff, the school they had both attended until the age of eighteen, Borthy particularly admired Bruce's ability to attract the attention of girls – even those with a reputation for despising boys. One of these girls, Candace Connaught, whose father owned a riding stables, and whose strawberry-blonde hair exactly matched the coat of the Highland pony she rode at Pony Club events, was a magnet to boys but utterly dismissive of any young male who dared so much as to address a chance remark to her. "Yeah, sure," she would say in response to any such approach, and then, without saying anything more, would turn away and busy herself with more important business than the awkward teenager who had plucked up the courage to speak to her.

Borthy himself had been amongst those who had dared to approach Candace. It had cost him a great deal of sleep, as he lay awake planning how he might engage her in conversation and how, one thing having led to another, they might find themselves seated next to one another in the back row of the cinema in Perth, a place well-known to the planets whose orbits determined the fortunes of love. He had finally decided that the best thing to do was to compliment her in some way, as he had read in a magazine an article that gave that particular advice to the reader. "Women like compliments – extensive psychological research has confirmed that. Factor compliments and flowers into your dating plans and you will never be disappointed. Fact."

That counsel had made a deep impression on Borthy, who had never gone out with a girl and whose secret fear was that he would die before he had the chance to do so. Knowing that Candace would be competing at the Strathearn Pony Club

Day, he made sure that he was there too, ready to address her as she groomed her pony before her event.

Candace looked at him. She had been aware that there was a boy watching her, but had given no indication that she had noticed him. But eventually, as Borthy edged closer to her, her irritation had broken through her affected indifference.

"Do I know you?" she asked, glancing at him briefly before returning to her task of grooming.

She then answered her own question. "Oh yes, you're at Morrison's, aren't you? Bobby something."

"Borthy. I'm called Borthy."

Candace ignored this. She was not intending to call him anything and so this information was hardly needed.

There was a brief silence. The hills towards Comrie were layers of blue. There was the smell of cut grass in the air. A loudspeaker cackled into life, announcing the next event. Somebody laughed somewhere.

Then Borthy spoke. "I really like your hair," he said.

Candace's hand, holding the grooming brush, faltered in its sweep of the pony's flank before resuming its task.

Emboldened by the fact that the earth had not opened to swallow him, Borthy continued, "I like the way it matches your pony. It makes you look the same."

The grooming hand came to a halt. A head was turned. Another head turned, too, as the pony gave Borthy a cold stare.

"You trying to be funny or something?" said Candace.

"No," stammered Borthy. "I wasn't. I meant it."

"So you think I look like a horse?"

Borthy was appalled. His voice rose several notes, and he struggled to lower it. He had always tried to sound like Sean Connery. He had practised and practised, and now, just at the moment when it was all so important, it was all failing him. "Of course not. I never said that. I didn't. I said that your hair is sort of the same colour as your pony. That's all. I said I like that."

Candace turned her back on him. She did not even say "Yeah, sure" but was completely silent. From the depth of his misery, Borthy struggled to apologise, but was ignored. He walked off, burning with a shame that lasted for several days and was not alleviated in any way when Bruce later told him that he had been at the Pony Club dance that evening and had danced with Candace Connaught – at her request.

"She was eying me up," he said. "She usually doesn't do that sort of thing – as you know. But she really wanted to dance with me. I had to let her. It's unkind to keep girls hanging around."

Borthy struggled to conceal his envy. "And?"

Bruce shrugged. "A close number. You know – cheek to cheek. Hah!"

Borthy's eyes widened.

"And you know what?" Bruce continued. "I licked her hair."

It was a few moments before Borthy could speak. Then he said, "While you were dancing?"

"Yes. Up close and personal. I licked the hair just above her ear. And you know something? It tasted of strawberries."

Borthy closed his eyes. That such things could happen in Crieff . . . but not to him. Life was so unfair. Here was he, with whom Candace Connaught would never dance, and here was Bruce, who had actually licked her famous strawberry-blonde hair. It was all so unfair.

7

Borthy Arrives

Poor Borthy, thought Bruce, as he heard his old friend come up the final stairs to his landing. Poor Borthy, with his wistful look and his perpetual air of injured longing – as if he knew that he was missing out on so much. There had been a time when Bruce had been bemused by that – Borthy was a loser, poor fellow, and the world was full of people like him . . . *wall-to-wall losers* as Bruce had once put it – and laughed at the pithiness of his observation – but he would no longer find that sort of thing amusing, because this was the new Bruce, who inexplicably felt quite different about people like Borthy Borthwick . . . Except that in reality the change was not so inexplicable: that extraordinary event in Dundas Street – that ultimate electrifying moment, as it had been described – had been the beginning of a new chapter in Bruce's life, a chapter of which the full implications were only now beginning to become apparent.

Bruce opened the door to a grinning Borthy Borthwick. It was a very particular sort of grin – almost apologetic – and it brought back so much, from such a long time ago: Borthy standing on the sidelines at the tennis club, waiting for an invitation to play mixed doubles – an invitation that rarely came his way, and then only to play with the novices; Borthy at some birthday dance at the Hydro, wearing a kilt and Prince Charlie jacket when everybody else was in jeans; Borthy, as a boy of eight, being rescued in the swimming pool during the boys' under-ten one hundred metres breaststroke when he had swallowed water and somehow lost his way while traversing the pool.

"Yo, Bruce!" said Borthy.

Bruce smiled. Nobody said *yo* any more, but Borthy was the sort of person who would start saying *yo* well after everyone else and continue to say it for years after everyone had stopped staying it. This, however, was the new Bruce, and so rather than reply, sarcastically, *Yo yourself*, he said, in a voice devoid of any irony, "Yo, there, Borthy."

Borthy began a high five. Bruce swallowed. Borthy obviously did not know that you *never* did high fives in the Edinburgh New Town; you just did not. What, after all, was the point of conserving such a large area of Georgian architecture if people were going to walk around saying *yo* in it and giving each other high fives? But, once again, not wishing to embarrass Borthy he responded with the appropriate gesture.

"Good to see you, Borthy," he said. "Come in."

"Thanks," said Borthy, gazing at Bruce in admiration. "How are you doing, Bruce?"

Bruce nodded. "I'm alive," he said.

Borthy nodded. "Aren't we all?"

They went into Bruce's living room.

"Cool," said Borthy, looking about him. "This is really cool, Bruce."

Bruce tried not to wince. Poor Borthy; he always got the words wrong. He tried so hard, but somehow . . . "Yah," said Bruce. "It's done me fine." *Done* . . . He had thought that his flat was ideal, and he had been proud of it, but life was different now. He no longer needed all this – this surround-sound stereo system, this minimalist post-IKEA furniture from the Danish Living shop in Bruntsfield, this large Bellany watercolour of a seagull sitting on a sailor's shoulder that he had bought in an auction at Lyon & Turnbull; this plaster head of Athene he had brought back from Lefkas a few years previously when he had gone on an Ionian Sailing Adventure cruise with those girls he had met in the Cumberland Bar. None of that meant much to him now, even if it was capable of impressing – as it clearly did – somebody like Borthy Borthwick.

"I'll show you where everything is," he said. "You'll need to know, if you're going to be living here. Kitchen things. Detergent. Bin liners and so on."

Borthy looked apologetic. "I wasn't planning to use your stuff, Bruce. I'll be buying my own."

Bruce shook his head. "You're going to be my guest, Borthy. You can use anything you find in this place – food, bed linen, drink – anything. What's mine is yours. Even my clothes – if they fit."

Borthy swallowed. He was at a loss for words. "Jeez," he said, his voice cracking with emotion.

"That's what friends are for," Bruce said.

Borthy looked puzzled. "You didn't tell me where you were going. You said up north somewhere . . ."

"Yes," said Bruce. "Up north. I'm going to a monastery up there."

Borthy struggled with this. "Work?"

Bruce looked away. Borthy was so slow on the uptake, he thought; why would anybody go to a monastery for *work*? But then he reminded himself: it was wrong to to be impatient with people like Borthy, who had only managed to get a degree in media studies, or something like that, from some third-rate university in England somewhere – a place that Bruce had never even heard of, although he thought that there was an airport there. Perhaps the airport and the university were one and the same place. Was there a Heathrow University? Hah! thought Bruce. BA (Heathrow). Hah!

But then he stopped himself. That was unkind – and that was not the way he thought now. Not after Dundas Street. The new me, he thought, doesn't mock people who have degrees in media studies, even if most of them are real thickos. He stopped himself again: he should not use that word, which was so unkind. *Thickos are my brothers*, he thought. That sounded more like it.

Borthy waited.

"Actually," said Bruce. "I'm going to spend some time there."

"How long?" asked Borthy.

Bruce shrugged. "A year? Five years? The rest of my life?"

Borthy laughed. "Oh, good one, Bruce. You? In a monastery? Yeah, I believe you."

Bruce fixed him with a stare. "I'm deadly serious, Borthy."

"But, you . . . What about . . .?"

Bruce held Borthy's puzzled gaze. "What about what?"

Borthy looked embarrassed. "What about . . . you know?"

Bruce bit his lip. Is that what I've become? he asked himself. Is that what people think of me? Bruce Anderson, the Lothario? Is that what I am in the eyes of others? He felt shame, and it burned about him: it was a new sensation for Bruce, and it was surprisingly painful.

"That's all in the past," he said quietly.

Borthy said nothing for a while. Was this new Bruce Anderson the real Bruce Anderson? he asked himself.

"You mean you . . .?"

Bruce raised a finger in a gesture of silence. "All over, Borthy. Past tense. *Finito*. Light seen."

Borthy let out a long low whistle. Then he muttered "Jeez" softly, before adding, "What happened?"

He wondered whether Bruce had taken something. Perhaps he was having medical treatment and all this was a side effect. How else might one explain it? How else?

8

Changed, Changed Utterly

"What I'm going to tell you," Bruce began, "may be difficult to believe, but it's true, you know. This is absolutely true." He paused. "But I don't want too many people to hear about it, if you don't mind."

Borthy put a finger to his lips in a gesture of silence. "You can rely on me, Bruce. You know that."

Bruce did know. At school, Borthy had always had a reputation for discretion, even to the extent of accepting punishment for letting down the geography teacher's tyres when it was not him but Magnus Stoddart who was responsible. Borthy had known the identity of the true culprit but had declined to incriminate him. That respect for juvenile *omertà* had not gone unnoticed.

"I know you're not a clype," said Bruce. "You never were."

Borthy acknowledged the compliment. But what was this? Had Bruce done something illegal?

"It's just I don't want too many people to know," said Bruce. "They may know that I was struck by lightning – I don't care too much if they know that – but I don't want them to know . . . to know how I *feel*."

But for Borthy, the most sensational aspect of this was the lightning. "You?" he gasped. "You were struck by lightning? As in . . . *bang*?"

Bruce nodded. "In Dundas Street."

Borthy shook his head in amazement. "Struck dead?"

Bruce sighed. "Obviously not, Borthy . . ."

Borthy grinned. "Of course. Stupid of me. What I meant

was struck as in struck by a serious bolt. From the sky? That sort of thing?"

Bruce described what had happened. "It was all over very quickly. One minute I was walking down Dundas Street and then, suddenly, *zap*! They found me in the middle of the street, unconscious. I woke up in the ambulance – or at least I think I did. It was all a bit confusing."

"And painful?" asked Borthy. "Did it hurt?"

Bruce thought for a moment. "It was odd. I had a headache for a while, and I was bruised all down one side. But that was more from the impact of landing after I had been thrown up in the air. They said they were a bit surprised that I hadn't broken anything."

"Jeez, Bruce," Borthy said. "It's unbelievable. Not that I'm doubting you – it's just the most amazing story."

"Well, I was lucky," said Bruce. "I could be dead right now. Dead. But I'm not, you see. And all that seems to have happened is that my hair stood up for a while and I had a rather odd burn mark on one leg – a sort of fern pattern on the skin. Apparently, that's a typical feature of lightning strikes. You get this odd pattern, as if a fern has been tattooed on your skin."

Borthy shook his head. "I'm really glad you survived, Bruce."

Bruce looked at Borthy. I have been so unkind to him, he thought. I've ignored him. I've laughed at him behind his back. I've thought, *poor Borthy*, and said to myself *Thank God I'm not him*. And here he is saying that he's glad that I survived. Well, at least I have time now to make up for all of that – and for everything else. Who gets that sort of chance in life?

"The odd thing," Bruce continued, "is that I felt completely different. It's hard to describe it exactly, but I saw everything in a different light."

Borthy frowned. "You mean, your tastes and so on?"

Bruce thought about this for a short while before he continued, "I suppose I like some of the same things." He glanced around the room. "That Bellany, for instance. My furniture. Nothing changed when it came to that sort of thing." He paused. "But it was a bit different when it came to music. I tried to listen to my playlists, and I found I didn't like them."

"How odd is that?" said Borthy.

"Yes. You know Creedence Clearwater Revival? 'Proud Mary'?"

Borthy grinned. "You always liked that."

"Well, I don't any more. Nor 'Bad Moon Rising'."

"So what do you like?"

Bruce smiled. "Gregorian chant. The theme from *Zorba the Greek*. And one or two other things – things I wouldn't have listened to before . . . before Dundas Street."

Borthy waited for him to elaborate, but he did not. So Borthy pressed him. "Such as?"

Bruce looked down at the floor. "*The Sound of Music*. You know that song they sing when they're about to leave Austria? 'Edelweiss'. I've been thinking of that tune a lot – hearing it in my mind."

Borthy was staring at him. "You've changed, haven't you?"

Bruce nodded. "Yes, I have."

"And you're going away because of that? Just because . . . just because your music's changed?"

For Borthy, this was a new experience; Bruce, the confident one, the social success, the role model, now seemed uncertain and vulnerable.

Bruce had been standing near the door. Now he gestured towards the kitchen. "I was going to make coffee. Would you like a cup?"

Borthy nodded, and the two of them made their way into the kitchen. Borthy looked around appreciatively at the array of appliances. "You've got everything here," he said.

Bruce looked around the kitchen, as with new eyes. "There's too much stuff," he said, as he slipped a coffee pod into the machine.

"Can you ever have too much stuff?" asked Borthy.

Bruce was certain you could. "You get stuff because you think it'll make you feel better. It doesn't. It ties you down. And the more stuff you get, the more tied down you are."

"But you need some stuff," Borthy argued. "You can't go through life having no stuff at all."

The coffee machine was now making a purring sound and began to discharge a thin dribble of dark liquid.

"I love the smell of fresh coffee," remarked Borthy. "Do you like it, Bruce?"

Bruce said nothing.

"So that's why you're going away? To get away from everything – having too much, *et cetera, et cetera*?"

Bruce opened the fridge to find milk. He answered the question over his shoulder. "That might be one of the reasons."

Borthy considered this. "You really mean it?"

"I do, Borthy. I really mean it. This is something that I need to do."

They drank their coffee in silence. Then, as Bruce took his friend's empty cup from him to put in the sink, he said, "Offering you the use of this place is my way of saying something."

Borthy looked slightly embarrassed. He was not sure about the new Bruce.

"It's a way of apologising," Bruce continued.

This puzzled Borthy. "For what? What have you got to apologise for?"

Bruce shook his head. "I don't know where to start," he said quietly.

9

Wedding Plans

Big Lou's wedding had been a moving affair, attended by just over eighty friends and family members. She would have been content with a registry office ceremony – "At our time of life, wouldn't it be more appropriate?" – but had gone along with Fat Bob's desire to be married with all possible formality. This had come as a surprise to Lou, who had had no idea that Bob was fond of Old St Paul's, an Episcopal church known for its traditional liturgical tastes and its liberal use of incense, incantation, and holy water. By special arrangement with the clergy of that church, Big Lou and Fat Bob were to be married by a friend whom Bob had known for years, the Reverend Andrew Mactaggart, whose current parish was in Fife.

They had gone to speak to Andrew some weeks before the wedding and had discussed the service with him.

"The Scottish Prayer Book, 1929 version?" Andrew had asked. "The traditional wedding service, Bob?"

Bob nodded. "Aye, Andrew," he said. "You ken weel what I like. None of this computer-speak, if you dinnae mind!"

Andrew understood. "It's hard to improve on that gorgeous Cranmerian language," he said. "Think of the way the marriage service begins: *Dearly beloved, we are gathered together in the sight of God and in the presence of this congregation . . .*"

Fat Bob nodded. "Aye, you hear that, Lou? Those words have real weight to them. Beautiful. Solemn."

Big Lou was happy enough. "I've no objection," she said.

"And then it goes on to speak of that first miracle wrought

in Cana of Galilee," Andrew continued. "Again, the wording is very poetic."

"You cannae go wrang wi' a bit of poetry," said Fat Bob.

Andrew agreed. "I recall what W.H. Auden said about the new wording," he said. "When they introduced the functional English of the new service, they threw away centuries of linguistic richness. Centuries. He thought that a tragedy."

"I agree," said Fat Bob. "This Auden guy is spot on there, Andy."

"And readings?" asked Andrew.

Fat Bob hesitated. "Kahlil Gibran?"

Andrew smiled. "Many people like Gibran. He has his moments, of course, and he touches upon the great things of life. Love. Friendship. Family. I wouldn't rule him out."

Fat Bob looked thoughtful. "But I'm not sure what you think, Lou? Do you like Gibran? *The Prophet*?"

Big Lou hesitated. "We didn't read him much up in Arbroath."

Fat Bob nodded. "Aye, well, how about something you like?"

"I like that passage about charity," said Big Lou. She turned to Andrew. "You know the one? About charity being greater than faith and hope? You know that one, Andy?"

"I should hope I do," replied Andrew. "It's from *Corinthians*." He quoted the words.

"That's it," said Bob. "*And the greatest of these is charity*. And if I have not charity . . ."

"I am become as sounding brass," Andrew completed.

Fat Bob nodded. "True," he said.

"I think it is," said Andrew, adding, "Of course, charity has a special meaning in that context. The modern word is a bit different. Charity at that time meant love of humanity. That's something very special."

"Good," said Fat Bob. "Let's have that."

Andrew looked enquiringly at Big Lou. "Happy enough, Lou?"

"I am," she said.

"Well, then," Andrew continued. "And the hymns? Have you given thought to the hymns?"

"'To be a pilgrim'," said Fat Bob. "And mebbe 'For those in peril on the sea'."

Andrew frowned. "The first of those may be appropriate," he said. "You are, after all, embarking on a journey together. I'm not sure about 'For those in peril'." He paused. "I'm not sure what the appropriate hymn would be for one like you, Bob – a professional strongman."

"'Fight the good fight'?" suggested Lou, grinning.

Andrew smiled. "You may laugh," he said, "but I was at a wedding once where they sung that. The guests had great difficulty in keeping a straight face. Mind you, I believe there is indeed a patron saint of weightlifters – St Hyacinth, a Polish saint of the twelfth century. He was enormously strong. As was St Christopher, I imagine, who carried travellers with ease. He was said, incidentally, to have been seven and a half feet tall."

Fat Bob returned to "'For those in peril'". "I like it," he said. "And I thought we should think about folk who aren't in our fortunate position – storm-tossed folk."

"Perhaps," said Andrew. He glanced at Lou. "All right, Lou?"

Big Lou nodded. "I think you should give folk a tune they know," she said. "It's no good asking them to sing something obscure."

"Precisely," said Fat Bob. "I'm sure you agree with that, Andy."

And so it was that the shape of their wedding service was agreed. Now invitations could be sent out, inviting friends to attend the marriage, according to the rites of the Scottish Episcopal Church, with a reception afterwards at the Mansfield Traquair Centre near Broughton Street. These invitations were then dispatched to eighty-two people, of whom eighty-one accepted, the only person not responding positively being recently deceased as a result of a salmonella infection contracted in an Airbnb in Turkey. For the rest, people responded with enthusiasm, expressing delight that two people had found each other fairly far along the pathway of life.

"Marry late and you make no mistake," a friend of Big Lou's had said. "Look at Lou and what's his name, Desperate Dan, or whatever . . ."

"Fat Bob."

"That's the man."

"Yes, Fat Bob. Well, look at them. Both of them are getting a bit long in the tooth, and yet they are getting married with all the bells and whistles."

"Yes."

"She's had bad luck," said the friend. "A succession of useless men – one after the other. The Jacobite. The Elvis impersonator. The chef. None of them much good."

"No."

"And now Fat Bob, who seems decent enough."

"Big Lou deserves happiness."

"Don't we all? Have you ever met anybody who didn't deserve to be happy?"

This required some thought. Then came the response. "One or two, I suppose. Would you like me to name them?"

Names were given, and each was followed by a grin and a guilty nod of agreement.

"You see?" said the friend. "There are limits to charity, once one gets going."

10

At the Mansfield Traquair Centre

The ceremony over, with Big Lou and Fat Bob now being husband and wife in the eyes of the law of Scotland, and of all the known world, the privileged guests, not a few of whom had found themselves moist-eyed in in the church, made their way to the Mansfield Traquair Centre. Here the caterers, old friends of Big Lou's, had set out four long trestle tables laden with food for the newly-married couple and their eighty-one guests. A small ceilidh band, consisting of two fiddlers, an accordionist, a pianist and a drummer, had already tuned up and was playing by the time the guests entered the building. "The Lewis Bridal Song" had been followed by "The Auld Hoose" and "The Laird of Drumblair". That was just the beginning, though: long reels lay ahead as the afternoon progressed and the tireless band gamely encouraged the guests to their feet and onto the dance floor.

Matthew and Elspeth found themselves seated at the same table as Domenica and Angus. Matthew was in his kilt, as were his three small boys, Tobermory, Rognvald, and Fergus, all in their father's tartan, a dark green weave shot through with red. Each of the boys wore a miniature sporran of badger hair that Matthew had had made for them by a sporran-maker in Fife. The face of each boy quickly reflected the contents of the plates on the table before them, with chocolate, jam and powdered sugar soon leaving their trace on the juvenile features. Elspeth sighed: she had been unable to keep the triplets clean, and had now given up. Boys were dirty – they just were – and perhaps it was best to accept that as being their natural state, ordained into that estate by biology and destined to remain there until, in teenage years, they discovered the self-consciousness that might make them attend to their appearance.

They knew everyone at their table, as Big Lou had been careful to ensure that friends found themselves seated together. So Elspeth was seated next to Domenica, while Angus was beside Matthew, and the Italian socialite nun and Turner Prize judge, Sister Maria-Fiore dei Fiori di Montagna, with her close friend, Antonia Collie, were on the opposite side of the table facing Domenica. The triplets had been given a seat each, but had so far been keener to sit under the table where, unobserved by adults, they moved amongst the feet, untying shoelaces here, leaving traces of jam on socks and trousers there.

Matthew leaned across the table to engage Sister Maria-Fiore dei Fiori di Montagna in conversation.

"You must drop into the gallery one of these days," he said. "I've seen you walking past once or twice. I waved to you, but you were deep in thought and didn't notice me."

Sister Maria-Fiore dei Fiori di Montagna considered this. She smiled sweetly as she replied, "We do not always find what we are looking for. *Mirabile dictu*, that is frequently the way things are. Our eyes are fixed on one thing, and we fail to notice another. How many times has that happened?"

It was a rhetorical question, typical of the rhetorical questions and aphorisms for which Sister Maria-Fiore dei Fiori di Montagna was so well known. But Antonia took it as a question that called for an answer, and replied, "Twice, in my experience."

They looked at her.

"Last week," she continued, "I was walking along Dublin Street, climbing the hill, you'll understand."

"We must climb such hills as they are before us," interjected Sister Maria-Fiore dei Fiori di Montagna.

Antonia Collie looked impatient. "Yes, yes," she said. "Nobody said you shouldn't climb hills." She paused, and before Sister Maria-Fiore dei Fiori di Montagna could resume, she continued, "I was walking along Dublin Street, as I was saying, and I almost tripped up over a hole that had appeared in the pavement. There was nothing to mark it – no barrier – nothing."

"Hills," said Sister Maria-Fiore dei Fiori di Montagna, "are often lower than we think they are going to be. A high hill may be a low hill once one starts the ascent."

"You'd think the council would make sure that holes had barriers around them," said Antonia. "If you dig something up, you should warn people."

"Why were they digging?" asked Domenica.

"Gas," said Antonia. "Somebody smells gas and they have to dig things up. They might be considered negligent if they don't. But the point is that I almost fell into the hole."

Matthew sought to continue his conversation with Sister Maria-Fiore dei Fiori di Montagna. "I hear that you've been looking at some of the nominees for this year's Turner Prize. How are things going?"

Sister Maria-Fiore dei Fiori di Montagna looked furtively about her. "I shouldn't really be talking about it, you know."

"Of course not," said Matthew. "But anything you say to me . . . well, I understand about confidentiality."

"It would go no further?" asked the nun.

Matthew reassured her. "Not a soul," he said. "I shan't say a thing."

Sister Maria-Fiore dei Fiori di Montagna leaned forward. She lowered her voice. "The most frightful rubbish," she said. "Rubbish on an ocean-going scale."

Matthew nodded encouragement. "I can just imagine," he said.

"Not a single one who can paint. Not one," said Sister Maria-Fiore dei Fiori di Montagna.

"So what are you going to do?"

"I have a plan," said Sister Maria-Fiore dei Fiori di Montagna. "I'm going to create an artist from scratch. I'm going to invent him, and then make sure he's added to the list of nominees. He will, of course, be completely made-up, but his work will be cutting-edge rubbish – and therefore a very strong possibility for the Turner Prize."

Matthew smiled. "Like Ern Malley?"

Sister Maria-Fiore dei Fiori di Montagna looked at him blankly. "Ern Malley?"

"One of the greatest artistic frauds of the last century," Matthew said. "Ern Malley was an Australian poet who didn't exist. It sounds as if your Turner Prize nominee will be very much the same thing."

Sister Maria-Fiore dei Fiori di Montagna was intrigued. "Tell me about this Malley person."

"It's a highly amusing story," Matthew began. "It starts in Melbourne in the nineteen-forties."

Matthew was aware that Angus was listening too and he raised his voice so that Angus could hear.

"Ern Malley came into existence because of intellectual pretension," he began. "Without intellectual pretension, the story would be nothing."

"Just like many examples of conceptual art?" said Angus.

Matthew nodded. "Yes, exactly. But let's imagine: Melbourne, back in 1943. Melbourne is far away from the literary centres of the English-speaking world, but there are people there who want to establish an Australian literary identity. *Angry Penguins* is a literary magazine that receives a letter from a woman about poems written by her brother, Ern."

They waited.

"And?" asked Angus.

"Well," said Matthew. "Let me tell you what happened."

11

A Modernist Poet

"You can imagine what it was like to be interested in modernist poetry in Adelaide in those days," said Matthew.

Angus frowned. "I'm not sure if I can."

"Frustrating," said Matthew. "The real literary world was elsewhere – thousands of miles away. While Eliot, Auden, MacNeice were pushing out the boundaries, quite a few Australian poets were still going on about gum trees. You know the sort of thing."

Angus smiled. "And painting them too, I imagine." He paused. Not every Australian painting of the time featured gum trees. "Sidney Nolan had started to change all that."

Matthew nodded. "Yes, he was a much-needed breath of fresh air. Although he left the country."

"Yes," said Angus. "He absented himself from the forces during the War. He would have been sent to Papua New Guinea."

Matthew was silent. Would he have gone elsewhere had he been faced with being sent to Papua New Guinea? Who amongst us could be sure? One should not be too harsh in the judgement of others, he felt.

"You know he did thousands of paintings?" Angus continued. "Some great rubbish. Some masterpieces. I saw his Ned Kelly series in Canberra when I went there some years ago. Very atmospheric. Haunting, even." He paused. "But in poetry? Fiction? It wasn't the most exciting of times."

Matthew shrugged. "Maybe not. Yet there were people who were making waves. In particular, a young man called

Max Harris – a big champion of modernist poetry. He set up a literary journal with a backer in Melbourne. They called it *Angry Penguins* – a laughable title now, but quite the thing in those days. Angry young men, I suppose, was the idea. Anger over the conformism of the country, the pub culture, the cultural cringe – everything, really. Very different from Australia today – which is a terrifically creative place. The arts thrive there. And it's the nicest country there is – after Scotland, of course."

Angus laughed. "Wha's like us? as they say."

"Scottish exceptionalism," observed Matthew. "Alive and well and all about us."

"I've never quite grasped the notion of exceptionalism," Angus said. "When people talk about it, I just nod. Maybe it's time to find out what it is." He paused. "Unless you're similarly in the dark, of course. You might be one of those people who uses words they don't understand – or which we have understood wrongly."

"Oh, I know about that," said Matthew. "The other day I heard somebody say that somebody was a sight for sore eyes. I thought they were being uncomplimentary, but the opposite turned out to be true. I'd always thought that when you were a sight for sore eyes you were dishevelled, or something like that. But I think it can actually mean that you're an attractive sight – a picture of perfection."

"It might be said ironically," suggested Angus. "In other words – you're a sight for sore eyes – not! The *not* is implicit in every ironical observation."

"Not," said Matthew. "When people use the word *ironically* these days, they mean *oddly enough*. They don't mean to use it in that other sense."

"Wicked," said Angus, and laughed.

"What's wicked?"

"I mean, that's another example of a change in meaning.

Bad has come to mean *good*. *Fake* has come to mean anything you don't like."

"*My* truth," said Matthew. "That's a really sinister development. The false can be true if it's yours. Magical thinking."

"That's the post-factual world," Angus observed. "The triumph of subjectivity. Was Allan Ramsay a great artist? Was Michelangelo? That all depends on what *you* think of them."

Matthew sighed.

"The concept of truth lies at the very heart of civilization," Angus continued. "Take it away, and what have we left. Anarchy. A fight for survival. The disappearance of all morality. Human life becomes a nightmare.'

"So when somebody in authority lies, then . . ."

"It's the end," said Angus. "If he or she gets away with it. It really takes away the foundations of *everything*, you know. Of civilization, for want of a better term." He looked at Matthew. They believed in the same things, he thought. He was older than Matthew, but Matthew understood. "We were talking about Scottish exceptionalism. Enlighten me, Matthew."

"Exceptionalism is the belief that you're different. You think that the normal rules don't apply to you. Or you think that your interests outrank everybody else's. It's a sort of divine right belief – but a bit different, I suppose."

"I've read about American exceptionalism," said Angus.

"Yes, the Americans suffered from it. They thought America was quite different from everywhere else, and could do as it wanted. And so did the British – for a long time. Remember the British Empire? You needed a healthy dose of exceptionalist belief to create something like that."

"Yes, I suppose so. The *God is an Englishman* view of the world?"

Matthew smiled. "Yes. And did we think He was Scottish? Did the French think He was French?"

Angus considered this. A French God would be a comfortable sort of figure – not too demanding in his proscription of adultery, for instance, and very accommodating when it came to overindulgence in the pleasures of the table. A Scottish God, however, would probably be Calvinist and rather strict. He would be a God of the *weel, ye ken noo* variety, not at all soft on sin. Closed on Sunday, more or less definitely.

"I think we make God in our image," Angus said, "even as we assert that He made us in His image."

Matthew was looking at Angus intently. He was reflecting on the fact that there were certain questions we seldom asked our friends, and one of them was *Do you believe in God?* People found that question embarrassing – too personal, perhaps, like asking somebody about a medical complaint. He had no idea whether Angus had any religious belief, and yet surely it was important to know that about a friend – it was such an important part of a life, after all. So he asked him.

Angus took a sip of wine. "Yes and no," he said. "I happen to believe there's some greater purpose, if you will, in life. I'm not always sure what that is, but I *feel* it, you know. And since I happen to have been born where I was born, at the time when I was born, then a particular spiritual means of expression is available to me – is part of my story, so to speak. And so I participate in that willingly. I respect what it stands for and I respect those who profess it."

"But inside?" Matthew pressed.

"Inside should, as far as possible, be the same as outside," answered Angus.

12

Angry Penguins

Sitting at their shared table at Big Lou's wedding reception, Angus and Matthew had in their conversation touched on exceptionalism, truth, art, and spirituality. Now they came back to Ern Malley, one of the great modernist poets of twentieth-century Australia – although, unfortunately, he had not actually existed.

Angus was thinking of Australia, and what it had been like when Ern had lived – or not lived, to be precise. "Now," he said, "I suspect, we look back on those times with a certain nostalgia – an age of innocence, perhaps. Pre-guilt; pre-regret; pre-cynicism." He suddenly looked wistful. "I rather think I would have liked to live in Australia then – before people doubted themselves."

Matthew looked thoughtful. "It would depend who you were," he said.

"Maybe," said Angus. "I suppose it wasn't all that easy being a woman, with all that unchallenged masculinity about. Or gay. Or to be a different colour from the majority. All of that."

"Same as just about everywhere in those days," said Matthew. "We're lucky, aren't we, to live in an era of antibiotics and relative tolerance?"

Angus smiled. "Both of those are under threat, don't you think? Antibiotics through overuse and resistance, and tolerance . . . Well, the threat to that is human nature and the desire that people have to silence others. There's an unbroken line between the persecutions of the past – in which Scotland joined in enthusiastically, let us remind ourselves – and the online mob of the present. Unbroken. It's the same moral energy finding expression in each case – only the nature of the victims has changed."

Matthew was thinking of the editors of *Angry Penguins*. "They were quite brave, actually – Harris and his friends. They knew that they were considered pretentious. They knew that there were plenty of people to whom they were – well, an affront, I suppose. People who challenge an existing view of things are often very much resented."

Angus sighed again. "Which is what happens to traditionalists today, don't you think?"

Matthew looked thoughtful. "You mean that traditionalists are cold-shouldered?"

"Yes," said Angus. "There comes a point, you see, where positions that were once seen as radical or revolutionary become the new norm. The consensus shifts. And then those who were outside, so to speak, but who are now inside, treat the former insiders as outsiders. A new establishment comes into existence. It's an old story. Those who were oppressed don't take long to become oppressors themselves."

Matthew said, "Harris and his friends were ridiculed by people I suppose one might call *hearties* – rugby-playing types."

This amused Angus. "Rugby players are not necessarily . . . how shall I put it – anti-intellectual?"

Matthew raised an eyebrow. He remembered his contemporaries at school who made it into the First XV. Hamilton, a winger, known as the Armpit; Grieve, a stalwart of the scrum, built like a fridge and with cauliflower ears; Maclean, a Borderer with a broken nose and so tone deaf that he could not even manage a recognisable rendition of "Flower of Scotland" – none of them struck him as being interested in the arts. Hamilton became a potato farmer in East Lothian;

Grieve ended up running a car hire business; Maclean joined the army, became a helicopter pilot, and was a major now. None of them, he imagined, were particularly sympathetic to modernist poetry.

"They threatened to throw Harris into the river," Matthew continued. "It was their idea of an intelligent response to his poetry."

"And did they?"

"Yes, they did. Muscular philistinism, one might call it."

"I suppose it's ever thus," said Angus.

"Yes, I'm afraid it is," said Matthew. "But to get back to Malley: there were a couple of people who decided to be a bit more subtle in registering their opposition to modernism. And this is where the letter from Ethel Malley came in. She wrote to Harris to tell him that she had found a manuscript when sorting out the possessions of her late brother, Ern, who had died of Grave's Disease. The manuscript consisted of a series of poems. She said that she had not known that her brother had written poetry – he had latterly been an insurance salesman, after working for a time as a mechanic.

"Harris read the poems," Matthew continued, "and he was pretty impressed with them. He showed them to a colleague, who was of the same view. They decided that they had discovered a major new poetic talent."

"Who was, nonetheless, dead?"

Matthew nodded. "Dying is a good career move for any young poet," he said. "You can't go wrong by dying. Byron. Rupert Brooke. Dylan Thomas. The list is quite a long one. Thomas made it to thirty-nine, I think." He remembered something. "I think they're now saying he died of pneumonia rather than drink. Drink is often part of the poetic legend. I don't think it was alcohol that did Brooke in, though. He was bitten by a mosquito, and the bite became infected. Septicaemia."

Angus brought up the question of Hugh MacDiarmid. "He lived to a ripe old age, didn't he – and yet he enjoyed his whisky. Glenfiddich, I think."

"The point about rules," said Matthew, "is that the exceptions outnumber them. And Byron."

"Malaria, wasn't it? Another mosquito. Mosquitoes: the enemies of poetry."

The band had started to play, although nobody was dancing yet. Big Lou and Fat Bob were standing by another table, shaking hands with their guests. They looked so happy, Angus thought, and he smiled to himself with pleasure: if anybody deserved happiness now, it was Big Lou, that hard-working, good woman who represented all the old values of Scotland's farming community. The world, he felt, had become a cold and casual place; Big Lou, with her warmth and the couthy qualities instilled in her during her girlhood at Snell Mains near Arbroath, was the very opposite of that.

"They published the poetry," Matthew went on, "in a special issue of *Angry Penguins*. They described it as the work of a major new Australian poet – although it consisted of cobbled-together nonsense, including sections of a military manual on mosquito control."

Angus let out a delighted laugh. "Wonderful," he said.

"And then the papers managed to find out who had written it. Two young men from Melbourne. They had composed the whole *oeuvre* in an afternoon."

"*Angry Penguins* was not amused?"

"No," said Matthew.

Sister Maria-Fiore dei Fiori di Montagna had been listening closely. Now, she observed, "Exposure of falseness can never be false. Nor, for that matter, can the false be true."

Angus and Matthew exchanged glances. "That might require some reflection," said Angus.

"Identifying that which requires reflection is itself a matter of reflection," said Sister Maria-Fiore dei Fiori di Montagna.

Antonia wrinkled her nose. "Sparkling wine makes me want to sneeze," she said. Then, turning to Sister Maria-Fiore dei Fiori di Montagna, she added, "And don't turn that into an aphorism, *carissima. Basta,* dear floral one."

Angus looked away awkwardly. A wedding reception was no place for a lovers' tiff, but, he went on to say to himself, that was exactly the sort of occasion where tiffs were most likely to occur. Like all things that were ever thus, this then, thus, was thus.

13

Minor Disagreements, Germs, Promises

As this conversation about Ern Malley took place at Angus and Domenica's table, on the other side of hall, the younger guests, seated around a low-level juvenile table of the sort to be seen in primary school classrooms, were contemplating the spread of sugary cakes and unhealthy aerated drinks that Big Lou had asked the caterers to provide for the children. The infantile guest list was not a large one, but included Finlay, Big Lou's adopted son; the triplets, Rognvald, Tobermory and Fergus; Bertie, who had been allowed to bring his friend Ranald Braveheart Macpherson; Bertie's tormentor and would-be Nemesis, Olive; and Olive's lieutenant and Greek chorus rolled into one, Pansy. There was also a boy with glasses, Tommy, who lived in Drummond Place, his sister, Henrietta, also with glasses, and Bertie's young brother, Ulysses, who was now able to walk although he was still to make significant progress in toilet training and in learning to refrain from biting.

Bertie's heart had sunk when he had seen Olive sitting several pews ahead of him in the church.

"Look over there," he had whispered to Ranald Braveheart Macpherson. "Do you see her, Ranald?"

Ranald followed the direction in which Bertie was pointing his finger. When his gaze settled on Olive, he gave a low groan. "It's her," he whispered.

"Maybe she's here by mistake," said Bertie. "You never know."

"And Pansy too," said Ranald. "They must have been

invited because I can see her mummy sitting next to her. And her dad, too. My dad says that Olive's dad drinks even more than he does."

"Maybe that's why they're at the wedding," said Bertie. "Some people just go to weddings to drink lots."

Ranald looked thoughtful. "My dad does that," he said.

Bertie nodded. "So I've heard, Ranald."

They managed to avoid Olive and Pansy coming out of the church, but when they reached the reception there was to be no escape.

"You and your friends are going to be sitting at a nice wee table specially for you," said Big Lou, as she greeted them at the Mansfield Traquair Centre. "And we've got lots of cakes and sweets for you. And Irn-Bru too. Lots of that."

Olive and Pansy were already at the table when Bertie and Ranald arrived to take their seats.

"So, Bertie Pollock," said Olive, fixing Bertie with a triumphant gaze. "Here you are at a wedding after all."

Bertie did not know how to respond. He and Ranald stared silently at Olive.

"I must say that I'm pleased to see you here," Olive continued. "After all, it's a good opportunity for you to practise."

Bertie continued to look at her suspiciously.

"I don't think he even knows what you're talking about," interjected Pansy. "You know how stupid boys are."

Olive considered this for a moment. "You may be right about boys in general, Pansy," she said. "But I think Bertie knows fine well what this is all about."

"I don't," muttered Bertie. "I don't know what you're talking about, Olive."

Olive's eyes narrowed. "Oh, you don't, Bertie Pollock? You say you don't? Well, let me tell you." She paused, her gaze fixed on Bertie as if she were sizing up a victim. "Should I let you know what I was thinking?"

"Yes," urged Pansy. "You tell him, Olive."

"I was thinking of how this was good practice for you on how to behave at a wedding. That's what I was thinking."

Pansy rubbed her hands together. "You have to know what to do," she said. "So you've been able to watch what's going on here and see what you'll have to do when—"

"When you and I get married," Olive crowed. "Because I can tell you one thing, Bertie. That's one wedding that's definitely, totally going to take place."

"Totally," echoed Pansy. "Probably right here."

Olive frowned. "I'm not sure that I want to commit myself to hiring this actual hall. I'll have to wait and see how they do things today."

"If they're good enough, then you can," Pansy suggested.

"Yes," said Olive. "We'll wait and see. But the important thing is that you should watch it all very carefully. I don't want any mistakes at our wedding – when it takes place."

"But I don't want to marry you," Bertie said quietly. "I never asked you, Olive."

"You did so!" hissed Olive. "And don't you forget: I've got it in writing. You signed, Bertie Pollock – and you can't go round signing promises to marry people and then pretend you didn't."

"That's not the way it works, Bertie," said Pansy. "Even your stupid friend Ranald Braveheart Macpherson knows that."

"He's not stupid," muttered Bertie.

"You're the stupid one, Olive," said Ranald Braveheart Macpherson.

Olive spun round. "You'd better take that back, Ranald Braveheart Macpherson," she spat. "If you don't, you'll be kicked out of the Mansfield Traquair Centre. I'll tell Big Lou and they'll throw you out."

Pansy rose to her feet. "I'm going to go and tell her right now," she said.

Olive restrained her. "Not just yet, Pansy. If Ranald apologises we'll let him off this time."

Bertie nudged his friend. "Just say sorry, Ranald," he whispered. "It's not worth it."

Ranald's grudging apology was accepted by a smirking Olive. "Now," she said, "we can get on with enjoying this party before the dancing starts."

She looked at Bertie. "I hope that you and Ranald know how to do a Non-binary Gordons," she said.

Bertie looked at the floor, as did Ranald. He was just about to reply that he was not sure, when Pansy suddenly let out a piercing scream.

"Olive!" she shouted. "Look what that horrible little boy has done!"

They all turned to look at Ulysses, who, unnoticed by any of the other children, had just finished licking every cake on the large plate of iced cakes that the caterers had set out for the children.

"Disgusting!" shrieked Olive. "Look at your disgusting little brother, Bertie. That's your fault. He's totally your fault."

Ulysses beamed at his accusers. "Cake," he said. "Nice."

Olive shrieked again. "What are you going to do about that, Bertie? You'd better do something quick."

"I don't mind eating them," said Bertie nonchalantly. "Do you, Ranald?"

"Not at all," said Ranald. "I don't mind getting a few germs from Ulysses."

"They say our food is too clean anyway," Bertie said. "If you don't get a few germs now and then, you get allergies."

"Bertie's right," said Ranald Braveheart Macpherson, helping himself to one of the cakes. "Look, I'm eating this and I'm not getting sick, am I?"

Olive's mouth pursed in fury. "You wait, Ranald Braveheart Macpherson. You just wait. Those germs take a bit of time to work, but you'll almost certainly be dead really soon."

"Exactly," said Pansy. "Totally dead. By four o'clock tomorrow afternoon, Ranald Braveheart Macpherson. You just see."

"Half past three, max," added Olive.

On the other side of the hall, Domenica looked across towards the children's table. "How nice to see the youngsters enjoying themselves," she said to Angus.

Angus nodded. "Like little angels."

"Childhood," commented Sister Maria-Fiore dei Fiori di Montagna. "A time of innocent pleasure and pleasant innocence."

Antonia Collie sighed. She had already had two glasses of Italian sparkling wine. "Oh really," she said.

"*Carissima*," whispered Sister Maria-Fiore dei Fiore di Montagna, leaning forward, "*Chiudi il becco, per piacere.*"

It was not the language one expected from a nun, but at least, as Domenica noticed, Sister Maria-Fiore dei Fiori di Montagna had added *per piacere*. These things make a difference.

14

The Reel of the Fifty-First

The wedding reception at the Mansfield Traquair Centre lasted until eight o'clock that night. By that time, the dancing had been going on for three hours more or less without interruption, the ceilidh band gamely working its way through its repertoire, and the guests fortifying themselves against exhaustion with draughts of chilled lager, drams of whisky, or cups of tea. Jackets were removed, sporrans transferred to the sides of waists, and heeled shoes abandoned on the floor. It seemed to Domenica, who, with Angus, sat out two dances in three, that some sort of mass catharsis was taking place – that reserves of pent-up energy, long suppressed in the sedate climate of Edinburgh, were being released with sudden and profound abandon. So might dervishes whirl to induce a state of heightened spiritual awareness – finding, as did these dancers, a sense of communion with something just beyond their immediate surroundings.

At eight, Big Lou caught the eye of the leader of the band, and nodded. She had discussed with him the point at which the party might end, and he was certainly ready. Fat Bob, though, was keen for a final dance – just one more Gay Gordons, he said, and then the curtain could come down. The band leader smiled, and agreed. He announced the dance. "Ladies and gentlemen, boys and girls, Bob and Lou have given us all a wonderful party, but every party has to come to an end. So take your partners, please, for a final Gay Gordons."

The guests paired off, willingly, or stoically, according to the extent of their enthusiasm for Scottish country dancing. Angus rose to his feet with a sigh that he quickly suppressed under Domenica's look of disapproval; Matthew, who liked dancing and who, as a teenager, had undergone long hours of lessons in Scottish country dance, needed no encouragement to lead Elspeth to the floor; Bertie, who looked about for an escape route but found none, was dragged onto the floor by Olive, while Ranald Braveheart Macpherson was similarly press-ganged by Pansy.

"You just pay attention to me, Ranald Braveheart Macpherson," warned Pansy. "I'll show you the steps – all you have to do is follow them. I'll lead. You just do what I say."

Ranald glared at her. "That's not the way it works, Pansy," he said. "I'm seven, remember – I'm not stupid. I was watching the Gay Gordons earlier on. The man takes the lady's hand and twirls it round before they do that sort of round and round dance. I saw it."

Pansy shook her head, almost in pity. "Oh, you are so *yesterday*, Ranald. That's not how it works these days. Men do what women say in dances. That's what happens these days – sorry, but that's where we are."

Ranald looked about him. He could refuse to dance. He could just sit down. Pansy thought she could tell him what to do, but she could not *force* him to dance the Gay Gordons.

"You can't force me," he muttered. "I don't have to dance the Gay Gordons if I don't want to."

Pansy glared at him. "You'd better be very, very careful, Ranald Braveheart Macpherson," she said.

Ranald swallowed hard. It was difficult to stand up to Pansy, who was almost as bad as Olive; but you had to do it, he decided, because otherwise life in Edinburgh would become unbearable.

"No," said Ranald. "I'd prefer not to dance, Pansy."

Pansy's eyes narrowed. "I'm giving you one last warning,

Ranald," she said.

Ranald hesitated. Bertie was already on the floor with Olive, and Pansy was a formidable foe. He sighed. There would be other opportunities to take a stand.

On the other side of the room, seated around one of the smaller tables, two middle-aged couples had decided to sit the final dance out. They had danced some of the earlier dances, including a demanding "Duke of Perth" and a "Reel of the Fifty-First", but now they gave the appearance of being somewhat dispirited.

They had been invited because they were regular customers of Big Lou's in her coffee bar, and when she had found that she had a few spare places at the wedding, she had decided to include them on the list. The men were her customers – their wives had been in the coffee bar once or twice, but she barely knew them. The men were, of course, Mackie McIntyre and his old friend, Iain McDonald, the Chairman and Secretary respectively of the Association of Scottish Nudists, a national organisation with its headquarters in nearby Moray Place, one of Edinburgh's most prestigious addresses. The association occupied two floors on the north side of the elegant Georgian crescent, and enjoyed sweeping views over the gorge of the Water of Leith below and, in the distance, beyond the Firth, the blue hills of Fife.

Mackie was married to Jane, a cookery writer, and Iain was married to Catriona, a veterinary surgeon who specialized in skin diseases in West Highland Terriers. All four of them were prominent naturists, having met in the movement, Mackie and Jane at a meeting of the International Nudist Federation in Geneva, and Iain and Catriona at the Scottish and Irish Nudist Games in County Wexford.

Now Mackie watched the couples assembling for the final Gay Gordons. "It's not quite the same," he remarked, a tinge of sadness in his voice.

"The band's been good," said Iain.

Catriona agreed. "Really good," she said. "That fiddler is wonderful."

"Yes," said Mackie. "But what I mean is that the dancing hasn't been as much fun as it was in Largs. Remember when we all went down to Largs, to that campground, and we had that dance on the last day? Remember that? We did an eightsome together with the Sinclairs and . . .", he searched his memory, "that couple from Melrose. Remember? They'd never been to a naturist gathering before. He wanted to wear a sporran, but was persuaded otherwise."

"Everyone has his or her way of coping with initial awkwardness," said Catriona. "And the weather was glorious. And we danced outside on the grass."

"Such happiness," mused Mackie. "Those days seemed to glow, didn't they?"

"The past has that aura," Iain said. He paused before continuing, "Do you think Scotland has changed? Have we lost the innocence we once had?"

"Was it innocence?" asked Jane.

"I'm not sure," said Mackie. "Maybe it was. But the point is that we have always been a country where people have felt happy within themselves. They may not have had much, but they felt love for their country and that made them happy. It's very curious."

"Not curious," said Iain. "Clothing is the metaphor here. Clothing obscures the spirit underneath. Clothing is an addition. Take your clothes off, and how do you feel? Liberated. If only more people in Scotland would take their clothes off."

"Oh, we all know that," said Mackie.

They looked at one another, and for a few moments a current of sympathy flowed between them. It was sympathy that meant so much, thought Mackie. David Hume and

Adam Smith had explained that in their system of moral philosophy. *Sympathy*. And if you were naked, sympathy was so much easier to feel, because sympathy needed no clothing, no artifice, no disguise.

15

The Perfect Bacon Roll

Were it not for the responsibility of running her coffee bar, Big Lou would undoubtedly have gone off on honeymoon – had Fat Bob suggested such a thing. But she did have that responsibility and Bob, in spite of several hints, subtle and otherwise, intended to implant the idea in his mind, had failed to produce the desired suggestion. So she had eventually reconciled herself to the fact that the trip to Norway that she would so much have loved to make, would simply not take place, and that instead of waking up on a honeymoon cruise she would instead find herself starting the day, as usual, in her flat in Canonmills, and proceeding with her regular routine. That involved preparing breakfast for Bob and her adopted son, Finlay, and then, after Finlay had been dropped off at school in Stockbridge, making her way up the hill to Dundas Street. There, in the small food preparation area behind the stainless-steel bar of her coffee shop, she would start preparing the bacon rolls that she knew her regular customers would order when they began to arrive in dribs and drabs from eight onwards.

Lou knew that to some extent it was these bacon rolls that prevented her from ever getting away on holiday, or, indeed, on honeymoon. The making of a bacon roll is not the most complicated task facing any cook, but it is one that, if it is to be done well, requires a certain set of skills that some people simply do not have. Big Lou had often thought about this, and had decided that the most important of these skills was a *feeling for bacon*. She had talked to Angus about that once and he, perceptive and sympathetic friend that he was, had immediately understood what she meant by that phrase.

"A feeling for bacon, Lou? Yes, I think I know what you mean."

Big Lou explained further. "I'm not boasting, Angus. I'm not saying that I'm one of the best cooks in Scotland or anything like that."

"Of course you aren't, Lou. And look, I think I know what you mean. The world is full of soggy bacon rolls."

Lou nodded. "Aye, you're right there, Angus. People think that all there is to a bacon roll is a roll – any old roll, in fact – and a couple of rashers of bacon. I have had some terrible bacon rolls in my time."

"And so have I," said Angus, shuddering at the memory. And now one or two of these rolls came back to him, just as the madeleine cakes came back to Proust, but without the warm connotations that the cakes had for young Marcel.

"I had to go down to London," Angus continued. "I was on a committee that met in London once a year and they used to send me a rail ticket – second class – to go down for that. I had a bacon roll on the train, and it was an utter travesty. Soft white bread – tasteless – and floppy, discouraged bacon, pink and limp, and far too salty, as I recall. The grease from the bacon had soaked down through the roll, making it even limper. It was a perfect storm of a bacon roll – *panis horribilis*, so to speak. Ghastly."

Big Lou shook her head. "And I imagine it wasn't cheap."

"Certainly not," said Angus. "I forget what it was exactly, but not much change out of five pounds." He paused. "Of course, those who were travelling first class got that travesty of a bacon roll free, but even that is overpriced."

Big Lou looked sad. "If only people would stand up to that sort of thing. If only they would stand up to people selling them that sort of unhealthy rubbish."

Angus thought about this for a moment. "Actually, Lou, can *any* bacon roll – even a well-made one – be considered healthy?" He gave her a sideways glance; he did not want to offend. "It's just that bacon . . . well, I thought we were being encouraged to eat less of it. I don't think it's the healthiest of meats. And white rolls – well, they're not all that good for us. And they're full of the wrong sort of carbs."

For a few moments Big Lou did not reply. Then she said, "Everything in moderation, Angus."

"You mean it's all right if one eats bacon infrequently?"

Big Lou nodded. "Yes. No more than once a day."

Angus considered this. "Once a *day*, Lou?"

Big Lou nodded. "My aunt used to make bacon rolls for the *orra man* on the farm. She made one in the morning when he arrived for work, one at lunchtime, and one for him to take home for his tea. He lived just outside Arbroath, you see – not far from Snell Mains. He was a good man – and a great accordionist. He sang bothy ballads."

"And ate rather a lot of bacon rolls?"

"He didn't think it was too much."

"Is he still with us?" asked Angus.

Big Lou shook her head sadly. "He's deid," she said. "Poor fellow."

"Ah," said Angus. He was not proposing to be tactless, but what could one expect?

"He just made his ninety-second birthday," went on Big Lou. "He was a keen curler, and he dropped down on the curling rink. It was the way he wanted to go."

Angus said nothing at first. Then he asked Lou what were the criteria of a good bacon roll.

"Slightly crisp bacon," she said. "But not too crisp. You often find it too crisp in the BT sandwiches, or is it BLT sandwiches?"

"BLT," said Angus. "You shouldn't get that mixed up."

"Acronyms," sighed Big Lou. "There are so many of them these days, what's a body to do? Yes, anyway, the bacon should be just right – neither overdone nor underdone. And it must not be too salty. Folk use far too much and the result is that all you taste is the salt. Then the roll itself should be crispish. Not too dry – a dry roll is no good at all – but you want a bit of firmness. And you must have butter. Some people say that you don't need to use butter, but you do. You have to have butter."

"Oh, Lou," said Angus. "My mouth is watering."

"Purely Pavlovian," said Lou.

Now, as she opened up the coffee bar on the Monday following her wedding, she thought of how the bacon rolls tied her down because there was nobody who could make them for her. James, the young man who worked in the coffee bar several days a week, only arrived at ten, and she had been unable to find staff who were prepared to come in for an early shift. And even if she did find such people, would they be able to make a good bacon roll? Lou doubted it. She could try to train them, of course, but Big Lou had discovered something about people that she had not known before: they did not want to learn, because an awful lot of people, in her experience, thought they knew everything already.

So she sighed, turned on the coffee machine and the oven, and started her day: day three of her married life – and Fat Bob was still fast asleep back in Canonmills – as far as she knew.

But he was not.

16

'The lightning is all about me'

At nine-thirty that morning Bruce came into Big Lou's coffee bar. This was a surprise for Lou, who had not seen him since he was struck by lightning. She knew that this had happened, of course, as the incident had been widely reported and Bruce had been given a full page in the *Daily Record* as well as one in *The Scotsman*. There had been other articles too, including one in the *Oban Times*, in which Bruce, in addition to being asked about his unfortunate experience, had also been invited to give a playlist of ten favourite tunes and propose a guest list for an ideal dinner party. Sean Connery, he had written; Billy Connolly; Tom Hanks; Nicola Sturgeon; Ruth Davidson; the Pope; Hillary Clinton . . . But now here was, looking very similar to the way he had looked prior to the lightning strike, even if there was something slightly different about his hair.

Big Lou had never really approved of Bruce. She was modest, and Bruce was anything but that. Big Lou rarely bothered to look in mirrors – Bruce could seldom resist them. Big Lou occasionally used a moisturiser, and even then tended to prefer a thin layer of petroleum jelly (the moisturiser used by her grandmother, and her grandmother's mother before her). Bruce, by contrast, used moisturiser every morning and evening, preferring an expensive brand developed in a laboratory in Geneva for which he paid roughly forty times the price of petroleum jelly.

Big Lou greeted Bruce warmly. Those who have been struck by lightning are in some way taken out of the common herd in which the rest of us mingle. It is as if they have been touched by divine fire and should be addressed with all the respect that should be accorded those whom the gods have singled out in any way.

"Bruce," exclaimed Big Lou. "This is a very pleasant surprise, so it is. And you look so well . . ."

Bruce inclined his head. "No complaints, Lou," he said.

Lou waited for Bruce to say something about his experience, but he did not. And so she said, "A bacon roll?"

Bruce said that this was just what he needed. "I'm meeting somebody," he said. "I suggested that we meet here."

"Well, there are plenty of tables free."

Bruce looked about him. "A doctor," he said.

Big Lou wiped her stainless-steel counter top with a white cloth. "Oh, yes?"

"He's doing research on lightning victims," Bruce went on. "He wants to find out about my experiences for a book he's working on. I want to help him."

"Of course you do," said Big Lou.

"And others too," Bruce continued. "I want to help other people, Lou. I really do."

There was something about the way that he spoke that made Big Lou hesitate. Was this the same Bruce she had known – the pre-lightning-strike – Bruce, who had been such a complete narcissist? Who had had a succession of girlfriends – foolish girls who *threw themselves* at him but never lasted for every long. One should never *throw oneself* at a man, Big Lou thought – and she had seen that happen quite literally, at a dance in Arbroath a long time ago, when a woman known in the area for her desperation to find a man – any man – had thrown herself at one of the local farmers who happened to be single and in need of a wife. She had knocked him over, fracturing his arm in the process. No, you should *never* throw yourself at a man.

"I've addressed issues in my life," Bruce said. "I've come

to realise that I was wasting my time. I've been far too self-obsessed, Lou."

Big Lou drew in her breath. "Well, Bruce, this is . . ." She trailed off, uncertain how to articulate the doubts and questions she had.

"I know you will find it surprising," Bruce said. "And I wouldn't be surprised if you were sceptical, Lou. But I mean it, you know."

Lou hastened to assure him that she did not disbelieve him. "Folk can change," she said. "I've seen it happen before."

"Well, there you are. And these people who changed – I assume they weren't even struck by lightning."

Big Lou grinned. "No, they weren't." She thought for a moment. "One of them got religion. He—"

Bruce interrupted her. "I'm going up to Pluscarden," he said.

Big Lou gasped. "To the abbey? You're going to become a monk? You?"

Bruce kept his voice even. "We are all looking for something, Lou."

"Oh, I know," said Big Lou. "But you . . ."

"Are you suggesting I don't know what I'm looking for? Is that what you think?"

She shook her head. This was becoming a very difficult conversation, but fortunately, at that precise moment, a tall man in a lightweight linen jacket entered the café and looked about him. His eye fell on Bruce.

"Mr Anderson," he said. "Bruce Anderson?"

"The very same," said Bruce.

"I am Dr Livingstone," said the man.

"If you sit down," Big Lou said to Bruce, "I'll bring your coffee to the table. And your bacon roll." She paused, and now addressed the newcomer. "What will you have, Doctor?"

Dr Livingstone turned to her. "An Americano," he said.

They went to the table, where Dr Livingstone fixed Bruce with a piercing stare. "I want you to talk to me as a researcher. You are not my patient, you know," he said. "Forget that I am a psychiatrist."

"I had already forgotten it," said Bruce.

"Good," said Dr Livingstone. "Now we can start: have you ever dreamed of being struck by lightning? Ever?"

"It's nothing to do with my dreams," said Bruce quickly. "That lightning was a sign. The lightning was all about me."

Dr Livingstone smiled. "How interesting," he said. And then he added, "Do tell me more, Mr Anderson."

"Bruce," said Bruce.

"Of course," said Dr Livingstone.

He threw a discreet sideways glance in Bruce's direction. *The lightning was all about me?* English was a stressed language only to a limited extent. But sometimes stress was crucial. "The lightning was all about *me*" was solipsistic; whereas "the lightning was all *about* me" was descriptive of being surrounded by lightning – as one is, no doubt, at the moment of being struck. You could never be sure about words, especially when words were used to describe the ineffably shocking. He remembered, curiously, unexpectedly, that sentence from *Catch-22* about how Kid Sampson, felled by a propellor, had *rained* all over. Impersonal verbs should not be personal – except sometimes, it seemed. He shuddered as he struggled to put the image out of his mind. To be struck by lightning, it seemed, although troubling, could be a better fate than some, not that one would wish quite so many volts on another – except sometimes, perhaps.

17

The Pronunciation of Gullane (Again)

That morning, not all that far from Big Lou's coffee bar, on the eastern side of Scotland Street, behind a Georgian window, with its white-painted astragals and its Palladian proportions, Stuart Pollock sat across the breakfast table from his mother, Nicola, ex-wife of an unfaithful Portuguese wine producer, proprietrix of the Glasgow pie factory now trading as Inclusive Pies, and grandmother – now mother-substitute – to the two small boys, Bertie and Ulysses.

The adults were by themselves. Ulysses had had a disturbed night – he had been projectile vomiting – and was having a long lie-in to catch up on sleep; Bertie had gone out with their neighbour, Angus Lordie, to walk Angus's dog, Cyril, in the Drummond Place Garden. It was the school holidays now, and although both children had been enrolled in a holiday club, it had not yet convened and several days at home were in the offing. Fortunately for Stuart, his mother provided full-time care for the boys, and indeed had moved in, leaving her own flat in Northumberland Street to be on hand for the boys' needs. Nicola had been happy to take on that role when Stuart's wife Irene had gone to study for a PhD in Aberdeen with her close personal friend, Dr Hugo Fairbairn, now Professor Fairbairn, author of that classic of child psychotherapy, *Shattered to Pieces: Ego Dissolution in a Three-Year-Old Tyrant*.

If Stuart had been relieved to see Irene go, then Nicola had been overjoyed. She had never approved of her son's wife, and had endured years of condescension from her. When the marriage had run into difficulty – all of it Irene's fault, Nicola was convinced – she had seen this as the chance for the hauden-doon Stuart at last to make something of his life – and he had done that – to an extent. Aberdeen was far enough away for a fresh start, Nicola thought, although she would have preferred it had Irene gone even further afield – to Shetland perhaps – there was a lot to be said for Unst – or even the Faroes. And there was always Iceland, of course, or Northern Scandinavia, although, *faute de mieux*, Aberdeen would do.

But now Nicola sat at the table, a pained look on her face, her mouth half open, as if she had been about to say something before being abruptly interrupted.

"She's what?" she stuttered. "She said she's what?"

"Coming back," said Stuart.

He was holding his telephone before him, and now he scrolled down the screen, his expression darkening as he did so.

"This is what she's written," he said. "Listen. 'I have decided to spend two months of the summer in Edinburgh, and so I shall be arriving towards the end of this week. Don't worry about being there to let me in, as I still have my key. I'll have the spare room. I can bring sheets if necessary. Let me know. And, by the way, you'd better let that . . .'" Stuart's voice trailed off.

"That what?" Nicola pressed. "You'd better let that what?"

Stuart swallowed. "I don't like the way she puts this," he said.

"You can say that again," said Nicola. "I've never liked the way she puts *anything*. What does she say, Stuart?"

Stuart read out the rest of the message from Irene. "'You'd better let that woman know that I'm coming and that she can go back to her own flat.'"

He looked at his mother apologetically. "I don't think she means to be rude."

Nicola laughed. "But that's exactly what she *does* mean," she said.

Stuart bit his lip. "She goes on to say why she's coming to Edinburgh. She wants to do some work in the National Library of Scotland. It's to do with her PhD thesis."

Nicola's lip curled. "Hah!" she said. "We could all do a PhD and go off to Aberdeen, couldn't we? Or Florence, for that matter. Or Paris. Or anywhere, really. Anywhere where we happen to have a lover, that is. *I'm off to do a PhD.* Wonderful. And who will look after the children, might one ask? *That woman* – that's who."

"Mother," said Stuart, trying to calm her. "There's no point—"

Nicola cut him short. "And so she imagines that I'll move out now that she's coming back for a few months? Well, Stuart, you need to take command of this situation."

"I know, Mother, I know. I've been thinking—"

Again, she stopped him. "You've been thinking? The time for *thinking*, Stuart is most decisively over. You need to get back to her and remind her that she no longer has any claim to this house. Your marriage is over, Stuart, and she can't come along and move back in when she wants to."

"I suppose so."

"Good. So, send a reply right now. Tell her that she's very welcome to come back to Edinburgh and that there are many Airbnbs from which she may select one to rent. Preferably on the other side of town. Burdiehouse, perhaps. Or Niddrie. Or even North Berwick or Gullane. It's very invigorating down there."

Stuart nodded. The mention of Gullane had reminded him that while Nicola pronounced it correctly – as *Gillin* – Irene had always insisted on calling it *Gullin*. That was because she considered *Gillin* to be a middle-class pronunciation, and therefore not one favoured by those with a finger on the common pulse.

"*Gillin*," he muttered.

"Yes," said Nicola. "*Gillin*. And don't you start, Stuart."

"I wasn't going to start."

"The etymology is clear," said Nicola. "We may not know what *Gullane* means, but we do know that it's Welsh."

"Yes," said Stuart. He was not really paying attention now.

"Because everybody round these parts spoke Welsh at one time," Nicola went on. "Or English. They did not speak Gaelic."

Stuart did not disagree.

"So, it's *Gillin*," concluded Nicola.

"I didn't say it wasn't," said Stuart.

Nicola had not quite finished. "May I ask you, Stuart: what is wrong with being middle-class? What is wrong with saying *Gillin* rather than *Gullin?*"

Stuart shrugged. "It's thought to be a bit . . . well, middle-class." He paused. "Not that I think it helpful to go on about things being middle-class. Or any sort of class, actually. We're all the same, aren't we? We're all Jock Tamson's bairns. Nobody is any better, or worse, than anybody else." He thought of Burns, and "A Man's a Man For a' That". That said it all, Stuart felt.

"I agree," said Nicola. "But *middle-class* is still used as a term of abuse, isn't it? By middle-class people, of course. Who pours scorn on middle-class attitudes? Middle-class social commentators, leading middle-class lives – that's who. Isn't that rich?"

Stuart sighed. "Oh well," he said. He knew that his mother was talking about Irene, who often expressed her contempt for the middle-class from which she had sprung. He looked at his phone. A further message had arrived from Irene. Now he read it out to Nicola: "'And I have enrolled Bertie in a camp. This is a sort of re-education camp for middle-class children. It's going to be at Carlops for ten days. They've confirmed his place.'"

Nicola's mouth opened in astonishment. "Re-education?" she stuttered.

"Perhaps she's joking," said Stuart. But he knew that Irene did not joke about such things. He groaned inwardly. He hated conflict.

For Nicola it was different. This was *war*, and the air was filled with the wail of the great war pipes of her ancestors. She was fighting for her grandchildren now, and nobody, neither Stuart nor even Irene herself, should be in any doubt about her determination. She was a lioness prepared to protect her cubs.

18

Energy Fields; Low Amperages

Matthew and Elspeth had originally not intended to take the boys to Big Lou's wedding, fearing that they would find it impossible not to interrupt proceedings. Although it would have been James' day off, he nonetheless offered to baby-sit, and they almost accepted. But then Big Lou had told them that she particularly wanted children present, and they had changed their minds.

They were grateful to James for his offer – and for everything. His handling of the boys was inspired and based on the principle of exhaustion – by far the best philosophy for the upbringing of small children. Each day had its projects, one after the other: he had built them a treehouse recently, and the boys themselves had constructed, under his supervision, a fort of sorts in the rhododendron bushes that were steadily encroaching over the four acres that surrounded the house. They had also made a pond, stocking it with carp, and they had dug a trap for elephants, although they had, to date, caught none. They loved him, of course, recognising, as small children so astutely will, a readiness to enter the anarchic imaginative world in which they spend the first few years of life. James had the gift of *fun* – something, Matthew observed, that you either had or you did not. It was genetic, he felt: those without that charismatic gene could try as hard as they might to enthuse others but would be destined to fail, no matter how hard they tried. Look at actors, he said: the ones who seem wooden will never be believed – they just won't. They don't have it.

"You can learn it at drama college, surely," said Elspeth.

"No," said Matthew flatly. "You can't. Look at the effect James has on the room when he comes in the door. Have you seen it? It's electric."

Elspeth knew what he was talking about. "He's lucky." She paused. "Do you think it's his teeth?"

Matthew thought about this. James had perfect, white teeth, which were revealed by a winning smile. Nobody could be indifferent to such teeth, Elspeth said, looking discreetly, but with some wistfulness, at Matthew's own, distinctly average dentition.

"I don't think it's just that," said Matthew. "He has an *energy field*. Some people just do." He paused. "You notice it with public figures – politicians, for instance. Some may talk sense, may seem thoroughly nice people, but just come across rated at one point three amps, at the most. No energy field. Undetectable. It's not their fault – it's just one of those things."

Elspeth smiled. Every so often Matthew would get on his hobby horse and sound off about various politicians and their high – or low – amperage, and their more egregious failings. He would try to be charitable, but there were still a few people whom he claimed he would never, under any circumstances, let in the house. It was not exactly an enemies list, of the sort that the late President Richard Nixon was alleged to have nurtured, but it was not far from it. Elspeth believed that the list currently had four names on it, two of whom she could imagine deserved their interdiction, while two were, she thought, being treated a bit harshly. She had once pointed out to Matthew that the chances of any of those on the list turning up at their house at Nine Mile Burn were infinitesimal, and he had replied that the list was not meant to be taken literally, but was, rather, a statement of disapproval. And you never knew, he said: sometimes people came into contact with one another in the most unexpected circumstances. He had met somebody whose great-aunt had in the nineteen-thirties bumped into Hitler while walking in a forest. She had been taken aback but had politely said, "Good afternoon, Mr Hitler." These things happened, and they showed that the idea of encountering the well-known was not entirely fanciful.

But now, on the day after the wedding, as Matthew and Elspeth sat over breakfast in their kitchen, he turned to her and said, "You know that guy who was wearing that plum-coloured jacket – rather like a Watsonian blazer? He was sitting at the next table but one."

Elspeth had noticed him. "Yes, he was with Shelley McElhose. She's my dental hygienist. But she's also a distant cousin of mine, remember. Third cousin, I think – or something like that. You've heard me mention her. That's her partner – Iain, I think he's called. He's a welder on the rigs. He does two weeks on, two weeks off. Shelley says she doesn't mind his being away because it gives her a bit of peace."

"Well," said Matthew, "I was talking to him when the band was taking a break. I'd met him before, you know. I can't remember where. It was somewhere."

Elspeth waited. "Talking about what?" Men talked about very mundane subjects, she always felt. It must be very dull to be a man, she thought – rather like being a crow or a common gull in an aviary full of colourful and rare South American birds.

Matthew hesitated. If there was a rule that one didn't talk ill of the dead, then there was another rule that forbade speculation as to the period that a recent marriage might last. And yet that had been the general tenor of the brief conversation that Iain had had with him at the wedding reception – a time and place when one might have thought the exclusionary rule applied with particular rigour.

"I thought he was being a bit tactless," he said now. "A bit

. . . How shall I put it – a bit *unsubtle*, perhaps."

Elspeth smiled. Poor Matthew, she thought. I love him so – enough to have actually married him, *and* conceived triplets with him – although that was a zygotic issue rather than the result of any deliberate choice – and yet he could be so . . . so *Edinburgh*. There, she thought: I have thought it. I have recognised what everyone knows about Edinburgh, but is too polite to spell out: the fact that Edinburgh, for all its claims, and for all its charms too, was ultimately rather *Edinburgh*.

"Tell me, Matthew," she urged. "Tell me what he said."

Matthew still felt uncomfortable. "I suppose he'd had a bit too much to drink."

"What did he say?" she repeated.

"And I suppose he's a bit rough and ready."

Elspeth burst out laughing. "A bit of rough?"

"That's not what I said," protested Matthew.

"Then say what he said rather than tell me that you didn't say what you said I said you said – which I didn't say, by the way."

Matthew closed his eyes. English was a strange language. Marriage was strange too.

19

Kitchen Confidential

"All right," said Matthew. "I'll tell you what Iain said at Big Lou's wedding. But don't, whatever you do, tell anybody – promise?"

Elspeth felt vaguely annoyed at being sworn to secrecy like this by her own husband. Of course she understood the confidentiality of the matrimonial kitchen, which was almost as sacrosanct, she felt, as the confidentiality of the matrimonial bedroom. Yet it was implicit, she felt, that what was said to one spouse might quite properly be divulged to the other by the spouse to whom the information was vouchsafed. That was how it worked – and everybody understood that. Of course, if one partner in a marriage was bound by professional secrecy, then confidential information conveyed under such a seal could not be shared with a spouse. Doctors should never tell their spouses or partners what they learn in the course of their professional life – and nor should lawyers or accountants. And although most, if not all, doctors respected that, unfortunately some lawyers and accountants did not; but that was another matter altogether.

Now she said to Matthew, in a slightly reproachful tone, "You know that I'm discreet."

He was apologetic. "Of course. Sorry. It's just that . . ." He sighed. "I wish he hadn't said it."

She struggled to conceal her irritation. "Said *what*, Matthew?"

"He said that it was going to end in tears."

"The marriage?"

Matthew nodded. "He said that we were all due for a big surprise when the truth came out about Bob. He gave me a knowing look and then, I'm afraid, he refused to say anything more. I asked him what he meant, but he just looked enigmatic and shook his head."

Elspeth frowned. She found it difficult to decide whether to discount this – people said all sorts of things at weddings, particularly after a few glasses of sparkling wine, and much of what was said could be written off as idle gossip or as shots fired, sometimes indiscriminately, in some ancient family squabble. Funeral teas were much the same: in one recent case in Glasgow, the Police Scotland riot squad had been called in – all forty members of it – to break up a disagreement at a wake between rival sides of a family. A water cannon had been brought over from Edinburgh and had helped to restore order, although it was a close-run thing. The armoured hearse kept for such obsequies had undoubtedly saved the day, with its puncture-proof tyres and its bullet-proof windscreen.

"It's most inconsiderate of him," Elspeth said. "You shouldn't tantalise people like that. Either you tell them everything, or you say nothing."

Matthew agreed.

"I think I'm going to ask her to tell me. She'll know."

Matthew was alarmed. "Her? That cousin of yours – the dental hygienist?"

"Shelley McElhose. Yes. Her. I could suggest we meet for lunch. I could ask her. She'll tell me."

Matthew became agitated. "No," he said, his voice rising. "You mustn't do that. You mustn't, Elspeth."

"Why not? If she doesn't want to tell me, she won't. I'm not going to twist her arm, or anything like that."

He shook his head. "No, definitely not. It's none of our business. If there's some bit of sordid scandal about Bob, I don't want to know it. Why should I? Or you, for that matter?

Other than out of vulgar curiosity."

Elspeth drew in her breath. "But what if it's something Big Lou should know? What then? We've known her for ages – years, really – and we know what a good person she is. What if this information that Iain has is something she truly needs to know? Wouldn't you tell her?"

Matthew did not disagree – at least immediately. But after a few minutes of silence, he came up with his response. "I don't think that it always helps to tell people everything. Let's say that Bob has some murky secret in his past. Let's say he treated somebody badly – that could be it, you know. Let's say that it is. But what if he's a different person now? People change, you know. Why drag up the past?"

"Oh, I know that people change," said Elspeth. "Sometimes they do. But sometimes they don't. It all depends, doesn't it?"

Matthew shook his head. "I just don't want to get involved. We could wreck everything. We can't assume that it would be the right thing to pass on whatever this thing is. We just don't know enough about any of this. Iain may have something against Bob for all we know. A grudge, perhaps. You know how vindictive people can be. Surely you see that?"

But Matthew was adamant. "Just don't," he said. "Keep out of it." And with that, he changed the subject, and started to talk about Edward McCosh, an artist who had a painting coming up at the next Lyon & Turnbull auction. "He paints in the style of the Dutch Masters of the seventeenth century. He does stunning studies of ornamental birds in a landscape. They're wonderful. When you look at them, you think you're looking at something by Melchior d'Hondecoeter or someone like that. But he's a contemporary – and he lives just outside Edinburgh. A master among us – waiting to be more widely discovered."

Elspeth knew his work. "They're very peaceful," she said. "That's the moral message behind them." She paused. "I think serious painting always has a moral message – even if it's a celebration of the everyday things of life."

"Oh, I agree," said Matthew.

Elspeth made a remark about the Peaceable Kingdom theme. "The lion shall lie down with the lamb – in some paintings."

"It can," said Matthew. "And it does."

Elspeth was thinking. She disagreed with Matthew about not trying to find out what Iain meant by his remark at the wedding reception. She had made up her mind: she would telephone Shelley and suggest that they meet for lunch. She would put her cards on the table. She would ask what it was that Iain knew, and tell Shelley that the two of them – she and Shelley – had a *duty* to warn Big Lou if she was in any way threatened. She would remind Shelley that women needed to stand by one another and that the masculine desire not to get involved – which was the position that Matthew, quite unreasonably, was adopting – was simply no longer acceptable. "Things have moved on," she would say, and it would be a rash person these days who would argue that they had not.

20

Lunch with a Dental Hygienist

Shelley McElhose was a woman of thirty-one, a dental hygienist who had qualified at Glasgow Caledonian University, and who had practised in Inverness and Fort William for several years before taking a job in Edinburgh. She was the eldest of the three children of a Mallaig fishing trawler owner, Robbie McElhose, a man whose prosperity had blossomed when he had inherited a second trawler and the fish quotas attached to it. He had been unstintingly supportive of his daughters' education, and had sent all three of them to Kilgraston School in Bridge of Earn, where their academic abilities had been assiduously encouraged. After leaving the school laden with academic honours, Shelley enrolled for a degree in oral health, while her sister, Flora, went on to study law at Dundee. To complete the picture of academic achievement, the youngest of the three, Julie, had completed a master's degree in Mandarin at the School of Oriental and African Studies in London. She was now employed in a department of an Edinburgh investment firm, where she wrote reports on the Chinese iron and steel sector.

Robbie was particularly pleased with Shelley's achievements, and had wept with pride when he and his wife attended her graduation in Glasgow.

"And she can do something useful," he said. "Dental hygiene is the way forward for Scotland, make no mistake. Those boys up in Mallaig . . ." These were his fellow fishermen, known as "the boys". "Some of them have frightful problems with their teeth. They could do with a bit of this dental hygiene from Glasgow Caledonian, I can tell you."

When Shelley took up with Iain, Robbie's reaction was lukewarm, at best. "I'm sure he's a nice enough fellow," he said, "but I know some of those people who work on the rigs, and I was hoping that you'd do a bit better, if you see my meaning, Shelley."

She had been careful not to hurt his feelings, but she was not going to pay any attention to this. Parents were like that – they often wanted something slightly better for their children, without realising that the only question a parent of a daughter should ask about her partner was: *is he kind?* That was enough. Nothing more was needed.

In fact, in Shelley's case it was a bit more complicated than that. What Robbie felt – but was not expressing – was a doubt that Iain was his daughter's intellectual equal. And that doubt was perhaps well-founded. Iain was nowhere near as bright as Shelley, as was apparent from the one-sided conversation that was the norm between them. Shelley would make a comment and wait for a reaction from Iain, who would often simply grunt in a non-committal way. It was far from being an equal relationship in matters of the mind.

Shortly after Matthew left to drive into work that morning, Elspeth found herself standing by the telephone, poised to dial Shelley's number. She found that her hand was shaking as she picked up the receiver. What she was doing was something that Matthew had very specifically asked her not to do. But he had not discussed it with her before he more or less forbade her – and that was the general tenor of the language he used, even if he had not used the word *forbid*. A husband had no right to do that any longer: you could not tell your spouse what to do. You could ask for something not to be done, but you could not say "I forbid you".

And so, in a spirit of principled resistance, she decided that she would call Shelley and arrange to see her. And Shelley, it transpired, was only too eager to meet for lunch. "I really like to get out in the lunch hour," she said, "but I often have nowhere to go. I don't like to sit by myself in some café somewhere. So I'm really pleased that you phoned. We need to catch up. You heard that Auntie Elsie died?"

Elspeth had. "She was a real character," she said.

"She had awful teeth," said Shelley.

"Oh well, she made it to eighty-nine."

They agreed to meet at the Canny Man's in Morningside, which would not involve too long a drive for Elspeth and where they could have a light lunch before Shelley went back to her dental studio.

After a brief catch-up on news of the extended family, much of it to do with cousins whom Elspeth had never met and indeed, in some cases, never heard of, Elspeth said, "I need to speak to you about something very difficult, Shelley. Woman to woman."

Shelley gasped. "Oh my God," she said. "You too?"

Elspeth looked blank.

"I mean, you're having matrimonial problems," explained Shelley. "Same as so many people you meet."

Elspeth laughed nervously. "Oh no, everything's fine between Matthew and me. It's just that . . ." She hesitated, and then she told Shelley exactly what Matthew had said to her. Then she waited for the reaction.

Shelley sighed. "Men," she said.

Elspeth waited. *Men* was an eloquent comment, but a little bit more detail would be required.

"It's true," said Shelley. "Iain first spoke to me about it a few weeks ago. He told me that there's this man who works on the rigs with him – an electrician, he said – who's really got it in for Fat Bob. He said this man – the electrician – told him that he knows that Fat Bob had an affair with his wife. *Had.* Past tense. But he hasn't forgiven him and he said that he has seen Fat Bob with another woman down in Leith. He said he's seen them together three or four times – even after Fat Bob became engaged to Big Lou. He says it goes to show what sort of man Fat Bob really is. He's quite happy to two-time right up to the wedding – and afterwards, apparently."

Elspeth absorbed this in silence. Then she said, "And he's sure this is still going on?"

"That's what he said."

Elspeth shook her head. "That's awful. We all thought he was so nice."

"Yes," said Shelley. "But we all love Big Lou. It really hurts to hear this sort of thing. But I suppose there's not much one can do about it."

"Should we tell her?" asked Elspeth. "Should we warn her?"

Shelley looked up at the ceiling of the café. "I think that if we left it, it's always possible he might stop seeing this other woman and he and Lou might sort things out. But if we interfere at this stage, then it could bring everything crashing down. At least not doing anything means there's a chance."

"A very small one," said Elspeth.

"But still a chance."

Elspeth looked doubtful, but decided that Shelley probably had a point. "I suppose so," she said.

21

Airbag Issues

They finished their lunch and, after they had parted with inchoate plans to meet in the Canny Man's again, Shelley returned to her probing of gums and her scaling and polishing of teeth. Elspeth had driven into town from Nine Mile Burn and had parked the car some distance away, not far from the Dominion Cinema. There were endemic roadworks, with barriers and temporary traffic lights, and so rather than heading for Morningside Road she decided on a circuitous route that would take her home along Colinton Road. And it was there, as she drove past the tennis courts beneath Craiglockhart Hill, that a cyclist swerved out in front of her. Elspeth reacted quickly, but in such a way as to take her straight into the path of an oncoming bus.

The bus driver braked and managed to avoid what would otherwise have been a head-on collision. But this swift response was not enough to prevent Elspeth from veering off to the left and only coming to a halt when she hit a lamppost with a thud of crumpling metal. The impact inflated the airbag, and she found herself pushed back against the seat, struggling for breath.

A man cutting his garden hedge dropped his electric clippers and ran to her assistance.

"My dear, are you all right?"

Elspeth struggled to free herself from the embrace of the airbag. Witnessing this, the man reached into his pocket, extracted a penknife and punctured the bag. A prolonged hiss, almost a sigh, uncompressed her.

"Thank you," she said. "You're so kind."

It was an Edinburgh accident. People were polite, even *in extremis*.

"Not at all," said the man, adding, "Any time."

He wondered whether to introduce himself. "I'm . . ."

Elspeth began to rise from her seat, but immediately lowered herself again as she felt the stab of sharp pain across her chest. She gasped. The man looked at her with concern.

"An ambulance?" he asked. "Shall I phone for an ambulance? Please allow me."

She nodded silently. He made the call on a phone he had extracted from a back pocket.

"They said to wait," he said, adding, apologetically, "and the police are coming too."

Ten minutes later the ambulance could be heard on its way, siren wailing. There was no sign of the police.

"It's not their fault," sighed Elspeth's rescuer. "They're snowed under with paperwork."

"It's not an emergency," muttered Elspeth. "They don't need to make such a fuss."

"They need to get you to hospital," he said.

The ambulance arrived. With brisk efficiency two paramedics helped Elspeth from the car and onto a stretcher. She winced with each movement.

"We'll get you in quickly," one of the paramedics said. She smiled. "They'll give you something to make you feel a bit better."

Elspeth wanted to cry. She looked out at the car before the ambulance door was closed. It seemed crumpled and dejected. She wiped a tear from her eye. It hurt to breathe. *I'm going to die*, she thought suddenly. *This is how it ends. In an ambulance; on Colinton Road; in summer; with the sky empty of clouds and a man cutting his hedge and this kind woman in her green uniform holding my hand. This is how it will be.*

And she thought of Matthew, and of her boys, of Fergus, Rognvald and Tobermory, and of the house at Nine Mile Burn and of how she loved it and how she had gone off and seen Shelley in defiance of Matthew's wishes. He would never do anything that I asked him not to do, she thought. And yet I have done just that, and now he will find out that I have ignored his wishes.

The ambulance moved off. Elspeth lay back, in spite of the pain that came with every movement.

"Where does it hurt?" asked one of the paramedics.

Elspeth opened her mouth to answer, and felt another sharp pain. It hurt to describe the hurt. She pointed to her chest.

The paramedic gently drew back Elspeth's blouse. "Airbag?" she asked.

Elspeth nodded.

"I wouldn't be surprised if you'd broken a rib," said the paramedic. "That sometimes happens with these things. They save your life, but can occasionally break a rib."

They arrived at the Royal Infirmary. Wheeled in on a stretcher, Elspeth was taken into a treatment room, a curtained-off area off a corridor. A nurse came, and called her *hen*, an old-fashioned Scottish term of endearment. Elspeth found it comforting. It made dying easier, she thought.

Then a doctor arrived and examined Elspeth's side and chest. "I'm concerned that you seem a bit breathless. Perhaps we should give you an X-ray, which we wouldn't otherwise do. It looks to me as if you've broken a rib. That can be pretty uncomfortable."

Elspeth waited half an hour for her X-ray, which was then interpreted by the first doctor who had seen her.

"Fracture," she said. "Seventh rib. Undisplaced – which means the bones are still in alignment. That's fortunate. There's no collapsed lung, as far as I can see. Altogether . . ."

She smiled as she looked at Elspeth. "Altogether not too bad. Nothing we need to treat."

The painkillers administered to Elspeth were having their effect, dulling the stabs of pain to a numbed, bearable throbbing. She closed her eyes with relief and fished for her phone in the bag that had accompanied her to hospital. But as she started to dial, she thought, *How can I tell him?* She could not, and without giving it further thought, she decided not to tell Matthew where she had been, and what she had been doing, when she had the accident. She did not mean to lie, but her mind was cloudy – perhaps through a combination of stress and co-codamol. She keyed in Matthew's number and he answered almost immediately.

She told him she was in hospital, but that it was nothing more serious than a cracked rib.

Matthew's voice broke with concern as he asked her where the accident had happened.

She hesitated for a moment. Was there any reason for him to know? "I'd been to the supermarket," she said. "I was coming back. It was on Colinton Road."

That was half true, she thought. And then she told herself, *I have lied to my husband.* It was undeniably true: she had lied, but, as often happens, lies don't stop the traffic or halt birds in their flight: they go out into the world with impunity, unchallenged because people are too tired or browbeaten to object, or because they have lost the ability to discern where the truth lies. And the skies don't fall either: so, when Elspeth was helped out to the car park by Matthew, solicitous and anxious, to be driven home, she saw that the heavens above were still there, in spite of her egregious lie. But that sky had seen so many lies told beneath it, millennia of mistruths, and had perhaps become inured to them.

22

Babar, Apollo, Contrition

That evening, although it was meant to be his evening off, James insisted on taking care of the boys, corralling them into their bath and then reading them their bedtime story – not only one, but two Babar books. There were tears from Rognvald when the old king of the elephants ate a poisonous mushroom and succumbed – tears that proved infectious, as Tobermory and Fergus soon joined in. This led to a prolonged discussion about mushrooms, death, and the role of prime ministers in a constitutional monarchy, which James assumed was the prevailing governmental system in de Brunhoff's Land of the Elephants. The story, with interruptions and questions, lasted a long time.

The help provided by James allowed Elspeth to go to bed at seven – at Matthew's insistence – and, with the aid of the drugs provided by the hospital, to fall asleep by eight. Matthew brought her dinner in bed – vegetable consommé, fortified with a drop of sherry, and scrambled eggs on Marmite toast – fare that he thought ideal for one only just discharged from hospital and advised by the doctor to take things easy for a few days.

"You really must rest," he said, as he placed the tray on her bedside table.

Elspeth smiled weakly. "I will. I promise." And thought: what right have I to promise anything, who went off this morning and did the very opposite of what he imagined I had promised not to do? Although I did not actually promise: I never said that I would not try to find out what Iain knew about Bob. I never actually said I would not, and if Matthew interpreted my silence as acquiescence, then that's not my fault: you are under no moral obligation to correct the misapprehension of others, even of your husband. She closed her eyes, and tried to remember the name they gave that sort of reasoning. Casuistry? Sophistry? Were they much the same thing? Did the classification of a wrong make any difference?

Matthew sat on the side of the bed while she ate her dinner. The consommé was improved by the sherry and when she had finished it she went on to the scrambled eggs. Matthew had chopped up pieces of smoked salmon and mixed them in with the egg.

"I know how much you like Marmite," he said. "I hope that that's all right."

"It's perfect," she said. "The comfort food par excellence. Eggs and Marmite are naturally complementary flavours."

"Americans don't like Marmite," he said. "Canadians too, in spite of being a parliamentary democracy. Like Plato's prisoners in the cave, they don't know what they're missing. It's hard to believe, but they think it's disgusting – I was at uni with a guy from Connecticut who said that he thought that Marmite was grease when he first saw a bottle of it. He put some on his bicycle chain."

Elspeth began to laugh, and immediately winced from the pain. "Don't make me laugh," she said. "It hurts."

He leaned forward and placed an apologetic kiss on her brow. "I won't say anything more about Marmite," he said. "Nor Vegemite – the Australian version. I quite like Vegemite, but I still prefer Marmite."

"It's what you're brought up with," said Elspeth. "A lot of things we like because we've been brought up to like them."

"No choice, then?"

"Some, but not as much as we'd like to think."

"Oh, well. I remember being told at school that Poussin's paintings were cold. We had an art teacher who said that, and I wrote it down in my art notebook. *Poussin – cold painter*. I accepted his judgement. And then, a lot later, I was in London and I went to the Wallace Collection. I saw *A Dance to the Music of Time*, and I stood there and fell in love with it." He smiled. "Really in love. Like I'm in love with you."

She caught her breath. "That painting . . ." she began.

"It has those figures dancing in a circle and then, up in the clouds, there's Apollo in his chariot – in the clouds. Apollo is all golden."

She closed her eyes. *Like I'm in love with you . . .* And I've lied to him.

"Apollo is one of my favourite gods," Matthew went on. "Have you got a favourite?"

Elspeth opened her eyes again. She stared at her plate, with its traces of scrambled egg round the rim. "Diana, I suppose."

"Good choice." He smiled again. "Actually, that's a pathetic thing to say: good choice. I sound like a waiter in a restaurant who says *Good choice* after you choose the sea bream."

"But sea bream *is* a good choice." Anything – even sea bream – was a welcome diversion from the guilt she felt.

"Apollo's terrific," Matthew went on. "You know, I've just read a poem about him. Angus wrote it. Could I read it to you?"

She nodded. She did not want to talk too much, because it hurt her, and if Matthew wanted to read poetry to her, she would be happy to listen. He sometimes did that, and she enjoyed it.

He left the room and returned with a piece of paper. "Listen," he began. "'Apollo'." He began to read:

Glittering Apollo, usually depicted
In complimentary terms, capable with his lyre
Of charming leopards, quieting tigers,
Subduing angry seas, encouraging Poseidon
To forget about the ships he planned to sink;
A hypnotist, perhaps, who preceded
The discovery of hypnosis and its tricks
By several millennia, or more;
He, that same Apollo, of impeccable taste,
Welcome in any cultivated salon
Still thought each day of Hyacinth,
Felled him with his discus, accidentally,
Wept bitter, inconsolable tears,
Cried buckets for his innocent friend,
As Achilles later wept on that desolate beach
For the loss of Patroclus; scholars
Sought to sanitise and make safe this loss,
Argued friendship and love were different things,
In classical times at least: so patently untrue,
Identified as such even by the innocent,
Who know what's what, and always have.

Matthew lowered the book. "It was a terrible accident. The wind blew his discus off course and it killed Hyacinth. Apollo felt terrible. That's why Angus says he wept . . ."

"Cried buckets," interjected Elspeth. "There's something very moving about that expression: *crying buckets.*"

Matthew agreed. "It's heartfelt. You only cry buckets if you mean it. Real tears."

He looked at Elspeth fondly. He thought she looked tired. He leaned forward and kissed her again. "I should let you get some sleep."

She felt drowsy. She would tell him tomorrow morning, she decided. She would say, *I'm really, really sorry. I wasn't thinking.* She would tell him how much she loved him and how she would never again hide anything from him, or engage in sophistry, for that matter.

There were so many words that would have to be uttered; words that would be like flowers sent in apology, filling the room with the scent of contrition.

23

Matthew Answers Elspeth's Phone

After she had finished her dinner, Matthew took Elspeth's tray back into the kitchen, where he found James sitting down to a meal of pizza and Greek salad, a graphic novel propped up in front of him. James made the pizza bases himself, then covered them with toppings that varied according to his mood, but that always contained olives, anchovies, and a liberal helping of garlic. Matthew knew, of course, that James was capable of making more elaborate dishes – he was, in fact, a remarkably good cook – but when catering just for himself, he did not seem to bother. Pizza was easy, filling, and left few pots and pans to be washed up.

"Boys settled?" asked Matthew.

"All three are fast asleep," replied James. "Rognvald was out before I finished the story. Tobermory was not far behind."

"It's very good of you to have taken over," said Matthew.

James made a gesture to indicate that thanks were not needed. "How is she?" he asked.

"I think it's pretty painful," answered Matthew. "They've given her some fairly powerful painkillers. Something called co-codamol. It's a combination of paracetamol and codeine, I think. The poppy's in there somewhere. Thirty milligrams of codeine in each tablet. I think that's more than you can get over the counter."

"And is it helping?"

Matthew said that he thought it was. "It's making her drowsy, which is all to the good."

"I had pethidine once," said James. "When I was in hospital.

That stuff works, I think."

Matthew pointed to the book James was reading. "Is that a graphic novel?" he asked.

James did not answer the question. "I bought it by mistake at an Oxfam shop. It's in Spanish, which I don't really read. I'm trying to work out what it's about, but I'm not sure that I'm getting anywhere."

"I had to watch a Japanese Noh play once," Matthew remembered. "In Japanese. One of the characters came back from the dead as a wisteria bush. Or so the programme notes said. That's when I realised that Japanese Noh plays might not be for me."

There was the sound of a phone ringing. Matthew looked around, and saw that it was Elspeth's – she had left it on the kitchen table. He picked the phone up, looked at the screen, and frowned. James watched him. Matthew, not recognising the caller's number, was not sure whether to answer. After a few moments, though, he took the call, and found himself speaking to Shelley McElhose.

"Elspeth?"

"No, it's Matthew. It's Elspeth's phone, but it's me."

"Matthew! How nice to hear you! This is Shelley – Elspeth's cousin."

Matthew spoke politely. "Of course."

There was a brief silence before he continued, "I'm answering Elspeth's phone because she's had an accident."

There was a shocked silence at the other end of the line. Then Shelley said "Oh, no, is she . . .?"

"She's fine," said Matthew. "She cracked a rib. But they say it'll knit together and she'll be fine. She was at the infirmary, though."

"Oh, Matthew – I'm really sorry." Shelley hesitated. "This afternoon? This evening?"

"After lunch," said Matthew. "She phoned me from the

infirmary at about half past three. It happened just after two, I think."

He heard Shelley gasp at the other end. It was, he thought, a bit of an overreaction: he had told her that Elspeth had not been badly hurt.

"She's right here at home," he said. "She's sleeping at the moment, but she's back home. They've given her painkillers. They don't do anything for an ordinary cracked rib, they told me."

"It must have happened just afterwards," Shelley said.

"After what?"

"After we had lunch. We were at the Canny Man's."

Matthew frowned. "Today? You and Elspeth?"

"Yes. This lunchtime. As I said, we were at the Canny Man's. Didn't she mention it to you?"

Matthew took a few moments to reply. "No," he said. Then, as some instinct came to conceal his dismay, he added, "Or, I mean, maybe. I don't know."

"Can she talk right now?" asked Shelley.

"No," said Matthew firmly. "It hurts when she talks."

"I know," said Shelley. "I knew somebody who cracked two ribs – one on each side. He said that he almost fainted from the pain."

Matthew was thinking of what Shelley had said. Now he asked, "It was a catch-up lunch? That must have been nice."

Shelley giggled. "Girly talk."

"I saw you at Big Lou's wedding," Matthew said. "Did you enjoy it?"

"Who wouldn't? We've always loved Big Lou."

Matthew kept his voice even. "And Bob? Had you met him before?"

This time there was a pause at the other end of the line. Then Shelley said, "No, I hadn't met him."

"He seems a great guy," said Matthew.

He waited. The delay lasted for almost thirty seconds. Then Shelley said, "Maybe. But I don't really know him – do you?"

"No, I don't," replied Matthew. He had had his answer.

He was about to say something else when Shelley spoke again. "I was phoning Elspeth to tell her that there's a flower collection for our great-aunt who died not long ago. Not for actual flowers, of course, but for a donation to charity. It's going to go to Shelter. I meant to tell her at lunch, but forgot. Will you tell her to get in touch with me for the details?"

"I shall," said Matthew.

"Well, I shouldn't keep you," said Shelley. "Give Elspeth my love – lots of it."

Matthew promised that he would, and then rang off. James had closed his graphic novel. "I'm not going to finish this," he said.

Matthew acknowledged this remark in an absent-minded way. He had rather a lot to think about, and he felt sick to his stomach. He did not feel like discussing Spanish graphic novels with anyone. He left the kitchen and went out into the garden. It was a clear night, and the sky was filled with stars. He looked for Sagittarius. There it was.

He began to walk along the path that led to the treehouse, which was a dark shape against the night sky. Off to the north, behind the crouching form of the Pentland Hills, was the glow that came from Edinburgh. The stars in that direction were not so visible because of the light.

He thought about what Shelley had told him. There was nothing to prove that Elspeth had gone to see Shelley specifically to elicit that information. But the timing suggested that, and it could not have been an innocent lunch, because, otherwise, surely she would have mentioned it to him. All she had said was that she had been to the supermarket and the accident had occurred on her way back. So it looked as if she was hiding the lunch from him – because she was ashamed that she had done something he had not wanted her to do.

The fact that she had met Shelley for lunch was not the real issue, of course: what mattered – what hurt – was that she had effectively misled him about her movements before the accident. And if she had done that, then there might be other things on which she had misled him – and might be misleading him still. That was what hurt – and the pain, it seemed to him, was as bad as the pain of a cracked rib. Worse, perhaps.

24

Canine ESP

Irene arrived by taxi at mid-morning, having alighted at Waverley Station from the Aberdeen train. Her trip had been uneventful, apart from a brief argument with the ticket inspector who had assumed that the man sitting next to her was her husband. This required her to deliver a short rebuke – gently administered, she felt – on the subject of bias in assumptions – a rebuke that he took with professional resignation. After the ticket inspector had gone, the man sitting next to her had muttered, *sotto voce*, but just audibly, "I'm really glad I'm not married to you." Irene had heard him, but had not engaged; there were always ignorant and unaware people on trains, she reminded herself; the whole country was full of them, in fact. She sighed as she thought of the major task that the Scottish Government had on its hands.

As her taxi swept along Great King Street, Irene felt a pang of anticipation. It was good to be back in Edinburgh, even if she liked Aberdeen, and had settled into a fulfilling routine there. The climate was an issue, of course, but Irene had quickly discovered that people who lived in Aberdeen used a simple expedient to deal with the temperature and the biting winds: they simply wore an extra layer of clothing. The men often wore two jackets and two overcoats, and the women not infrequently donned three cardigans before they went out in the morning. The resulting bulk might have made them all look particularly well-developed, but one became used to that quickly enough. In times of high energy costs, of course, this tactic was particularly useful. No house in Aberdeen had central heating, but the wearing of extra clothing circumvented this problem and the bills were accordingly small. Indeed, many households in Aberdeen had a negative bill, in that the electricity providers found that it was they who owed money to the customer rather than the other way round. This was puzzling, and the electricity companies were looking into the issue – so far without success. Unheated bathrooms, with their ice-cold water, could be a challenge, of course, but showering was always possible if one resorted, as some did, to the wearing of a wetsuit of the sort worn by divers and long-distance swimmers. Irene had not yet done that, but Hugo Fairbairn did.

She and Hugo were happy, although he had, admittedly, become progressively quieter over the past twelve months – the result of work pressures, she thought. His chair had few administrative duties attached to it – it had been conferred as a personal chair – but he had twelve postgraduate students working under his supervision, of whom Irene was one. She was an exception, of course: he did not cohabit with the other eleven.

Now, as the taxi turned into Drummond Place, she saw a familiar figure opening the gate that led into the garden. This was Angus Lordie, taking his dog, Cyril, for his mid-morning walk. Irene had always found Angus civil enough, in spite of his being, in her view, irredeemably old-fashioned in his outlook. His painting was ridiculous, she felt – there was no cutting edge to it – none at all. What *statement* did a portrait make? None, she thought; all that it did was to stroke the ego of sitters and underline what they saw as their achievement. Portraiture emphasised power and possessions. It was all about pride and affirmation of position.

It was true that Angus could paint, in the sense that he could use paint to imitate what he saw before him. But that was all that it was – in Irene's view, representational art was simply the copying of what was already there – and that could be done as effectively, and much more cheaply, by a camera.

She had once discussed this with Angus and it seemed to her that her criticism must have been exactly apposite, as he had become quiet, bitten his lip, and had offered no defence – no *apologia pro vita sua.* You could always tell when somebody did not have a leg to stand on – and Angus was as good an example as any. And as for his dog – Irene was firmly against the keeping of animals. Again, it was all a question of power and possession. People who had dogs kept them because they were subservient. The dog was there to do one's bidding, to *affirm* one's status. A dog was a thing, like any of the other things that we surrounded ourselves with, to boost our sense of our own value. It was so clear, so obvious. And yet people went on about companionship and loyalty and even love. Such delusional nonsense.

That dog, Cyril, she reflected, was particularly objectionable. Irene disliked Cyril's confidence – his bright eye and his cocked head – qualities that she saw as being particularly male. Toxic caninity, she thought, and shuddered.

Meanwhile, they went through the gate into the Drummond Place Garden, Angus suddenly noticed that Cyril had stiffened and that the hair along his back had begun to bristle. At the same time he uttered a low growl, a bass rattle that Angus knew signalled that the dog had sensed something threatening.

Angus looked about him. The most likely cause of such behaviour was the presence of a squirrel or, possibly, a cat – two creatures that Cyril felt it was given to him in life to keep in their place. But there was no trace of either, and Cyril now seemed to be straining on his leash to face backwards.

Angus turned round. He saw a taxi rattle past; he did not see Irene within.

"Something bothering you, Cyril?" he asked. "That's only a taxi, old pal."

Cyril's growl grew louder as he watched the taxi pass.

Angus was amused. "You've seen plenty of taxis," he said. "Nothing to see there, Cyril."

Had Angus attended the previous week's lecture in the Arthur Conan Doyle Tuesday Lecture Series, at its headquarters in Palmerston Place, he would have heard a renowned parapsychologist, Dr Julia Polcetti, talking about her work on telepathic awareness in animals. She had investigated the frequently reported experience of cat owners in finding that their cats anticipated their return home after a period of time away. The evidence was there, she said: animals could pick up things that we could neither see nor hear. And we could too, she said, if we opened our minds to the possibility.

And this, it seems, was what Cyril was doing as he growled at the passing taxi. That taxi was not innocent, as far as Cyril was concerned. That taxi represented a clear and present danger.

25

The Whiff of Battle

Nicola became aware of Irene's arrival not through the operation of any sixth sense but by looking out of the window onto Scotland Street below. When she saw the taxi draw up outside the door of the common stair, her heart sank. In spite of Stuart's prompting, Irene had not given them a date for her arrival, nor had she confirmed that she had arranged for the renting of a flat. This had caused Nicola some concern, and she had quizzed Stuart as to what he would do if Irene simply presented herself at 44 Scotland Street.

"She won't do that," he said. "Don't worry."

But Nicola had worried, and now, as she saw Irene emerge with an unwieldy suitcase, her anxiety deepened. An unwelcome guest who arrives with a small suitcase is one thing – one who arrives with a large suitcase in tow is quite another. Irene's suitcase was extremely large.

She did not wait for Irene to ring the bell, but took up her position on the landing outside the flat's front door. She had not read von Clausewitz's *On War*, but had the great strategist been there, he would have approved of her tactics. It was important, he advised, to have an advance position to repel an enemy, but to have a clear route for retreat should that become necessary. This she had, in the slightly ajar door immediately behind her.

She took a deep breath as she heard Irene struggling up the stair, the suitcase banging against the walls and the iron-work bannisters. She had decided to be firm, and would be. She was not intimidated by Irene – why should she be? She saw through Irene's tactics: the other woman characteristically went on the offensive before anything was said – it was a form of pre-emptive strike. In many cases this wrong-footed the opposition, but Nicola was determined it should not do that now. She would play Irene at her own game; the first salvo would come from her, taking every advantage of the fact that she would be *above* Irene as she approached the landing. The high ground – again as von Clausewitz would point out – confers important advantages, whether one is talking about artillery or, as in this case, verbal sparring.

As Irene hove into view, struggling with her outsize suitcase, Nicola called out, "Well, this is a surprise! I thought you agreed with Stuart that you would tell us when you were coming."

It was hardly a welcome, by any stretch of the imagination, and it stopped Irene in her tracks. She opened her mouth to speak, but was cut off by Nicola.

"And you told us you'd let us know where you were staying."

This was largely untrue, but it had its effect. Flustered and irritated in equal measure, Irene struggled to reply.

"I did no such thing," she said. "I never . . ."

"It's very difficult," Nicola pressed on. "It's hard to plan for the boys when there's this uncertainty. Children need certainty in their lives. Certainty and stability."

Irene's jaw dropped. And then, having absorbed these first defeats, she mustered her forces for the counter-attack.

"I don't need to be reminded about the needs of children," she said. "It may have escaped your attention that my doctoral studies are about childhood. Perhaps you didn't know that."

"Oh, I knew that," Nicola shot back. "But theory and practice are two different things, I believe. Anyway, let's not argue. Please come in for a cup of tea. Then I can phone for a taxi to take you on to the flat you've rented. Where is it, by the way? Stuart said that he sent you the name of a very helpful agent. It always pays to go through agents, I find."

Irene ignored this. Picking up her suitcase again, she climbed the remaining stairs with her mouth set in a grim line of determination. Once in the kitchen, she sat down at the table to recover her breath while Nicola filled the kettle.

"Where is your place?" Nicola enquired over her shoulder.

"What place?"

"The flat you've rented. I hope you've found somewhere comfortable – and not too expensive. Edinburgh has become a bit pricy, I think. I'm glad I don't have to rent somewhere."

Irene waited a moment before she replied. Then she said, "I don't have somewhere. I intend to stay here – at home."

Nicola stood quite still. She had anticipated this. Work out what the other side is going to do before they do it, counselled von Clausewitz. Nicola had done that.

"I'm so sorry," said Nicola. "There just isn't room here. What a pity. It would have been so cosy having the five of us all together, but there we are. Architectural limitations are architectural limitations, I always find. Sorry about that."

Irene was not to give up so easily. "But . . ." she began. She got no further.

"Excuse me," Nicola went on. "I don't want to be ungracious. You've had a long journey and now you find yourself with nowhere to stay. That can't be easy. But at the same time, there simply is no room here."

"There's a spare room," said Irene. "Don't think I don't know that."

Nicola remained calm. "The thing about spare rooms," she said, "is that they cease to be spare once somebody has moved into them. So, in relation to this so-called spare room to which I think you are referring, it is a *former* spare room. I live in it now. So sorry."

Irene bit her lip. "We'll see what Stuart says about that," she muttered.

"But it was Stuart's idea," said Nicola brightly. "I moved in at his suggestion. I look after the boys, you see – your sons, in point of fact. I have . . ." She paused, wondering whether a rapier stroke of such killing efficacy was justified. She decided it was. *This situation has escalated rapidly, moving to nuclear level quite quickly.* "I have had to pick up the pieces, you see."

Irene glowered.

"Not that I resent it," Nicola continued. "What grandmother would fail to answer such a call when the mother herself dies or is incapacitated . . . or leaves the nest prematurely, so to speak, because of, well, emotional interests elsewhere? What grandmother would not step forward, I ask you? They must have thought something similar at the time of the Battle of Britain. Only it wasn't the grandmothers who flew the Spitfires, but those brave young men." *That was a bit much,* Nicola thought, *but this was an extreme situation.*

Irene was staring down at the floor. She looked up slowly. When she spoke, her voice was quiet – not the voice of the aggressor, but that of the vanquished. "I don't know why you dislike me so much," she said. "You've never approved of me, have you? Right from the beginning, you wrote me off, didn't you? And it never occurred to you that I might be doing my best by Stuart and the boys. You never thought of that, did you? And it never occurred to you that when I left Stuart it was because he never paid me any attention. There are two sides to every story, but perhaps you don't see it that way." She paused. "And now, I'll go back to Aberdeen. I don't want to be somewhere where I'm not welcome."

There was nothing in von Clausewitz about this, and Nicola stood where she was, unable to respond.

26

A Damascene Moment

Nicola wavered. She had been completely resolute up to that point, but Irene's apparent collapse, as unanticipated as it was sudden, had unnerved her. What Irene had said about her attitude to her was indisputably correct. She had never liked her; Irene had read her mother-in-law's attitude correctly. But had she bothered to ask herself why Nicola felt that way, she might have developed some insight into her overbearing attitude, her relentless ideologically-motivated nagging, and the Himalayan heights of the condescension she had shown in her dealings with others. She had done none of that, but Nicola reminded herself that, for all her faults – and who amongst us is without fault? – Irene still had all the hopes and fears that go with being human. She remembered what her friend Charlie MacLean, the whisky writer and connoisseur, a man of great understanding, had said of one seemingly rather difficult character of his acquaintance: *He's only trying to do his best.* It was a simple observation, but it drew on deep wells of sympathy, and it had made a great impression on Nicola. Now, faced with a deflated Irene, it occurred to her that she should have uttered that mantra before she launched, so severely and unforgivingly, into her broadside against her former daughter-in-law. *As you did to the least of my brethren . . .* The words came back to her from somewhere, from her school years in the Borders, perhaps; from that lumber room of the mind that we forget about but in which so much of our deep self is located; *as you did to the least of my brethren . . .*

She sat down at the table, opposite Irene. She reached out and took the other woman's hand. At first Irene seemed to want to withdraw it, as if repelled by the unwanted intimacy, but Nicola held on, and Irene desisted.

"I am very, very sorry," Nicola found herself saying. "I've been harsh and uncharitable." She made a helpless gesture. "I couldn't help myself."

Irene said nothing. She was still staring at the floor, and when she looked up, Nicola saw, to her surprise, that her cheeks were moist. She clutched Irene's hand more tightly.

"Please don't be upset," said Nicola. "I really shouldn't have said what I did." And then she went further, the words coming to her lips without being weighed before their utterance. "We could start afresh, you know. We could . . ." She looked around for an expression that might embody what she felt she had to say, but all that came to mind was that trite phrase, *we should move on*. It was such a resounding cliché – a catch-all distraction employed by politicians eager to evade responsibility for misdeeds. "We should move on. I need to get on with the real job." It was a common enough smokescreen. So might Attila or Tamburlaine have spoken if confronted with the devastation of sacked cities: "We must move on; there are other conquests to be made." And now she almost said it herself; almost, before she managed, rather lamely, "I've been really rude."

There was a brief silence. Then Irene spoke, and the voice with which she spoke was one of defeat. "Thank for saying that. You think I don't feel these things, but I do. It's good of you to say what you said."

Nicola was still surprised by herself. Had she really said that? Had she apologised to Irene, of all people, when if anybody had any apologizing to do, it would be Irene herself? And yet she had meant the words she had used – they did not come from nowhere. There was such a thing as charity, even if it very easily became obscured by the smoke of our daily battle.

"Yes," said Irene. "It should have been obvious to me that neither you nor Stuart wanted me."

Nicola started to object. "Oh, you mustn't say that . . ." And yet of course it was true; it was completely true. They had not wanted her. Stuart was less forceful in his antipathy – Irene had, after all, been his wife – but he had . . . And here Nicola found the dreadful phrase slipped so naturally into her unspoken thoughts: he had moved on. That was the problem with clichés: they became so embedded in our minds that we found it hard to think, or speak, without them.

Irene interrupted her. "No, it's true. I've lost Stuart. And now I'm going to lose the boys too. My summer access was so precious, but—"

Nicola rose to her feet. "Stop," she said. "I've had an idea."

Irene looked up. Her eyes narrowed. Nicola did not notice that.

Nicola retrieved her phone from a shelf behind her. "I'm going to make a call."

"Stuart?"

"No," said Nicola. "Stuart's at work. I don't want to disturb him." She sat down, the phone on the table in front of her. She looked at Irene. "You remember Antonia."

Irene nodded. "Our neighbour? Of course I do."

"She lives round the corner now, in Drummond Place. She shares with that peculiar Italian nun – the one who goes to all the parties. You see her photograph in the social pages of *Scottish Field*."

"Yes, I know her. Sister Maria-Fiore dei . . . something-or-other."

"Sister Maria-Fiore dei Fiori di Montagna. Yes, her. She's become very well-known. She's now on the boards of the National Galleries and the Museum. She's the first nun to be on the museum board, apparently. And I'm told that she's been pestering the Lord Lyon to be appointed a pursuivant."

Irene waited for Nicola to continue.

"Anyway, she and Antonia have set up home together, as I said, in Drummond Place. It's a very nice flat they've got, and there's a lot of room in it. It's one of those rambling New Town flats with all the Georgian features more or less intact."

"They're fortunate," said Irene.

"Yes," Nicola continued. "I think they have a very comfortable existence. Antonia's still writing her history of the early Scottish saints – she'll never finish that, I imagine – and Sister Maria-Fiore dei Fiori di Montagna has got all her social climbing and general interfering to do. So they're pretty happy. Apparently, Sister Maria-Fiore dei Fiori di Montagna is a rather good cook. She spends a lot of time in Valvona & Crolla, buying provisions to make all sorts of Tuscan dishes. People vie for invitations to dinner there – it's quite the salon they have."

Irene smiled. "I love Italian food. I always have. You know I taught Bertie Italian? I started when he was three months old. I hope he hasn't forgotten too much of it."

As she made this last remark, Irene cast a glance at Nicola that suggested that she might just be the sort of grandmother to let a grandson's Italian slip. But nothing was said, and Nicola, anyway, was occupied with dialling Antonia's number.

Round the corner in Drummond Place, a phone rang, the tones being the opening bars of the overture to *Cavalleria Rusticana*.

Antonia answered. "*Pronto*," she said, smiling at Sister Maria-Fiore dei Fiori di Montagna, who was sitting opposite her, and who, with a conspiratorial wink, mouthed the word *Prontissimo!*

27

St Senga of Dunfermline

Forewarned by the telephone call from Nicola, Antonia was waiting at the door of the flat in Drummond Place. As the entrance to a main door flat, this gave out onto a small external landing, reached by a few stone steps from the pavement below.

"The Floral One and I are most intrigued," she said to Nicola. "A matter of some importance, you said. We've been speculating for at least five minutes as to what this might be."

"All will be revealed," said Nicola. "But I think I should speak to both of you together."

"Sister Maria-Fiore dei Fiori di Montagna is in the kitchen," said Antonia, gesturing for her neighbour to follow her into the flat. "She's making ciabatta, which she does divinely, I can assure you. Plenty of Poggio Lamentano olive oil, rosemary, sea salt. It sounds simple, but it requires a touch – which she has."

"Delicious," said Nicola. "I can't resist ciabatta. In fact, I can't resist anything."

Antonia laughed. "I, too, suffer from weakness of will. Sister Maria-Fiore dei Fiori di Montagna says that, like everything, that particular failing is a gift. She says our shortcomings are gifts in exactly the same way as our good qualities are. That is what she says."

Nicola nodded. She had heard enough of the nun's aphorisms to last her for years, but now was not the time to express her views on that.

They went through to the kitchen, where they found Sister

Maria-Fiore dei Fiori di Montgana putting the finishing touches to a large tray of neatly-dimpled ciabatta.

"Into the oven this will be popped," said the nun. "That which is uncooked is destined to be cooked, if it has been prepared with cooking in mind." She fixed Nicola with a stare, as if to challenge her to refute the wisdom of this observation. "So too is it with us – humble creatures that we are: the Lord intends certain things for you and me, and we must open ourselves to his plans."

Nicola gave an inward sigh. On the outside, though, she smiled, and then said, "We are raw dough, I think – or most of us are. We await the heat that will make of us the finished loaf."

Sister Maria-Fiore dei Fiori di Montagna heard this with delight. She clapped her hands together. "*Certo!*" she exclaimed. "That is very true, dear Nicola." She paused. "Your name . . . When I utter it, as I just have done, my mind goes inevitably to the saint after whom you are named. San Nicola of Myrna. That dear Turkish bishop."

"Actually, I'm named after an aunt who lived in Dunbar," said Nicola. "She had a bicycle shop there."

Sister Maria-Fiore dei Fiori di Montagna clapped her hands together once more, but perhaps with slightly less enthusiasm. "But how delightful," she said. "I love bicycles, although I have never owned one, nor indeed ridden one. But I do so love them. The way their wheels go round in perfect harmony with the pedals!"

"They wouldn't be much use if they didn't," observed Nicola drily.

If there was sarcasm in this response, Sister Maria-Fiore dei Fiori di Montagna either did not notice it or chose to ignore it.

"Dear San Nicola," she said, dusting the flour off her hands. "He was much-loved – and performed several remarkable miracles. You'll know, no doubt, of the boys in the barrel. The boys were chopped up and put in a barrel of brine, but San Nicola brought them back to life. It was remarkable. Benjamin Britten wrote a cantata about it – well, not just about the boys in the barrel, but about San Nicola and his doings in general. "And of course," she continued, "he was the original Santa Claus. He has a large cult in the Orthodox Church. Our poor, dear misguided Orthodox brethren – I cannot see why they can't accept Rome's authority. Oh, I know all about the squabbling over the *filioque* clause, but if only they saw reason and were prepared to accept the obvious – that Rome is right – then life would be *so* much easier." She paused. "His saintly bones are preserved in Bari – in the Church of San Nicola. We are so immensely fortunate to have his bones, even after all these years."

Antonia now joined the conversation. "At least nobody is saying that San Nicola did not exist," she said, a slight note of resentment in her voice. "You have no idea how many of the early Scottish saints I've been looking at have been declared to be apocryphal." She looked pained. "It's the fault of various Protestants. For some reason, Protestants have a certain animosity towards saints. The late Reverend Paisley, Pastor Jack Glass, and all the rest – they were so suspicious of saints. Such a pity."

"Envy," snapped Sister Maria-Fiore dei Fiori di Montagna.

"I'll give you an example," said Antonia. "I've been doing some research on a little-known Scottish saint, St Senga of Dunfermline. Have you heard of her, by any chance?"

Nicola shook her head.

"There you are, you see," said Antonia. "She has been allowed to become obscure because our medievalists just don't seem interested. They're prepared to spend any amount of time on the Vikings, trying to rehabilitate them, would you believe it? It's got mixed up with the constitutional issue. Our dear patriotic brethren are so keen on Scandinavia as a model for Scotland that they don't want people reminding us that the Vikings were the most frightful bunch. Hardly good political role models."

Nicola smiled. "I would love to be Swedish, personally. I admire them a great deal."

"Well, you can't be," snapped Antonia. "Ideology can't overcome geography. Nor can one aspire to be Finnish, for that matter, because it takes a very long time to learn Finnish, I'm told. A language with *fifteen* cases – I ask you! Anyway, I'm trying to do what I can to make up for all this neglect and, in some cases, active indifference. Take St Senga, for instance. We know very little about her, other than that she is believed to have ventured into Fife in an attempt to convert them. Many people have done that, and indeed there are some brave souls who still do. I believe Senga met with some success, but there are those who deny that she ever actually existed."

"There must be some references," said Nicola.

"Very few," sighed Antonia. "However, I have found one – a manuscript source that says *Sancta Senga erat*. That is all – just those three words. Now, some have suggested that this is an incomplete sentence, that there was something preceding the *erat* – because a Latin verb would have been at the end. But I examined the manuscript closely and have identified a full stop immediately after *erat*. So, the sentence did not say that St Senga *was* anything, it simply says that she *was*. In other words, it confirms that she existed."

"Punctuation can make all the difference," said Nicola.

"It can," agreed Antonia. "The only difficulty is that there are those who say the full stop in question is not a punctuation mark at all but a random spot of ink from the scribe's pen."

"Nonsense," said Nicola quickly, knowing that she needed Antonia's co-operation in what she was about to propose. "Patent nonsense."

28

Dr Livingstone Expounds

Big Lou took two cups of coffee over to the table occupied by Bruce and Dr Donald Livingstone. It was the quietest table in the coffee bar, and it was much appreciated by those who wanted a private chat. From neighbouring tables it was just possible to hear what was being said at it, but only if the rest of the coffee bar was quiet, which was rarely the case. It was a good place for lovers to meet, and exchange the sort of words – and looks – that lovers like to share. It was a good place for businessmen and financiers to sip a cup of coffee and do a bit of insider trading. It was a good place to unburden oneself of the issues which we like to offload on our long-suffering friends. It was much sought-after.

"I've always liked this place," said Bruce, after Big Lou had returned to the bar. "That woman – Big Lou, as she's called – is very popular. She just got married to a guy who goes round Highland Games tossing cabers and so on – a strongman, believe it or not."

Dr Livingstone raised an eyebrow as he looked over towards Lou. "Interesting," he said. "Does she mind the sobriquet . . .? I mean, the name – Big Lou. People are sensitive about these things."

"No, not as far as I know. And her new husband's called Fat Bob. I don't think he minds either. It's just the way things are."

Dr Livingstone smiled. "I used to be called David at school – for obvious reasons. And once I left medical school, people used to make the same joke all the time. They'd say, 'Dr

Livingstone, I presume' and then crease up with laughter – as if it was the first time anybody had ever said it."

"What was his name?" asked Bruce. "The man who found him?"

"H.M. Stanley. You know, I never bothered to find out what the H.M. stood for. I should, I suppose. He was an American journalist who was sent by his paper to find Dr Livingstone. Initials are funny things, aren't they? Some people use them as a substitute for a first name."

"Why do you think they do that?"

"Relative anonymity," replied Dr Livingstone. "Or perhaps impersonality rather than anonymity. Initials are formal – first names are usually more, well, personal. Initials tell you less about a person than the full name. J.B. Stetson, for instance – he was a famous hatter – sounds more remote than John B. Stetson."

Bruce wondered whether it might have something to do with being unhappy about one's name. "We had a boy at school who was called P.D. Collins. That was how he signed himself on any list. He was always P.D. Collins – and nobody knew what the initials stood for. If you asked him, he would ignore the question. He'd look away or change the subject."

"A disliked name can be a great burden in this life," said Dr Livingstone. "Poor chap."

"And then we found out – just before we all left school – what the initials stood for. He was Percival Desmond. People laughed a lot at that."

Dr Livingstone winced. "The damage done," he said. "Such damage we do to others."

Bruce looked away. "I was one of the ones who laughed," he said.

Dr Livingstone held him in his gaze. "I wouldn't berate yourself too much for that," he said. "We've all done things we regret – especially when we're young."

"I wouldn't laugh now," said Bruce.

"I'm sure you wouldn't."

For a few moments, Bruce was silent. At length he asked, "Can we become different people?"

"Do you mean can we change? Of course we can. Part of my job in the past has been to help people to change – or at least to adapt. There are some things that are very deep-seated that we can't do anything about, but we can change the way we deal with them. That amounts to a transformation of sorts."

"I feel very bad about a lot of stuff," said Bruce.

"We all do," said Dr Livingstone. He paused. "You do know, don't you, that I haven't come to see you in order to treat you? It's very important that you understand that. I'm here because I'm writing a paper for a psychiatric journal on the psychological implications of being struck by lightning. I'm trying to have a condition recognised, you see, and that's a long process. You have to persuade the profession that there is a recognisable and consistent set of symptoms – a standard pattern, if you will."

"So that the condition gets a name?"

"Exactly," said Dr Livingstone. "And that's not easy – particularly when it's relatively rare. So far, I've interviewed four people who have been struck by lightning and survived. One of them reported no changes in his life after the event. He said he was exactly the same as he had been before the lightning strike – apart from losing his eyebrows. They were apparently singed. Behaviourally, there was no change in what he did. Or what he thought, for that matter – although he became much better at mathematics, incidentally."

"And the others?"

Dr Livingstone became animated. "They were very interesting. They all reported feeling very differently about things. One changed his political opinions completely."

"Just because he was struck by lightning?"

Dr Livingstone hesitated. "Well, that's hard to answer definitively. You have to be sure of a causal link – you have to satisfy the *post hoc, propter hoc* test. People change their political views for all sorts of reasons. Growing older, for instance."

"That makes a difference?"

Dr Livingstone laughed. "Of course it does. In many cases there's a slow drift to a more conservative position across the lifespan. There's a saying that addresses that. It's not one I agree with, by the way. It's this: 'A person who is not a socialist at twenty has no heart; a person who's still a socialist at forty has no head.' I don't think that's true, actually, but it expresses a phenomenon that one might actually observe – the replacing of passion with caution. And I suppose that a cautious approach is more likely to be accompanied by thoughtfulness, although passionate people might argue that their passion comes from precisely that – from thinking about something that makes them feel passionately about it. I imagine that there are plenty of passionate socialists who feel that way precisely because they have contemplated and thought about the suffering of others. And that's something that I can very much sympathise with."

Bruce looked thoughtful. "Would this condition be called after somebody?" he asked. "Aren't some conditions named after people who had them?"

Dr Livingstone allowed himself an almost undetectable smile. "Would you like that?" he asked.

29

Capgras et al.

Bruce looked embarrassed. Dr Livingstone had implied that he might like the post-lightning-strike syndrome named after him. It was true that that possibility had crossed his mind – and indeed would have appealed greatly to the old Bruce, but not to the new person he felt himself to be. So he replied, "I wasn't thinking of myself, you know."

Dr Livingstone was tactful. "Of course not." He thought for a moment. "Of course, it's more often the discoverer of the syndrome who gets the credit, as it were. Capgras Syndrome was first described by a French psychiatrist called Joseph Capgras. And then there's de Clérambault's Syndrome, and Cotard's Syndrome too. There are quite a lot of these, I suppose, that immortalise the doctor who first identifies them. Not that I would want there to be a Livingstone's Syndrome, frankly. That's not my motive in any of this."

Bruce was interested. "This Capgras Syndrome – I've never heard of it – nor of any of the others. What do you do if you've got Capgras?"

"It's an unusual one, that," said Dr Livingstone. "In fact, all of them are pretty rare. Most of the time, we deal with much more mundane complaints. But Capgras is certainly interesting."

Bruce waited.

"Capgras Syndrome," Dr Livingstone explained, "is present when the patient believes that a person he knows – often a close relative or friend – has been replaced by a double. The patient says, 'Yes, that certainly looks like my wife, but it isn't, you know – it's somebody who looks exactly like her.'"

Bruce looked incredulous. "They actually believe that?"

Dr Livingstone nodded. "There's a very good account of it in a book called *Uncommon Psychiatric Syndromes* by two psychiatrists, Enoch and Trethowan. It's an illuminating read – if you're interested in the wilder shores of human behaviour. They have a whole chapter on Capgras Syndrome – and some its variants. Capgras-type conditions can get quite complicated. There's the delusion of intermetamorphosis, for instance, where the patient thinks that people are exchanging their identities. So, you think that John has taken on Harry's identity and Harry has taken on Frank's – and Frank has taken John's. Not simple."

"No, not simple at all."

"And then," Dr Livingstone continued, "there is often some delusion of persecution going on in the background. The patient believes that his persecutor has replaced the person close to him in order to be able to carry to out whatever persecution is being practised more effectively."

"And what do you do?" asked Bruce.

"There are drug treatments," said Dr Livingstone. "They may or may not help. If the background delusion is treated, then they may stop imagining that there is a double. It doesn't always work, but it may."

"And the other syndromes you mentioned?"

"De Clérambault's is rather worrying," said Dr Livingstone. "I've never encountered it, but it's not all that uncommon. It can have tragic consequences. It's where the patient believes that somebody is in love with him or her – somebody who may have absolutely nothing to do with the patient, who probably doesn't even know him – or her: women are prone to this too. It's often a public figure or somebody whom the patient sees somewhere and latches on to. Thomas Clouston, who was a very distinguished Scottish psychiatrist in the nineteenth century, described a case of this nature in a one-legged dressmaker who conceived of the idea that a random member of her church congregation wanted to marry her. There was, of course, no basis for this belief, but it was certainly held by the woman in question. These people really believe that the objects of their affections feel something for them."

"And the other one?"

"Cotard? That's even stranger. You have Cotard if you end up denying your own existence and the existence of the external world. The French call it the *délire de négation*, which is a good description of it. It leads to utter nihilism."

Bruce shook his head. "It's difficult to imagine what it's like to believe any of the things these people believe. It's bizarre."

Dr Livingstone laughed. "What's the Yorkshire saying? There's nowt so queer as folk? That's true, you know. But listen, there's an even more bizarre delusion. This one is exceptionally rare – probably non-existent today – but there was a time when it was quite common. Sometimes an odd belief can be socially transmitted – as in mass hysteria. You know how groups of people can suddenly get an odd idea in their heads all at the same time. It used to happen a bit in boarding schools, where you could get hysterical behaviour.

"This delusion is very colourful. It's called the glass delusion, and effectively what it means is that you believe you're made of glass."

Bruce looked incredulous. "You actually think that? That you're made entirely of glass?"

Dr Livingstone nodded. "Yes. It was quite well-known in the seventeenth century, although there were references to it before then. It's mentioned by Cervantes and Descartes, and there was a French monarch who suffered from it, Charles VI. He was very careful about not being bumped into in case he shattered."

"No!" exclaimed Bruce. "Your actual king of France? He thought he was made of *glass*?"

"And then there might have been something similar going on in the mind of Tchaikovsky, who was very worried that when he was conducting an orchestra, his head would fall off. He may have been suffering from something very similar to the glass delusion."

"Seriously strange," said Bruce. He stared at Dr Livingstone. "You don't think I've got anything like that, do you?"

Dr Livingstone laughed. "Oh, my goodness, no. I do think, though, that when one gets struck by lightning there is a chance there will be some lasting effects. These could be the result of disturbance in the brain pathways. That's one hypothesis. That's why I was keen to talk to you about how you feel you've changed as a result of your unfortunate experience on . . ."

"Dundas Street," said Bruce.

"Yes, Dundas Street."

Dr Livingstone took a sip of his coffee. "Tell me, then, how you think you've changed."

"Utterly," said Bruce. "I know it sounds corny, but I've changed utterly."

"Would you say that you're a nicer person?" asked Dr Livingstone. "Or have you changed for the worse?"

"Oh, for the better," said Bruce. "I used to be . . ." He hesitated.

Dr Livingstone gave him an encouraging look. "You need not be embarrassed with me," he said. "I've seen and heard just about everything. And there's nothing to be ashamed of." Then, seeing Bruce hesitate, he added, "I'm unshockable."

Bruce lowered his voice. "I used to be really hot. I used to admire myself in the mirror – sometimes for fifteen, twenty minutes at a stretch. I used to put this clove-scented gel in my hair. I used to think I was God's gift to women. I really did."

"And now?"

"Now, I want to lead a simple, chaste life. I want to grow

things. I want to work with my hands. I want to unclutter."

"Interesting," said Dr Livingstone. "And you think you'll find all this in a monastery?"

"I *know* I shall," said Bruce. "And that's not a delusion on my part."

"Hah!" said Dr Livingstone.

"Don't you believe me?" asked Bruce.

"Oh, I do," said Dr Livingstone. "My *hah* was not a *hah* of incredulity. It was a *hah* of recognition – perhaps even of sympathy."

"I hate myself," Bruce muttered.

"You mustn't," said Dr Livingstone.

"Okay, I disgust myself."

Dr Livingstone nodded. "That's better," he said, adding, "There is a distinction, you know."

30

A Swiss Army Knife

It was the last day of term at the Steiner School and the talk in the playground was all about plans for the upcoming summer holidays. Bertie was unsure what Stuart and Nicola had planned for him – there had been some talk of going away for a week or two in the Highlands, but nothing definite seemed to have been arranged. Bertie himself had asked whether it might be possible to have a holiday in Glasgow, but this suggestion had been met with silence and glances between his father and grandmother that he had found difficult to interpret.

Then Stuart had said, "That's an interesting idea, Bertie, but usually, if you live in a city already, you go somewhere different for your holidays." He paused. "That's not to say that Glasgow isn't a good place to go. I'm sure that there's a lot to do there."

"One could go down the Clyde," Nicola suggested. "There's the Waverley paddle steamer, and then there's . . ." She looked to Stuart for help.

"The People's Palace. And the Burrell Collection is not far away. And . . ."

"There's plenty to do in Glasgow," Nicola said. "But I think that we might go further afield." She looked fondly at Bertie. "You love Glasgow, don't you, Bertie?"

Bertie nodded. Glasgow was a promised land to him – it had always been a place of freedom and excitement – a place devoid of the constraints of life in Edinburgh, where you had to watch what you did, where there were people like Olive and Pansy around to criticise anything you said, even if life was, admittedly, easier since his mother had gone to Aberdeen and the psychotherapy and yoga had stopped. There was no yoga in Glasgow and very little psychotherapy, he had been told, and there were lots of jokes, too, because all the photographs he saw of Glasgow were full of smiling people. And they liked pies there, and everyone drank Irn-Bru, which was widely discouraged in Edinburgh for some reason.

But now there was a cloud – ill-defined and distant, but a cloud nonetheless – on Bertie's horizon. This was the remark that Stuart had made about the possibility of him being sent to some sort of camp outside Edinburgh. "Mummy thought you might enjoy it," Stuart said, glancing at Nicola as he spoke. "It's out near Carlops somewhere, Bertie, and they have all sorts of things for the boys and girls to do."

Nicola was silent. Bertie did not notice her eyes rolling up as Stuart spoke.

"Will it be a scout camp, Daddy?" Bertie asked. It had long been an ambition of his to go to scout camp. "Will we be able to cook sausages on a fire?"

"Vegan sausages possibly," muttered Nicola.

Stuart shot his mother a warning glance.

"I'm sure they'll have campfires," he said.

Nicola muttered again. "I'm not."

Bertie sensed that his grandmother had her reservations. "And will we be able to do some tracking?" he asked. He had read about tracking in *Scouting for Boys* and he was keen to try it. He had read how you could put sticks on the ground in the shape of an arrow to show people what route you had taken. He had seen pictures of how you could tie grass in a knot to leave a similar message. And then there were signalling flags: Bertie had always wanted to learn semaphore. A camp was just the sort of place where semaphore might be useful.

But most of all, a camp spelled the promise of a penknife. If you went on a scout camp you more or less certainly had to have a penknife, which would come in useful for all sorts of tasks. Perhaps this was his chance to be issued with the Swiss Army penknife that he had long craved with every fibre of his being.

"I expect I'll need a penknife," he ventured. "You can't go to camp without a penknife, I think."

He watched for the adult reaction. Stuart looked away, but Nicola smiled. "I think that's a very good idea, Bertie. I think you should definitely take a penknife to this camp."

Bertie's eyes widened with delight. "Do you really think so, Granny?"

"Yes," said Nicola, heedless of the warning glance from Stuart. "A penknife will be *de rigueur.*"

"What's that mean, Granny?"

"Compulsory," said Nicola. "Essential."

Stuart gave her a discouraging glance. "I'm not sure . . ." he began.

"Well, I am," said Nicola. "And I'll get you one. A Swiss Army knife is what you need. Is that correct?"

"Yes," said Bertie quickly, before the offer could be withdrawn. He could hardly believe his good fortune. A Swiss Army knife – at last!

Bertie did not hear the exchange that took place between his father and his grandmother later that evening.

"You are being deliberately provocative," said Stuart. "You know how that's going to go down with Irene. She'll go ballistic."

Nicola shrugged. "I don't care," she said. "I've had enough. I've bent over backwards to sort things out for her – arranging for her to stay with Antonia and Sister Maria-Fiore dei Fiori di Montagna. But when it comes to Bertie, I'm not prepared to give any ground."

"Well, I have major misgivings," said Stuart.

"He's a very responsible little boy," said Nicola. "He'll be careful how he handles it. And it'll only be a small penknife – it's hardly a machete."

"I know that," said Stuart. "But it's the principle of the thing. This camp that he's going to – well, you know what it'll be like. They won't approve of knives."

"Nor campfires, I suspect," said Nicola.

"Be that as it may," said Stuart. "Irene is Bertie's mother and she has joint custody. She has the right to send him during his time with her."

"He should be with her during her access time," said Nicola.

"I know," sighed Stuart. "But please, Mother: don't poke a stick at Irene. Keep things cool, please. Bite your lip."

"That's exactly what I've been doing," said Nicola. "I've poured a great deal of oil on the water. You needn't worry."

"I wish I knew a bit more about this camp," Stuart said. "She said something about an electronic detoxification programme. No mobile phones or tablets."

"That seems reasonable enough."

"Yes," agreed Stuart. "But she also said something about removing bourgeois expectations."

"Bourgeois expectations?"

"Yes."

Stuart looked out of the window. He was doing a mental calculation, working out exactly how many weeks, days and hours it would be before Irene returned to Aberdeen. The total seemed so dauntingly large. It was going to be a long, hot summer – metaphorically, of course.

31

Vitamin D Deficiency

"So, Bertie," said Olive, as she and Pansy approached him and a small group of other boys in the playground. "Where are you going for your summer holiday?"

"I'm not sure, Olive," he mumbled.

"You're not sure?" exclaimed Olive. "That's really serious, Bertie." And turning to Pansy, she said, "Isn't that amazing, Pansy? Bertie's not made any plans for his summer holiday. Oh dear, oh dear."

"I didn't say that," Bertie protested. "All I said was . . ."

"It's really bad luck," chimed in Pansy. "Poor Bertie! Imagine staying at home when everybody else is going to Disneyland and—"

"And Spain," interjected Olive. "We're going to a place called Benidorm. It's a very exclusive resort. I wish you could see it, Bertie – you'd love it. Such a pity. Only very fashionable people go there. Everybody wears sunglasses."

"It's famous for that," said Pansy. "I've seen pictures in magazines. All those people in their sunglasses, sitting in cafés. They all sit in cafés, you see. In the sun."

Olive interrupted her. "I don't think we should talk too much about it, Pansy. It'll only make Bertie sad. He's probably only going to somewhere like North Berwick. Or maybe even just Portobello. You don't need sunglasses for that sort of place. It's always cloudy in places like that and you wouldn't be able to see where you were going if you wore sunglasses there."

Pansy laughed.

Bertie was not alone, and now one of the boys who had been with him intervened. It was Tofu, the toughest boy in the school, and the one least in touch with his feminine side. "How do you know that Bertie would like to go to Spain, Olive?" he asked. "Not everybody wants to go to Spain, you know. And if Spain's such a great place, why did all those Spanish people go to South America in the first place?"

Olive spun round to face Tofu. "So have you ever been there, Tofu?" she retorted. "Have you? I don't think so. You go nowhere because your dad doesn't believe in aeroplanes. Don't think I don't know that. My dad says your dad wants us to go back to the Stone Age."

"Yes," said Pansy. "Your dad is really sad, Tofu. I saw a programme on television with lots of people like your dad in it. Greens. They were really sad, and they all died at the end. It was a vitamin D deficiency."

"Have you checked your dad's vitamin D levels recently, Tofu?" Olive challenged. "Have you? I don't think you have, you know. And you'll get a very nasty surprise when you do."

"I don't think there's anything wrong with your dad, Tofu," Bertie said. "I don't think he'll die for ages. Greens live until they're really old."

"Thanks, Bertie," said Tofu.

"Oh, poor boys," said Pansy. "Listen to them trying to make each other feel secure. It's so sad, Olive."

"And illegal," said Olive. She shook a finger at Tofu. "I've got some news for you, Tofu. Do you want to hear it?"

"Tell him even if he doesn't want to hear what you have to say, Olive," said Pansy. "He's in denial. All boys are in denial, but Tofu specially."

"Yes," said Olive. "And I will tell you, you know. I'll tell you because it's best for you to know things about yourself – especially if you're in denial – which you are."

"Big time," agreed Pansy. "Boys are often in denial. They

can't help it, I suppose."

Tofu made a face. "I don't care what you say. I'm not ashamed to be a boy. We like being boys – don't we, Bertie?"

Bertie was not sure whether he wanted to get drawn into this debate. There were some arguments, he knew, that you simply could not win – and this, he had discovered, was one of them.

"I don't think it's nice to argue," he said mildly.

But Pansy was not of that view. "Did you hear what Tofu said, Olive? Did you hear what he said about not being ashamed of being a boy?"

Olive nodded grimly. "Incredible," she said. "But I suppose it's not your fault, Tofu. I know you can't help it. Especially since you've got all those warts on your hands. Warts love boys. Warts float around looking for a boy to grow on."

Tofu looked down at his hands. "I've only got one wart," he said. "And there's nothing wrong with having warts. It's a sign that you're strong."

Olive shook her head. "Oh, that's so sad, Pansy. Did you hear that? Tofu doesn't know what warts mean. He doesn't know. I find that really sad."

"Tragic," said Pansy.

"And anyway, Tofu, leaving aside the question of warts, you need to know something else."

"Tell him," Pansy urged.

"You've been cancelled, Tofu. As a friend, I really have to tell you."

"With immediate effect," said Pansy.

Tofu looked anxious in spite of himself. "Who says?" he asked.

Olive smirked. "Who says? The public says. Social media, Tofu. You're cancelled."

Bertie looked alarmed. "What has Tofu done?" he asked.

Olive hesitated. "Where do we begin?" She sighed. "You

heard him, Bertie. You heard him say that there was nothing wrong with being a boy."

"I don't care," said Tofu. "I don't care if I've been cancelled."

"That's what you say," said Olive quickly. "But you'll find out soon enough, Tofu. You'll find out."

Bertie tried to change the subject. "I think I'm going to go to a camp. I'm not sure, but I think I am."

Olive looked interested. "Whereabouts, Bertie? Where's this so-called camp you're going to?"

"It's near a place called Carlops."

Olive let out a shriek of delight. "But that's marvellous, Bertie. I'm going to that camp too. And so is Pansy – aren't you, Pansy?"

"Yes," said Pansy. "That's the plan."

"We'll be able to show you what to do there," said Olive. "And if you're lucky, we can give you some of our food. We'll be taking lots of chocolate cake and stuff."

"Big time," said Pansy.

"I've been there before," said Olive. "We go on expeditions. You can be in our team, Bertie. I'll be leader and Pansy will be deputy leader. You can carry some of the stuff for us." She smiled at Bertie. "I'm really glad you're coming, Bertie. It's going to be really good fun. All of us together – except for Tofu, of course."

Bertie swallowed. He did not want to go to camp with Olive.

Now Olive thought of something. "I hope your friend, Ranald Braveheart Macpherson, isn't coming, Bertie? Have you heard whether he's coming?"

"I don't think so," said Bertie. "But why couldn't Ranald come if he wanted to?"

Olive gave Bertie a pitying look. "Oh, Bertie, you just don't get it, do you? Ranald is just so sad. Have you seen how spindly his legs are? They're like matchsticks. Nobody wants to play with somebody like him. We're prepared to be kind, aren't we, Pansy?"

"Yes," said Pansy. "We're really kind."

"But there are limits," Olive went on. "In fact, Bertie, I think it would be best if you dropped Ranald Braveheart Macpherson. It's not going to do your reputation any good at all, you know. If you want people to respect you, you're going to have to get better friends." She paused. "Like us."

Pansy nodded.

"And going to camp with us will be a start," Olive went on. "We can bond while we're there. I'm looking forward to bonding with you, Bertie – I really am."

"Me too," said Pansy, adding, "Big time."

32

Transparency

Matthew persuaded Elspeth to stay in bed for at least the whole day following her accident on Colinton Road.

"You heard what the doctor told you," he said. "A cracked rib is no joke."

Elspeth protested that it was only a tiny fracture, hardly visible on the X-ray. "And it's getting better," she went on. "These pills really keep the pain under control. It's not too bad at all."

Matthew shook his head. "You're really brave, you know. But you should stay where you are. James will look after the boys. He'll take them to their playgroup after I've gone to work."

He looked at her. He loved Elspeth so much, and he hoped that she knew it. Yet it occurred to him that she might not be sure of that because he had not told her – or at least he had not told her recently. Wives and husbands, it seemed to him, did not say that sort of thing: it was all left unsaid – assumed, perhaps, but not spelled out. That was the problem with life in general – we slipped into a rut in which we failed to state what we meant by the things we did. Our lives, Matthew thought, can become like silent films without the subtitles.

And if Elspeth was unaware of his feelings for her, that might explain why she should have concealed from him her meeting with Shelley. Perhaps she thought he had become indifferent to her, and that indifference licensed her, in a sense, to ignore his feelings and to do things that she knew he did not want her to do.

That distressed him because it meant that this whole situation of mistrust was his creation. If he had been a better husband – or a more demonstrative one, perhaps – then Elspeth would never have deceived him as to what she had been doing immediately before her accident. *Deceived him* . . . the words lodged in his mind as a thorn might lodge in flesh. Deceit was so corrosive, he thought. It could cause the bonds between people to shrivel and die. It was like weedkiller sprayed on a plant; like a upas tree with its toxic roots, destroying such growth as it encountered in the nearby soil.

He should speak to her – he knew that. A problem articulated was a problem halfway to being solved. His father used to say that to him, and his father was right, as he was about so much else. But he had never paid much attention to what his father said because . . . He wondered why he had ignored parental advice, and decided that it was because it was parental – that was why. He had not paid much attention to what his parents said simply because they were his parents and all children wanted in their heart of hearts was to make decisions that were their own, that were authentic to them. Lip service was paid to the wisdom of parents – and to the experience that parents had – but you had to be yourself, thought Matthew. You had to make your own decisions. And yet here I am, he thought, remembering what my father said to me about talking about problems rather than ignoring them. But he could still not bring himself to confront Elspeth with his inadvertent discovery of her failure to tell him about the lunch. He could not, because he imagined how painful it would be – for both of them. He would seem reproachful and she would feel as if she were a malefactor caught in the headlights of the righteous.

So he remained silent, as did Elspeth. She had gone to sleep the previous night – eventually, and only after a further dose of painkillers – with the firm intention of confessing to Matthew the following morning, but when the following morning dawned, she found that she could not face speaking to him about it. He would be hurt – of course he would, because they had always believed, even if they had not expressed this to one another, that they had no secrets. Married people, or people in a close relationship of any sort, should not have secrets from one another – or should they? She stopped herself. Did we really have to tell our partner *everything*? Surely there were at least some things that could be kept private – some thoughts that expediency, if nothing else, suggested we should not disclose.

She had once asked Matthew what he dreamed about, and he had blushed. It had taken her by surprise, and for a few moments she felt flustered and was, like him, silent. That was because her question must have prompted him to remember dreams that he might not want to disclose to her because . . . She hardly dared think about it. A girlfriend had once said to her that her boyfriend had told her about a dream that he had that was, well, not the sort of dream that a girlfriend would want a boyfriend to have. And while he thought that his candour was reassuring to her, in fact it had the opposite effect. That was because we all knew, Elspeth's friend said, that the things we do in dreams are the things we really want to do – or so the Freudians said, though of course you could argue that the human mind actually identified things that you did *not* want to do and then rehearsed them in dreams out of a sort of daredevil bravado. In this way, you could argue that the fact you dreamed of something meant that you would never do what the dream implied: it was simply a marker of the bounds of desire. And what did her friend know, anyway? She was always going on about popular psychology. That was probably why her boyfriend had confessed his dream in the first place: he was winding her up because he was fed up with popular psychological theories. Ultimately, Elspeth thought, dreams were just nonsense, and told us nothing about anything. They were random noise that meant nothing.

Now, as she lay in bed, listening to James exhorting the boys, his words rising above the incessant clamour of young voices, she decided that she would not, after all, tell Matthew about her lunch with Shelley. It would only upset him, and there was no reason for that. What she *would* do, though, was make a private promise to herself that she would never again conceal anything from him. In that way, she would not just be walking away from a difficult situation – she would be using it to strengthen her commitment to truth and . . . and what? Transparency. That was the word: we were all meant to be transparent now, and for a moment she imagined a roomful of transparent people, wispy as wraiths, rather like jellyfish glimpsed just below the water's surface, their internal organs visible through their insubstantial flesh, their transparent skin. She smiled at the thought – and the smile sent a shiver of pain across her ribcage. Not only was laughter contra-indicated with a cracked rib, but so, it seemed, was a smile.

33

Fungus Issues

If Elspeth had put aside her discomfort over her unfortunate non-disclosure (or lie by omission), the same could not be said of Matthew, who, as he crossed Dundas Street for his morning latte at Big Lou's, was revisiting in painful detail the moment when Shelley's innocent remark had so badly disturbed his equanimity. Was there a point in any marriage, he wondered, where one party realised that the unquestioning trust, or indeed love behind that trust, was possibly misplaced? Could you wake up one morning and realise that you no longer loved the person whose head was on the pillow beside you? Undoubtedly that happened, but Matthew had never imagined he would experience it himself. And he had not, of course, since he still loved Elspeth; now, though, there was a niggling doubt, a potential dawning of detachment. That would be terrible – almost inconceivable, in fact – and yet he thought that he was on the verge of feeling just that.

Matthew had been brooding on his situation, but had been unable to decide on any course of action. He suspected that he would end up doing nothing, and allow the whole issue to be forgotten. Most arguments and disagreements had a natural shelf life, and there was a lot to be said for allowing the normal course of events to overtake the problems of the past. And yet even if that happened, he feared that he would feel unhappy. He had been betrayed, and that left a wound that would be slow to heal.

And then something else occurred to him – something that was infinitely more disturbing. What if Elspeth had another reason not to tell him why she had been driving along Colinton Road – a road that she would normally have no reason to be on. What if she were having an affair? The lunch with Shelley might not be the main thing she wanted to conceal; she might have been driving along Colinton Road for a reason that she wanted to keep from her husband – and the most obvious reason for that would be she was meeting somebody else – another man.

For a few moments he stopped in his tracks, as the awful possibility dawned on him. The traffic passed up and down Dundas Street, indifferent to his anguish. He remembered a line in a John Betjeman poem he had read at school a long time ago. People laughed at John Betjeman, called him sentimental, but he could hit the nail on the head when it came to describing people's feelings; and he had written there about a man coming out of a doctor's surgery, his X-ray photos tucked under his arm, the bad news having just been conveyed to him within. And he surveys the passing crowd, whom he describes as indifferent, as *merciless, hurrying Londoners*. We are so often alone in our grief and our fear.

What if Elspeth were to leave him? He had never considered that possibility – not once – but now he did, and he wondered whether he would be left with the boys in that echoing, empty house. He saw himself sitting down to his bachelor's meal of ready-made macaroni cheese, exhausted by the effort of putting the triplets to bed, facing evening after evening of loneliness. One reassuring thing about marriage was that you no longer had to worry about inviting anybody out, but if he were to be left by himself he would have to get back to that – and all the anxiety it involves. Imagine having to do internet dating, and to subject yourself to critical appraisal before you even met. And even if a date were arranged, what would you talk to a perfect stranger about? Yourself? All he could say was that he worked in a gallery and knew something about pictures and had three very young sons. And her eyes would glaze over, because she would be bound to be looking for something much more exciting than me, he told himself, with my bit of hair that always sticks up no matter how hard I try to slick it down, and my tendency to get athlete's foot unless I'm very careful about changing socks and using that special antifungal powder.

Would *anyone* show the slightest interest in a person who used antifungal powder? Of course, one might not mention it, but then it might be discovered in the bathroom and she would say "So, what's this, then? Antifungal powder?" and he would have to claim that it belonged to a cousin who came to stay and who left it behind – a cousin who had fungus issues, but was trying to do something about it – as one should, if one has a fungal infection. And she would look at him with the look of one who can only too easily see through people who lie about antifungal powder. And he would be at a loss for words, because he was an unconvincing liar.

He reached the café still distracted by the thought of disaster. It was quiet inside, and Big Lou was sitting behind her counter doing *The Scotsman* cryptic crossword. She had almost finished it, but was struggling over 10 across, *Put paid to endless mixed-up saga, tasty and greasy epic without c! 6, 3.* She looked up, and put her newspaper to one side.

Matthew could tell that something was wrong. "You all right, Lou?" he asked. He nodded towards the newspaper. "You don't want to let these crosswords wreck your day, you know."

The solution came to her as he spoke. *Scotch pie.* Scotch was a verb, as much as it was an adjective. And 'pie' was an anagram of epic without the letter 'c'. Of course; of course. But it gave her no satisfaction.

"Lou?" he enquired. There was something very wrong – he was sure of it.

"Aye," she said. "You'll want your coffee."

"No," he replied. "I want to know what's wrong. There *is* something, isn't there?"

Big Lou hesitated. She glanced around the café, as if looking for an excuse to say nothing. But it was empty.

"There's nobody," said Matthew. "Come on, Lou. Tell me."

Big Lou took a deep breath. "Oh, Matthew," she said. "I don't know – I just don't know."

"Don't know what, Lou?"

She looked away, avoiding his gaze. "I know fine you shouldn't pay any attention to these things. I know that fine."

"To what, Lou?"

"To anonymous letters."

He sat down, reaching across the counter to take her hand. She allowed him to hold it, and he gripped it awkwardly for a moment or two before releasing it.

"Oh, Lou," he said.

"I dinnae have any idea what folk who write these things think they're doing," she said. "Maybe they think they're helping. Maybe they just want to cause trouble."

Her voice was rising, and he tried to calm her down. "If you've received an anonymous letter, Lou, I'd put it straight in the bin. That's where these things belong. And then think no more about it. Forget it."

"Even if it says your husband's seeing somebody else?" said Lou. "And even gives you her name? Betty? Even then?"

34

Signed in Green Ink

Matthew asked Big Lou if he could see the letter. She hesitated, and he was about to tell her that it didn't matter and that she should just destroy it anyway. But then she reached below the counter and brought out a single sheet of paper. It was typed, although the final line, *A well-wisher,* was written by hand, and in green ink.

Matthew's first thought was of his English teacher at the Edinburgh Academy, Mr Vansittart, an enthusiast for the novels of Anthony Trollope, who was also a foe of what he called "ridiculous beliefs of every stripe".

"Be aware of false beliefs," he said. "They are all about us: such as the proposition that those who write in green ink are lunatics."

And here was a letter signed in green ink.

"Green ink," he said to Big Lou.

She nodded. "A sign of lunacy. Well-known."

Matthew looked at her, but said nothing. This was too upsetting a moment to engage in a discussion of popular myths, and Mr Vansittart, he thought, would agree with him.

"Read it," said Big Lou. "Go on."

Matthew read out loud. "'Dear Lou,'" the letter began, "'You do not know me, but I have seen you once or twice in your coffee bar – a long time ago. I know that you got married recently to a man they call Fat Bob. He used to stay down here in Leith, where I stay. I know it's none of my business but I thought you should be told that although he recently married you, Bob has been seen down here a lot recently with a woman called Betty. You should see her. She has a tattoo on her right arm of Atlas holding up the world. I've seen it. He spends a lot of time in her house and the only conclusion I can reach is that he is having an affair with her. I can't stand by and watch a man cheating on a woman like that. We women have so much to put up with, and men think they can get away with it because we won't stand up for ourselves. Well, I say that it's about time we stood up to men like that and stopped them making our lives a misery. That's why I'm writing to you. I would give you my name, but Bob has been known to be violent and I'm not going to risk it. Sorry about that, Lou. And I'm sorry if this comes as a shock to you, but I think it's best for you to know.'" And then, in emerald green ink, *A well-wisher.*

Matthew handed the letter back to Big Lou with a groan. "This is awful, Lou. It's horrible."

Lou slipped the letter back under the counter. "Do you think it's true, Matthew?"

There was sorrow in her voice, and Matthew thought that, although she asked this question, she had already decided on the answer.

"I don't think so, Lou," he said. "This woman could be anyone. She could be . . ." He was about to say "a lunatic", because there was the green ink, of course, but he did not.

"Mental?" asked Big Lou.

"Possibly," said Matthew.

Big Lou shook her head. "It doesn't sound like that to me," she said. "I think the person who wrote this letter was as sane as you and I are, Matthew. I think this is not the letter of somebody who's mental. This person knows what she's doing."

Matthew bit his lip. That was exactly what he felt, but had yet to say. This letter was, he suspected, entirely truthful. He thought of something. "Did you look at the postmark?"

"None," said Lou. "The envelope was slipped under the door."

"Saving postage?" asked Matthew.

Big Lou shrugged. "I don't know."

"I see that she uses the word *stay* when she mentions being down in Leith. That's genuine. Edinburgh and Leith people always say *stay* rather than *live*. You never say, *Where do you live?* You say, *Where do you stay?*"

"I don't think that helps," said Big Lou.

"No," admitted Matthew. "It doesn't. I was just making an observation." He paused. He and Big Lou were old friends. He could speak frankly to her. "Do you think that Bob might be . . .?" He looked for a tactful way of putting it, and decided upon "Do you think Bob might be *seeing* somebody?"

Big Lou looked away. She was clearly upset, and Matthew regretted having asked her.

"I don't know, Matthew," she said eventually. "If you had asked me that up until two days ago, I would have said it was impossible. But over the last few days he has been out when I phoned the flat. And then, when he was due to collect Finlay from his dance lesson yesterday, he didn't turn up. I asked him where he was and he said that he had gone out for a walk and had forgotten that he was meant to be collecting him. But there was something in the way he said this that worried me. There was tension in his voice."

"That might have been because he had forgotten to collect Finlay," said Matthew. "That could have been embarrassment."

"Perhaps, but it made me think."

For a few minutes Matthew was silent. He was unsure what to say. Then he decided. "Would you like me to check up?" he said.

Big Lou turned to face him. "Do you think we should?"

Matthew nodded. "The truth of the matter, Lou, is that I've heard – very much at second-hand – somebody say something about Bob. It wasn't anything specific – just something to think a bit about."

"So you think we should do something?"

"It's up to you, Lou, but if I were in your shoes I'd want to find out whether there's any truth in what that letter says. And if there isn't any, you can ignore it. I suspect there's nothing."

"But you've just said that you heard something."

Matthew winced. "Sorry, Lou, I was trying to protect you, I suppose. This letter might be serious, I'm afraid. Might be. Who knows?"

Big Lou closed her eyes. "It always happens to me, doesn't it?" she said. "I'm not sure what I've done to deserve this bad luck I have with men, but—"

Matthew interrupted her. "You've done nothing to deserve that, Lou."

Lou was silent. Then she said, "All I want out of life is to get a small amount of happiness, Matthew. Not a lot." She checked herself. "That sounds like self-pity. Sorry."

Matthew shook his head. "It isn't, Lou. I don't think it's that at all. Not for one moment."

35

No Point in Girning

Matthew had never seen Big Lou in tears, and indeed would have imagined the very expression "Big Lou in tears" to be an oxymoron. In his mind – and indeed, in the minds of most of those who knew her – Big Lou embodied all those strong, stoical qualities invariably present in those who come from the Scottish agricultural hinterland. If you were from rural Angus, as Big Lou was, you did not complain about life; you did not go on about your victimhood; you did not burden others with your problems; and above all, you did not snivel. And yet here was Big Lou, from Snell Mains, that cold farm near Arbroath, wiping the tears from her cheeks.

Of course, she was embarrassed, and tried to conceal her fragile state from Matthew.

"Mustn't complain," she muttered, trying to keep her voice level. "There's nae point in girning."

Matthew felt his heart go out to her. "Oh, Lou," he began. "Oh Lou, you mustn't . . ." Mustn't what? Mustn't cry? He realised that, although a natural response to the distress of another, this was not what we should say in such circumstances. If you felt like crying, then that is exactly what you should do, as crying allowed your anguish to come to the surface, and exposure to sunlight was often just what anguish needed.

So Matthew corrected himself, and said, "Have a good cry, Lou. Why not?"

But Big Lou then said, "So you think I've got something to cry about?"

Matthew tried to soothe her feelings. "I don't know. There may be something in that horrid letter – or there may not. Perhaps you should just talk to Bob about it? Ask him whether he's seeing somebody else."

Big Lou shook her head. "I can't. Not without some proof. If it's all false, then I will have shattered the trust that exists between us. You can't go around asking your man – at random – whether he's having an affair. You just can't."

"All right," said Matthew. "Don't ask him. But then what? Are you prepared to ignore that letter? It's obviously making you cry."

And it was – again – as Big Lou began to sob afresh. And at that moment, as her sobs took hold, a shadow passed the window that gave out onto the descending steps – a shadow that might have been a large bird of prey – a hawk, perhaps, with outstretched wings – but was, in fact the shadow of Sister Maria-Fiore dei Fiori di Montagna, whose robes, fluttering about her as she negotiated the steps, were like the wings of a bird.

The nun swept in before Big Lou could compose herself, and saw at once her friend's distress. Matthew glanced at Sister Maria-Fiore dei Fiori di Montagna with irritation: this *bossy* nun was everywhere, it seemed – on the board of the National Gallery of Scotland, on the governing body of the Art College, on the council of Hibernian Football Club – everywhere. It was as if those in charge of such boards had discovered a new and essential criterion for a balanced membership – an Italian nun – and had ticked, with relief, the box that signalled their compliance with that diktat. And here she was, entering Big Lou's coffee bar as a galleon in full sail breezes into a harbour.

"Oh, Lou," exclaimed the nun. "*Disastro!* Are you all right, dearest one? *Sancta Maria*, you are crying? Can that possibly be so?"

It was a broadside, in a way, and it brought an end to Lou's sobbing.

"I'm all right now," she said to Sister Maria-Fiore dei Fiori di Montagna. "It was nothing much. You know how it is sometimes . . ."

That comment, of course, was not one that one would normally want to address to another with a reputation for the coining of aphorisms. And, indeed, it triggered an immediate aphorism from Sister Maria-Fiore dei Fiori di Montagna. "When it seems that there is nothing," she began, "it is often the case that there is something – behind the nothing."

"True," said Matthew. "I hadn't thought of that."

To which Sister Maria-Fiore dei Fiori di Montagna, replied, "The fact that we have not thought about something does not mean that others have not thought about it."

Matthew nodded. "That's true too," he said, adding, "As far as it goes."

Sister Maria-Fiore dei Fiori di Montagna now came up to the counter. Reaching out, she took Big Lou's hand, and held it gently, stroking her fingers with her own. *She's very tactile,* thought Matthew, *but Italians are a tactile people. They love stroking others.*

"Dear Lou," said Sister Maria-Fiore dei Fiori di Montagna. "Has something happened?"

Well, of course it has, thought Matthew. Lou wouldn't burst into tears in her coffee bar simply because it was a Tuesday.

"It's nothing," said Big Lou, dabbing at her cheek with a tea towel.

"No," Sister Maria-Fiore dei Fiori di Montagna contradicted her. "It's Bob, isn't it? You've found out about him?"

Big Lou's surprise at this remark seemed to suppress her sobs.

"You know about it?" she asked.

Sister Maria-Fiore dei Fiori di Montagna lowered her head, as might one do who has been discovered to be harbouring some momentous secret. "About Bob's . . . about his arrangements? I fear that I might have heard something from my contacts down in Leith."

Matthew looked on with amazement. *Contacts down in Leith?* Were there no natural bounds to the extent of Sister Maria-Fiore's influence?

Big Lou let out a groan. "It seems that everybody knows – except me. And I am just his wife."

Matthew intervened. "You have to be careful of tittle-tattle," he said. "Rumours may be baseless, and yet spread like wildfire." He looked at Sister Maria-Fiore dei Fiori di Montagna as he made this last remark.

Sister Maria-Fiore dei Fiori di Montagna turned to address him. "Dear Matthew," she said. "Big Lou is a strong woman. We should not protect her from the truth. We should help her."

"I don't see how we can do that," said Matthew.

Sister Maria-Fiore dei Fiori di Montagna disapproved of defeatism. "We can investigate the matter," she said firmly. "We can find out whether these rumours have any substance." She paused. "That is, if Big Lou would like us to." She paused again. "It is with knowledge of the facts that one is best armed, even if that knowledge is unwelcome."

Oh, really! thought Matthew. But he confined himself to saying, "I think we should keep out of Big Lou's business."

"The business of our friends is always our business too," retorted Sister Maria-Fiore dei Fiori di Montagna. "Our sister is our sister, and our sister's concerns are our concerns. None of us is an island. *Lo sappiamo per certo.*" She looked at Matthew as if he was making a contestable claim to insularity.

He met her stare. "But what exactly do you propose to do, Sister Maria-Fiore dei Fiori di Montagna?"

She had her answer at the ready. "To follow him," she said. She spoke briskly, as if to challenge Matthew to object to her plan.

Matthew was silent. What could be less likely to attract attention than a nun in full habit tailing a man like Fat Bob through the streets of Leith? He smiled at the thought.

36

At Valvona & Crolla

Two days later, in a different coffee bar altogether, that of Valvona & Crolla on Elm Row, Angus Lordie was waiting for the arrival of Roger Collins, the historian of medieval Spain, meticulous chronicler of Popes and Jacobites alike, and his long-time friend. They had met when Angus was at art college in Edinburgh and Roger, a neophyte medievalist, was writing an undergraduate dissertation on Alfonso the Wise; they were both on a walking tour of Spain and found themselves staying in the same bedbug-ridden youth hostel on a well-beaten track to Santiago de Compostela. Such memories provide a basis for friendship that a clean and convenient hotel can never give: Hilaire Belloc recognised this in asking Miranda, in verse, whether she remembered an inn, and the fleas that teased in the high Pyrenees . . . It would be difficult to wax poetic in that way about a room in a Hilton Hotel, with its thoughtfully-placed copy of *Be My Guest* and its notice about the charge that would be levied for cleaning should a guest smoke (guests who spontaneously combusted would, one assumes, not be asked to pay). Since that meeting, where they both cheerfully – and gratefully – made do with a dinner of a small piece of chorizo, hard goat's-milk cheese, and a bottle of Rioja, they had remained in touch, occasionally meeting for coffee and a discussion of matters of the day.

Both were disinclined to complain about the world. Angus was an optimist by nature, although he also claimed to be a realist, and Roger had too broad an understanding of history to believe that things were at any particular time all that much worse than they had been, or would be, at any other time. This meant that they wasted little time in bemoaning those things that old friends sometimes bemoan when they meet after an absence. Neither was at all like Joxer Daly in Sean O'Casey's *Juno and the Paycock,* who remarks throughout the play that the "whole world's in a terrible state of *chassis*". And yet sometimes that temptation must have been there as *chassis*, surely, could be seen at every turn when one contemplated the world. Of course, to make that observation about *chassis* ameliorates the situation, as laughter, in spite of surrounding gloom, indeed *chassis*, has been clinically proved to be therapeutic. The data is in: laughter, like vitamin B6, is an antidote to depression.

Roger was sitting at a table and waving to Angus as the artist came up the short flight of stairs leading to the coffee room at the back of the shop.

"Here we are," said Roger. "In spite of all the *chassis*."

Angus laughed. "Indeed, Roger. But a spot of *chassis* focuses the mind, one might argue."

They ordered coffee and Roger enquired about what Angus was painting. He always asked, and was usually regaled with a description of the latest portrait – of the sitter and his or her ways, and of the challenges of achieving a likeness without causing grave offence to the sitter and the sitter's family. But on this occasion, Angus had more profound matters to discuss.

"I want to do something more substantial," he said. "I've been talking for years about painting something . . . well, something bigger. A painting that *says* something."

Roger nodded. "I've heard you talking about it." He added, with a gentle smile, "Several times, in fact."

Angus looked sheepish. "Yes, like garlic, I repeat. But I never seem to actually put brush to canvas."

"We all do that," said Roger. "I have books I've intended

to write. In fact, when you think of the books that people form a firm intention to write but never do, well, the Great Library at Alexandria could never hold them. They are there, in the ether of ideas, in their countless thousands." He paused. "Have you ever met anybody who *isn't* planning to write a novel?"

Angus thought for a few moments. Now that he came to think of it, almost all his friends talked about their novel. Some even talked about writing a *great novel*, and, in one immodest case, about writing *the great Scottish novel*. But they never did; these were the mute, inglorious Miltons of Gray's "Elegy", or perhaps, more appropriately, the unrealised Robert Burnses *de nos jours,* still at the plough. He sighed. Was he in that company? It seemed to him that he probably was. He was the man you met in a bar who told you about his unrealised plans to do some great thing.

And there was so little time to do it. At twenty, you thought you would do it when you were thirty; at thirty, you thought you would do it when you had the wisdom and insight of your forties. But of course the forties are a busy time in the lives of most, and the great projects are put off until the fifties, and beyond, into the vague lists of injury time. And then, at some stage, the whistle blew, and it was too late to do the great things of this life.

He sighed again. Angus was not all that old; he had time, and he liked to think that he had the ability. But the problem was exactly the same as it was for those people who never wrote their novel: he had no plot, or, in his case, no subject. And the problem with having no subject is that you cannot deliberately invent a great theme: a great theme has to come to you; it has to *hurt* you into artistic expression. Great paintings painted themselves; they came from somewhere deep in the artist, some well of feeling, of passion, that demanded expression. They put themselves on the canvas, challenging others to look at them, to see what it was that they simply had to say.

Now he said to Roger, "*Guernica*."

Roger looked at him. "The village? The site of the outrage?"

Angus shook his head. "No, the painting."

"Ah yes," said Roger. "I've actually seen the painting. I stood for, oh, half an hour or more. It has a visceral effect."

"It's probably Picasso's most important work," said Angus. "It's one of the most recognisable pictures in the world."

"Along with what?"

Angus thought. "The *Mona Lisa*, I suppose. That might be the most famous artwork of them all. Or Botticelli's *Birth of Venus*. It's hard to imagine anything better known than those two."

"I agree," said Roger. "I must say that I always enjoy going into a gallery and seeing the effect that a famous painting has on people coming into the room. They stop and you see the delight of discovery on their face – their delight at seeing the real thing. They say to themselves: *Am I actually seeing this?* I observed that in the Uffizi. When people came into the gallery in which Venus stands forever on her shell, some of them actually screamed. It was as if they were at a pop concert and saw Paul McCartney or . . . or Elvis."

Angus laughed. "Screaming is an odd thing to do," he said.

"Except sometimes," said Roger. "There are occasions when it seems absolutely the right thing to do. I heard Pavarotti sing 'Nessun dorma' once. In Milan. Some people screamed."

"Or exhaled," suggested Angus, adding, "Opera fans exhale volubly, don't you think?"

"Of course," said Roger.

37

Ossian, and So On

Roger wanted to help Angus. He did not consider his friend a failure – Angus was far from that: he had more portrait commissions than he could handle and, though in demand, he charged only the most modest of fees, even painting some of his more deserving subjects on a *pro bono* basis. His work had been widely praised, and he had been elected an Academician of the Royal Scottish Academy. He might not be a contemporary Allan Ramsay or Henry Raeburn, fêted by the powerful and the influential, but, like those earlier portraitists, he was creating a very particular record of his time. Our age might have a plethora of electronic devices to encode each and every moment, but the portraitist's eye remained unmatched in its power to capture the essence of the human subject.

Roger knew that, and he appreciated the sometimes rather lonely artistic furrow that Angus ploughed. He hoped that Angus understood the value of what he was doing, but he had long since come to the conclusion that not all those whose work amounts to something believe that what they do is good enough, or even worth doing. The most accomplished among us, he felt, can be failures in their own eyes, simply because the standards they set for themselves were too high. There were plenty of artists of mediocre ability who thought their own work reached great heights; there were far fewer of real talent who believed that of themselves.

"You need," Roger began, "a—"

"Subject," Angus supplied.

Roger smiled. "The very word."

Angus looked up at the ceiling, as if hoping for inspiration from that quarter. After a few moments, he said, "Our problem in Scotland is that we have plenty of romantic stories. Look at Water Scott."

"Yes, indeed," agreed Roger. "Scott was not short of plots."

"And our history is hardly dull," Angus went on. "The Declaration of Arbroath. Bruce *et al.* Those Stuarts of yours and their ill-fated wanderings. Reivers by the score. Plots at every turn. And we have plenty of material that may not be romantic but is still pretty colourful, even heart-rending. Remember that painting *Lochaber No More* – the Highlanders on their way to Canada, or wherever? And the gritty, irrepressible character of the Clyde. You can't be indifferent to all that. But do we have a national epic for a painter like me to get his teeth into? I don't think so."

"Do you really need one?"

Angus said that he thought it could be useful. "One can get by without a national epic," he said. "But so many people have one and I think it's a pity that Scotland hasn't."

Roger looked thoughtful. "I suppose you're right. But have you *looked* hard enough? Perhaps we do have something lying about that fits the bill. I imagine it's easy enough to mislay the occasional national epic when one's mind is on other things."

Angus looked incredulous.

"There's the *Gododdin*, for instance," said Roger. "That was probably composed, even if in oral form initially, here in Scotland – the *ur*-Scotland, of course. It probably began round about where the castle is today." He paused. "Of course, it's in Welsh, which is what was spoken in these parts. The wrong sort of Gaelic, that is: P-Celtic rather than Q. People, you see, don't always speak the language other people want them to. Have you noticed that?"

Angus grinned. "Or they speak it in the wrong place."

Roger nodded. "That, indeed. The *Gododdin* is a series of eulogies to heroes sent down to deal with our neighbours down south. Unfortunately, they all came to a sticky end somewhere in North Yorkshire, near Catterick Racecourse. And you can't have a national epic in which your own side is roundly defeated. Odysseus has to get home, after all."

"Defeat is not a good idea," agreed Angus. "People, on the whole, like their heroes to win. And it sounds as if the Welsh have claimed that particular epic anyway."

"Of course, there are Irish stories that might be considered Scottish in an attenuated sense," Roger continued. "Ireland and Scotland were part of a common travel area way back – a sort of early Schengen zone. So early Scots, whoever they were, would have been familiar with the Ulster Cycle and so on. Those tales are mostly about drinking, fighting and stealing cattle; but those were popular Scottish activities in those days."

"One has to do something to pass the time," said Angus.

"What about Ossian?" asked Roger. "You might find something in all those bits and pieces that Macpherson collected . . ."

"Or invented," interjected Angus.

Roger nodded. "I see you're *parti pris* on that one."

"Well," said Angus, "with the best will in the world I can't imagine myself doing anything with Ossian. I've seen some of the previous attempts, and they're not edifying. *Fingal's Battle with the Spirit of Loda* is an example." He shuddered. "No, I fear that we're really short of epic material. There's what might be called a Scottish epic-deficit."

"You could invent one, of course," said Roger. "Every epic has to start somewhere and even if you found only one or two sentences of something, you could develop it. Have you heard of the story surrounding the beginnings of the Frankish royal dynasty? There's only one sentence about that – it's in *The*

Chronicle of the Pseudo-Fredegar. The founder of the dynasty, Merovich, was said to have been conceived as a result of his mother's encounter with a sea monster on a beach. These things are so colourful. And Tolkien, after all, wrote an epic from scratch. *Lord of the Rings* was meant to provide a saga for the English. Tolkien felt they lacked one and he might fill the gap."

Angus took a sip of his coffee. Roger was right; every epic has to start with an act of authorial invention, and if only he could think of something that had epic qualities but that did not involve too much . . . how had Roger put it? Drinking, fighting, and stealing cattle? Could there be such a thing as a national epic that did not involve violence? He tried to think of one that was entirely pacific, and failed.

And it was while he was struggling with that question, that he saw a couple enter the café and sit down at a table on the other side of the room. He recognised the man immediately, but not the woman. It was Fat Bob, and there was an unfamiliar woman with him. As they sat down at their table, the woman reached out and took Bob's hand and caressed it, fondly, wistfully, as a lover might do.

Roger noticed Angus's glance, and looked across the café. "Know them?" he asked.

"One of them," muttered Angus.

Roger could see that Angus was upset about something. Perhaps talk of national epics had that effect. He was about to change the subject, in an effort to lighten the mood, when they both noticed another person entering the café, hard on the heels of Fat Bob and his companion. This time, the new arrival spotted them and immediately made her way over to their table, with only a quick glance in the direction of Fat Bob to ensure that he had not seen her. And he had not. He had withdrawn his hand from his companion's, quickly, guiltily, out of clear concern that the intimacy might be spotted. Now he was staring fixedly at the tablecloth.

"You won't mind if I join you," said Sister Maria-Fiore dei Fiori di Montagna.

It was a statement rather than a question, delivered with the certainty that accompanies the former and is rarely a concomitant of the latter.

38

Seriously Cold

Borthy Borthwick said to Bruce, "Look, Brucie, let me drive you up to this abbey place you're going to – it's the least I can do."

Bruce thought, *The least you can do, Borthy, is to stop calling me Brucie. I am not Brucie. We're not six any longer.* But he said none of this, because now he spoke – consciously – with charity, and it would have been uncharitable to reproach poor Borthy Borthwick, with all his limitations, while he, Bruce, had so much going for him: looks, in particular, and that special way with women; the list was as long as the West Highland Way . . . He stopped himself. That was the *old* Bruce; the *new* Bruce did not think that way at all. And so he simply thanked his old friend for the offer and said that it would save him a great deal of trouble to be driven up to Elgin and to Pluscarden Abbey, where he was expected later that day.

Bruce had packed a single suitcase. "I won't need many clothes," he explained to Borthy. "I'll be wearing a habit up there, and they said they could give me working clothes for the garden – old trousers and boots – that sort of thing."

Borthy wrinkled his nose. "Old trousers? I'm not sure if—"

Bruce put up a hand to silence him. "There is nothing wrong with old clothing, Borthy. We don't need to adorn ourselves."

"*You* may not," Borthy said. "But then, you look good in anything. I need all the help I can get from clothes."

Bruce ignored this. "And anyway," he continued. "I told you that you could have any of my gear – remember?"

Now, with Borthy at the wheel of his beige Vauxhall Corsa – and Borthy was just the sort of person to drive a beige Vauxhall Corsa, Bruce had decided, until, once again, he withdrew his unkind thought – with Borthy at that wheel, they headed north to Morayshire. On either side of the road, Highland Perthshire now revealed itself to them like a travel poster: hills and forests and waterfalls tumbling down hillsides with boyish exuberance.

"I don't know when I'll see all this again," said Bruce, as he gazed out of the car window.

Borthy glanced at him. "Don't speak like that," he said. "You're only going to Elgin."

Bruce sighed. "I'm not sure that you understand, Borthy: I'm becoming a monk. I'm about to say goodbye to the world."

For a few moments, Borthy did not reply. Then he said, "Are you quite sure you want to go through with this, Brucie? It's not too late, you know. I can pull over and turn round. We could be back in the Cumberland Bar in a couple of hours. Or the Wally Dug. Or Bennets beside the King's Theatre – remember that place?"

Bruce was patient. "No, Borthy, I've made up my mind."

"Jeez," said Borthy, and left the subject at that. A few minutes later, though, he said to Bruce, "You remember that girl, Candace? Remember her?"

"Yes," said Bruce, cagily.

"You remember how you said you licked her hair at that dance? Just above her ear. Remember saying that?"

Bruce shook his head. "I never licked anybody's hair. Why would I do that?"

"Because she had this strawberry-coloured hair – that's why. It's only natural to want to lick strawberry-coloured hair."

Bruce shook his head. "Listen, Borthy, leave it – just leave it. That's all in the past. It's history. Medieval history, for heaven's sake."

Borthy was apologetic. "I'm sorry, Bruce, I keep forgetting. You've changed."

"Yes," said Bruce. "I have."

Borthy waited. Then he said, "I've been wondering about it for years, you know. I keep asking myself: could that really have happened, or did he make it up?"

Bruce frowned. "Why would I lie? Do you think I lied about that sort of thing, Borthy? Do you think I would actually make up a story that I'd licked some girl's hair?" He paused. "And do you think I'm the sort who goes around licking people's hair at the drop of a hat?"

"I didn't say that, Brucie. I didn't say you were that sort of guy."

"Because now," Bruce said, "I don't want people talking like that. I have promises to make."

"You mean they're going to ask you to promise not to lick people's hair?"

Bruce shook his head. "That's covered by a general promise. They don't have to spell it out. And I think you should just leave it, Borthy. Just let it go."

Borthy looked crushed. "I wasn't criticizing you, you know."

Bruce was still staring out of the window. "That's all right, then. Let's just move on."

"What do you get to eat in this place?" Borthy asked. "Regular food, do you think?"

"I have no idea," said Bruce. "Simple fare, I imagine. Oatmeal porridge. Fish, probably. Beans. Potatoes."

"And will they cut your hair?" asked Borthy. "Like Friar Tuck? That sort of thing?"

Bruce fingered his scalp nervously. He had not thought about that. "Not at first," he said. "I'm going to be a novice, and novices aren't fully signed up to the Rule."

"Just as well," said Borthy. He glanced at Bruce again. "Do they know – these monk guys – do they know you've been struck by lightning?"

Bruce shook his head. "I don't think that's relevant."

Borthy was not convinced. "But what if the effect of the lightning wears off? How do you know if lightning has a permanent effect? Did that shrink say anything about it?"

"Dr Livingstone?"

"Yes, the shrink you told me about. Him."

Bruce tried to remember exactly what had been said. "I think he said that if there were changes they would not be short-lived. He said there was a lot about electricity and the brain that they simply don't understand yet. He said that the way ECT works is still a bit of a mystery. They just know it works. Maybe it's the same with lightning: they know it changes you, but they don't know how."

The conversation continued, but on a different tack. And it did not seem long before Pluscarden Abbey came into sight, nestling in its glen, a tree-lined hillside above it.

"That's the place," said Bruce. "Right over there. See it?"

Borthy let out a whistle. "Big," he said. "And you know something about that building, Brucie? You want to know? It looks seriously cold to me. I'm not saying it's definitely cold – it's just that's the way it looks to me. Do these places have any heating at all, do you think? I don't think they do – because you can't heat a place like that without a big stash of the readies. Big time."

"I have no idea," said Bruce.

"I knew somebody who bought some electric socks once," said Borthy. "He was going up to northern Norway for an oil company and he bought these socks that had small batteries. They heated up. He said that he thinks they saved his toes from frostbite."

"I don't think it's that cold here," said Bruce.

"I hope not," said Borthy. "You don't want to lose your toes, Bruce."

Bruce resisted the temptation to give Borthy a withering look. Really! What a statement of the obvious: *you don't want to lose your toes.* Why did people like Borthy think it necessary to make such banal observations?

39

The Consequences of Frostbite

"No," said Borthy. "You need your toes, you know. We take them for granted, of course, but you just try walking without your toes. Just try it. You go all over the place. It's to do with your balance."

Bruce took a deep breath. The journey was not yet over, and he was not sure that he could tolerate Borthy's conversation without showing his irritation. But I have to, he told himself; I have to be kind to this poor chap, who's never really had a proper girlfriend and who drives everybody up the wall with his wittering on about toes and such things. Take another deep breath, Bruce; remember that this is the new you.

"Did you ever meet that guy who lived between Crieff and Comrie?" asked Borthy. "His place was on the left as you drove towards Comrie . . . no, hold on, it was on the right. Yes, it was on the right."

"Does it matter?" muttered Bruce.

"Does it matter? Does it matter losing your toes?"

"No, does it matter whether his place was on the left or right? I mean, in the eternal scale of things . . ."

Borthy looked puzzled. He negotiated a bend in the road. "In the eternal scale of things? I'm not with you, Bruce."

"It doesn't matter," said Bruce. "What about this guy who lived on the left or right of the Comrie road? What about him?"

"He was called Tom something-or-other. Mac-something, I think. My father knew him. He used to sell him hay for his horses."

Bruce sucked in his cheeks. "And?"

"No, just hay. He had some cows, I think, but one of them got that disease that makes them blow up and burst. There was something about it in the *Strathearn Herald*." He paused. "Somebody said humans could get it too. Have you heard of anybody bursting like that?"

Bruce sighed. "No. Not recently."

"But earlier on? Somebody burst some time ago?"

Bruce gave his answer between clenched teeth. "It doesn't matter, Borthy. What about this guy – the one who bought the hay from your old man? What about him?"

"Oh, him. Yes, well, he only had four toes. Yes, four. I think he had three on his left foot and one on his right. Or it might have been the other way round – I can't actually remember. You know how it is: you hear something, and the next minute you've forgotten what you heard."

Bruce attempted to steer the conversation back to toes. In spite of himself, he wanted to know about this unfortunate man on the Comrie road, with his paucity of toes and his bursting cows. Once he was in the monastery he could forget about these petty things, but until then it had somehow become important to know.

"So he had only four toes?"

"Yes. And you usually have ten. Most people have ten."

Bruce let that truism pass uncommented upon.

"Anyway," Borthy went on, "he told my dad what happened. He used to be a keen mountaineer. He'd done over one hundred Munros and had even gone to Everest – not to get to the top – he didn't have the money to do that – but at least to get up above Base Camp. You know there's this big ice field there. You go to Base Camp and it's the next stage up. Have you seen the pictures?"

Bruce nodded.

"You wouldn't catch me going up there," said Borthy.

"Not on your life! Base Camp, okay, although I wouldn't go there myself. Why bother? What's there to do but sit around in tents and get cold? No thanks. Would you go, Bruce?" Bruce shook his head. "Not to Base Camp, no. Definitely not." And yet, he thought, I'm going into a *monastery* . . .

"So this chap, Tom what's-his-face, goes up there and is taken by a bunch of Sherpas up onto this ice field. They find a place to spend the night and they put up tents and he gets into his tent, zips it up, and climbs into his sleeping bag. They have these special sleeping bags that have a very high thermal rating, you see. But his has a faulty seam down at the bottom and during his sleep he kicks through it without thinking, and his toes are exposed. He had socks on, but they'd come off and the next thing he knows is that he wakes up to find that he has bad frostbite on his toes. Disaster.

"They take him down – the Sherpas carry him because they feel a bit bad about it – not that it was their fault, but they're really conscientious about taking people up the mountains and they don't like it when they get frostbite. So they get him down, and there's this Belgian doctor at Base Camp and he looks at Tom's feet and shakes his head and says it's too late to save most of the toes."

Bruce winced. "Bad news."

"Yes. It took months for him to get back to walking properly, and even then he had to use a stick to steady himself."

"Not good," said Bruce.

Borthy became silent. Then he said, "Are you sure about this, Bruce? We'll be there in five minutes. If you want to turn back, all you have to do is say so."

Bruce did not reply immediately. He realised that this was a watershed moment in his life. He had once read a poem about such moments of decision – somewhere or other – when he was at school, he thought. Yes, it was there, at Morrison's Academy in Crieff, and Borthy might have been in the class too. They must have been seventeen, or thereabouts – it was just before they left. And the English teacher, whom they all liked, read a poem to them at the end of each lesson. What was it? Something about being at the junction of two roads and having to decide which one to take. Frost. That was him. Funny, that it should come to me, he thought, when we had been talking about frostbite. But that was how life was: everything was connected in some way or another; one thing led to another, and then to another after that. And then we came to a point where the road forked in an unambiguous and unavoidable manner and we had to decide.

"Just keep going," he said to Borthy. "Straight ahead."

"Oh, jeez, Bruce," said Borthy. "This is taking me back five centuries. Jeez."

"At least seven," said Bruce.

40

Early Rising

They were met by the Guestmaster, a man in his mid-forties
clad in the characteristic white robe of the Benedictine monk.
This was Brother Gregory, who repeated their names after each
introduction. "Bruce," he said, and then, "And Borthy? Yes?"

"He's really called Arnold," explained Bruce. "But nobody
uses that – for obvious reasons."

Brother Gregory gave Bruce a slightly reproachful look.
"We must be comfortable with our names," he said.

"I've always been called Borthy," said Borthy. "It stuck."

Brother Gregory smiled. "Well, you will be tired after
your journey." He looked at Borthy. "Will you be staying . . .
Borthy?"

"No," said Bruce quickly. "Borthy has to get back to
Edinburgh."

"I understand," said Brother Gregory.

"In fact, he has to go more or less immediately," said
Bruce. "He has a long journey ahead of him."

"So do we all," said Brother Gregory. "Well, thank you for
bringing our guest up."

"Yes, thanks, Borthy," said Bruce. "Safe journey back."

Borthy seemed disappointed not to be invited to stay, but
took it in good stead. He shook hands with Bruce, and then
with Brother Gregory, and returned to his beige-coloured
Vauxhall. Brother Gregory gestured to Bruce to follow him,
and the two of them entered the main door of the priory.

"How much do you know about Pluscarden?" asked
Brother Gregory.

Bruce hesitated. "A bit," he said. "It's very old."

"Parts of it date back to the fourteenth century," said Brother Gregory. "That's quite a thought, isn't it? I find it astonishing to think that God's work has been done here, in this very spot, for all those hundreds of years. Sometimes, I think of what these stones have seen."

They found themselves in a long cloister. "We might have a brief walk along the cloister before I show you to your quarters. Leave your case here and we can pick it up on the way back."

Bruce deposited his case on a small stone bench. "It's very quiet," he said.

"Cloisters usually are," said Brother Gregory. "And you will find that we do not engage too much in superfluous conversation here. We believe that quiet enables one to commune with God more effectively. Noise is the enemy of the inner voice. It can drown it completely."

Bruce began to say something, but stopped himself. *Noise*, he thought.

"We have hours of strict silence," Brother Gregory went on. "But at other times one may converse."

Bruce nodded. "I understand," he said.

"But," Brother Gregory continued, "the conversation you and I are having at present is perfectly justified by the needs of the situation. I would like to know a little about you, and you will need to find out a bit about what our life here is like. If you are to join us as a novice, you need to know something of what you are letting yourself in for. The monastic life is not for everybody, you know."

"It's definitely what I want," said Bruce quickly.

Brother Gregory fixed him with a gaze that was sympathetic, but penetrating. "I'm not sure that you can say that yet. You cannot make a decision without first knowing a bit more about what you are letting yourself in for. That is why we like people to spend a bit of time with us before they embark more fully on the whole business of becoming a full member of the order." He paused. "Are you used to getting up early, Bruce?"

Bruce nodded. "Yes," he said. "I'm always up by eight-thirty. I hardly ever lie in. Eight-forty-five at the latest."

Brother Gregory received this information passively. "I see," he said. "Our day starts a bit earlier than that, I'm afraid." He paused. Their steps sounded on the stone, a creaky, leathery sound.

"I used to get up at seven when I had to get a bus into work," said Bruce. "I can do early."

Brother Gregory clasped his hands together. "Yes," he said quietly. "We are early risers, I'm afraid. Most monks are. We rise at four-fifteen each morning."

Bruce gasped. "Four-fifteen?"

"Yes. One of the brothers comes and knocks at each monk's door and calls out *Benedicamus Domino*. Then the brother within the cell replies *Deo gratias*. One or two other things are said, and then the brother who is charged with waking up the brethren moves on to the next door, and the whole thing is repeated. Then we go on to Vigils. That, as you may know, is the Night Office, which consists of twelve psalms along with Psalms 3 and 34 that we say every day."

"I see," said Bruce.

"Then," continued Brother Gregory, "we move on to personal prayer for an hour or so, or to the *lectio divina*, which is a reading of a spiritual work of some sort."

"And breakfast?" asked Bruce.

"Oh, we do have breakfast," Brother Gregory assured him. "But that doesn't come until after Lauds, and the Angelus prayer. That's when breakfast is served. We have a special name for it – *pittance*. It is not a substantial meal. A slice of bread, perhaps, and some honey. The bees have their work to do – I sometimes say they have their Rule too, if you see what I mean."

"Oh, I see." Bruce thought: *coffee?* But he was not sure what the Benedictine attitude to coffee might be.

Brother Gregory was looking at Bruce. "Tell me, Bruce," he asked. "What brought you to this place? Is it true that you were struck by lightning?"

Bruce nodded. "In Dundas Street," he said, and added, "That's a street in Edinburgh."

"I see. And after the lightning strike?'

"I felt different," said Bruce. "I looked at my life and thought that I had been getting a lot of things wrong."

"Most of us can say that about our lives," said Brother Gregory. "We go through life getting a lot of things wrong. But tell me, have you read much about monasticism? Have you encountered Patrick Leigh Fermor's *A Time to Keep Silence*, for instance?"

Bruce shook his head.

"Paddy Leigh Fermor was a great man," said Brother Gregory. "I would have given so much to have met him, but that was never possible. He writes beautifully because he had a sound grasp of Latin. His prose is Latinate, you know, which gives it a very special feel, I think. That book is about visits he made to French monasteries. It is a very special book, in my view."

"I see," said Bruce.

"Or any of Christopher Jamison's books?" asked Brother Gregory. "He's the abbot of our house down in Sussex."

Bruce shook his head. "I think you will find that I have a lot to learn," he said.

Brother Gregory looked at him. "In saying that you have shown me there is one lesson you have already started to learn – the lesson of humility."

"I hope so," said Bruce.

41

An Astonishing Act by Bruce

Brother Gregory insisted on carrying Bruce's suitcase for him.

"It will be no burden," he said, as he picked up the case.

"But, please," said Bruce. "I should be carrying it."

Brother Gregory shook his head. "You are our guest – at present. In due course, there will be many tasks for you to perform."

Bruce smiled, and tried to wrest the case from the Guest-master.

"Please," said Brother Gregory, brushing aside Bruce's attempt. He put down the case and adjusted his cassock. Bruce looked abashed.

"It's important to be able to accept," Brother Gregory said. He glanced at Bruce in an encouraging way. There was no hint of reproach in his voice; just warmth. "Some of us find that hard – I know that – but graciousness in accepting the help of others is something that the least of us can develop." Here he paused. "And when I say 'the least of us', or even 'the weaker brethren', I do not mean other people, you know: I mean myself."

Bruce was silent for a few seconds before he said, "I'm very sorry, Brother Gregory."

The monk shook his head. "No apology is needed. But now that you have offered – by your gesture – to carry the case, then I, too, must show gracious acceptance. Please carry your case, if that is what you wish to do."

"I do," said Bruce and began to reach for the case. But

then he stopped. "Of course, if you want to carry it, then I shouldn't insist."

For a few moments, neither moved nor spoke. Then Brother Gregory said, "There are times when something very ordinary – a suitcase, even – can assume great symbolic significance. What matters then is not the suitcase, but the thing for which the suitcase stands."

Bruce stared at his suitcase. It was an expensive make – what he would have described as a designer suitcase. *Would have* . . . that sort of thing, he thought, is in the past. Now he felt ashamed. He had spent a large amount of money on a suitcase that did no more than the very cheapest piece of luggage could do. Suddenly, without considering his words before he uttered them, he blurted out, "I don't think I want my suitcase after all. I'd like to—"

Brother Gregory looked at him expectantly. Somewhere behind them in the shrubs around the cloister, a bird sang.

"I'd like to give it away."

Brother Gregory considered this carefully. "You would like to divest yourself of your suitcase?" he asked, his voice so quiet that Bruce had to strain to hear it.

Bruce nodded. His mind was made up. He was ashamed of his suitcase and everything that it represented.

"And the contents?" asked Brother Gregory. "Your suitcase will have some of your possessions in it, I imagine. What about those?"

Bruce hesitated. There was a certain amount of clothing, his shaving kit and hair gel, sunglasses and his laptop computer. He closed his eyes.

"I want to give everything away. There's some clothing, but you said there were work clothes for me here – and a habit."

Brother Gregory raised a finger. "Visitors do not usually wear a habit. Once you become a novice, of course . . ." He paused. "But every rule has its exceptions, and the abbot may give dispensation to wear a novice's habit in special circumstances."

"I would like that," said Bruce.

"And your computer?" asked Brother Gregory. "Most people are very attached to their computers and their . . . what do you call those things that people clutch to themselves as if their life depended on them?"

"Their iPhones," said Bruce.

"Exactly. Their iPhones."

"Yes, people become very attached to those electronic devices. Separating them from those gadgets is often impossible, I find. It becomes like an amputation. We had a visitor once who lost his iPhone in the vegetable garden. The poor soul was in tears."

"It can be hard," said Bruce. "You can lose all your contacts, you see."

Brother Gregory thought about this. "All your contacts? All gone? So, you are alone once more."

"Most people have a back-up," said Bruce. "So the disaster is short-lived."

"Of course," said Brother Gregory. "A back-up. Of course." He gave Bruce an enquiring look. "But what about this computer of yours – the one in your suitcase?"

"It's a MacBook Pro," Bruce said quickly. "It's quite new. It has the new M1 chip."

"Ah," said Brother Gregory. 'The M1 chip. I see." He lowered his gaze, as if aware that he was treading on delicate ground. "Surely you would not want to give that away? Clothes, yes – what are a few garments, after all? But a MacBook Pro with an M1 chip – well, surely that's a different matter?"

Bruce swallowed. "I said that I would give away the suitcase along with the contents. And that includes the computer. I wish to give it away."

Brother Gregory folded his hands in the sleeves of his habit. "I see," he said. "And does this decision come from the heart, do you think? Sometimes we are perhaps slightly impulsive in our desire to do something about our lives and we say things that may be helpful and well-intended, but that may lack the depth that comes with deliberation. It is important to distinguish between settled intention and impulse."

"It is," said Bruce.

Brother Gregory inclined his head. "I think that you understand what you are doing. I think that you have experienced something very valuable – an insight – and that it would be churlish of me not to acknowledge your moral choice. We shall certainly be able to find a use for all the items in the suitcase – and indeed for the suitcase itself. There are many who do not have a suitcase of that quality – or, indeed, a MacBook Pro. They will be very grateful."

"I can wipe the disc," said Bruce. "That way, it will be ready for its new owner."

Brother Gregory shook his head. "We have our own IT arrangements," he said. "They will handle that. Your computer will end up in very loving and appreciative hands."

Bruce bit his lip. He loved his computer, but now that he had decided to give it away, he felt a sense of freedom come over him. He did not *need* a MacBook Pro. He did not *need* an M1 chip – a much slower chip would be perfectly adequate for his needs. Who needed speed?

"And your contacts?" asked Brother Gregory. "Should we save them? Brother Mac can put them on a disc for you, or save them in the heavens somewhere." He waved a hand in the direction of the sky.

"You mean the cloud?" said Bruce.

Brother Gregory nodded. "Yes, I believe I've heard Brother Mac using that term."

Bruce was intrigued by this mention of Brother Mac, and

asked who he was.

"Just one of the brothers," replied Brother Gregory. 'You'll meet him in due course. He is a very useful member of our community. He is a carpenter, amongst other things. It is a useful – and calming – thing to work with one's hands on wood. But he's also very good with computers."

They left the suitcase where it stood and Bruce followed Brother Gregory as they made their way towards the guest wing. He did not look back. There was no looking back, he thought, and that doesn't worry me the slightest.

"Don't bother Brother Mac about my contacts," he said to Brother Gregory. "Wipe the disc permanently. Everything: emails, contacts, passwords, apps – the lot."

"Very wise," said Brother Gregory. "There's a great deal to be said for the *tabula rasa*."

42

The Entity

In the café at Valvona & Crolla, Fat Bob and his companion were still apparently unaware of the fact that they were being observed, admittedly with discretion, from a table at the far end of the room. That was the table at which Angus and Roger, having been engaged in a conversation about art and national epics, had been interrupted by the arrival of Sister Maria-Fiore dei Fiori di Montagna. No conversation joined by the celebrated socialite nun remained on its original tracks, and although Roger valiantly tried to return to the subject of the Ossianic verses of James Macpherson, and made several remarks about the potential of the courtly epic, *Fergus of Galloway*, his efforts were expertly headed off by Sister Maria-Fiore. With a dismissive wave of her hand, and the simple formula "Be that as it may", she precluded any further discussion along those lines with the disclosure, delivered *sotto voce*, that she had followed Fat Bob all the way from North Bridge and had seen him meeting the woman with him below the equestrian statue of Wellington.

"A very discreet place for an assignation," remarked Angus, with a smile.

Sister Maria-Fiore shook her head. "I take it from your tone of voice that you mean the opposite of what you say," she scolded. "That is a common habit here, I have observed. In Italy we mean what we say . . ." She paused. "Although we don't always reveal everything we think."

"Who does?" said Angus. "If all were revealed all the time, then social life as we know it would be impossible." He turned to Roger. "What do you think, Roger?"

Roger smiled. "I couldn't say," he replied.

This might have been an opportunity for Sister Maria-Fiore to coin an aphorism, but she resisted. "I'm only following this man out of a sense of duty," she said. "I believe that he is deceiving Big Lou, you see, and I don't think he should get away with it."

Angus sighed. "I fear that you're right," he said. "But I'm not sure about whether we should intervene. These matters are usually somewhat delicate." He gave Sister Maria-Fiore an enquiring glance. "It can't be easy to follow somebody and not be observed – particularly if one is, oneself, somewhat – how shall we put it? – conspicuous."

The remark was gently made, and Sister Maria-Fiore dei Fiori di Montagna did not take exception to it.

"I take your point, Angus," she said. "But I happen to have had experience of these things."

Angus looked doubtful. "Experience? You?"

Roger remained tactfully silent.

Sister Maria-Fiore had been talking quietly, but now she lowered her voice even further. Angus and Roger strained to hear what she said, as did two women at a neighbouring table who had been enjoying, in so far as they could hear, the discussion.

"You may or may not be aware," she began, "of the fact that the Vatican has an intelligence service."

Angus looked doubtful, but Roger smiled.

"Oh, that is well known," Roger said. "It has been operating for at least five centuries – somewhat longer, I would venture to suggest, than MI6 or the CIA. They're newcomers by comparison."

"Exactly," said Sister Maria-Fiore. "Of course, you've written on the papacy, Roger – you'll know all about it."

"It used to be called the Holy Alliance," Roger said. "Then

it became known as the Entity. It is still very much in business. It enjoys a very high reputation amongst intelligence services. It has, shall we say, excellent sources."

"That is quite true," said Sister Maria-Fiore dei Fiori di Montagna. "And although I am bound by certain obligations of secrecy . . ."

At the neighbouring table, the two women were now leaning out of their chairs at the maximum angle compatible with remaining seated.

"Although I normally don't talk about this," the nun went on, "in the circumstances I feel that I need to explain. I was, you see, at one point seconded by my order to serve with the Entity in Rome. I was . . ." She paused, and then, barely whispering, continued, "I was originally given a junior role in the administrative section, but Monsignor Rinaldi, who was at that time a senior figure in the personnel department – he's now Nuncio in Asunción – arranged for me to serve for several months in the field, as we call it. Of course, I can't tell you what I did there . . ."

"Quite right," said Angus.

"I am glad you understand," Sister Maria-Fiore dei Fiori di Montagna went on, "but what I can say is that I did manage to get some experience of following people of interest, as we called them. I also received training in codes."

Angus looked at Sister Maria-Fiore in frank astonishment.

"All that is in the past," she said airily. "But I do recall very well a particular lecture we had on the technique of merging with your surroundings. The message we came away with was very clear."

They waited as Sister Maria-Fiore took a sip of her coffee. As she put down her cup, she glanced down the room towards Fat Bob's table.

"They told us that it was a complete fallacy that one should try to look the same as everyone else. What you should do, they advised, is to *look different*. If you look out of place, then the last thing that anybody will conclude is that you are trying to conceal anything. You will immediately be relieved of any suspicion."

With the delivery of this surprising piece of information, Sister Maria-Fiore sat back in her chair and smiled. At the neighbouring table, the two women looked at one another in disbelief.

"No," said Sister Maria-Fiore dei Fiori di Montagna, "it is absolutely true. Stand out in order to disappear; fit in, in order to stand out."

Angus laughed. "So, if Fat Bob over there sets off down Leith Walk, and you trail after him – nobody, not even Fat Bob himself, will turn a hair? Is that what you're suggesting? Seriously?"

Sister Maria-Fiore dei Fiori di Montagna frowned. "You may mock, Angus, but if you care to accompany me, you will see what I mean. Nobody will pay the slightest attention to us."

"Remarkable," said Roger. "But possibly quite true. Shall we put the matter to the test?"

43

Down in Leith

"I am not entirely convinced," said Roger, "that we are quite as inconspicuous as we might wish to be."

He passed this remark as the three of them made their way down Leith Walk, Sister Maria-Fiore dei Fiori di Montagna in the vanguard, her habit billowing in the fresh north-easterly breeze coming in from the Firth, with, behind her, and walking abreast on the pavement, Angus Lordie, renowned portrait painter, in his high-waisted corduroy trousers and moleskin waistcoat, and Roger Collins, historian of medieval Spain, dressed less conspicuously than Angus but still rather more formally than was the norm for that part of the city at that time of day.

"True," said Angus. "But our floral friend seems convinced and . . ." He glanced at the two figures walking in the same direction almost one block ahead. "The man himself seems unaware of our presence."

"He seems only to have eyes for her," remarked Roger.

Angus agreed. "I would have thought there's absolutely no doubt but that those two are on close terms." He shook his head sadly. "Why did Bob get married if he was carrying on with somebody else? What's the point?"

"There's an adage about having your cake and eating it," said Roger. "Perhaps he falls into that camp."

Roger sighed. "I feel so sorry for Lou," he said. "Life hasn't been kind to her."

"No," said Angus. "And that's what strikes me about all this. Those who most richly deserve happiness often are the last to find it. Big Lou deserves better than some Highland Games strongman with a wandering eye."

"Is that what he does?" asked Roger.

Angus nodded. "He told me. Tosses the caber. Throws the hammer. And he has a day job too. He has a portfolio career. That's the expression people use these days – if they do more than one thing. A portfolio career involves lots of different jobs. You have to be a bit of a juggler."

"What was the term the Japanese used for people who stuck to one employer for their entire lives? Cradle-to-grave stuff?"

"Salarymen," Angus said. "A salaryman started with a firm after leaving college or university and never left it. They went into the office at eight or whatever, and came back late – by way of a geisha bar, apparently. They did this until they were sixty-five or so. And they got their salary every month, regular as clockwork. That was the bargain."

Roger looked thoughtful. "I suppose that everybody's life is a bit like that – a bargain, I mean. You don't always get everything you want, but you settle for what you have."

"And make the most of it," added Angus.

They continued on their way. Now they crossed the invisible boundary that separated the City of Edinburgh from its port, the former burgh of Leith. There was no sign to inform them of this transition – or at least not one that they noticed – but there was still a distinct change in atmosphere. Every port, even one whose glories are in the past, has a slight tang in the air, that mixture of salt and seaweed and diesel oil that drifts in from docks into the urban hinterland. Certainly that was so in Leith, where that particular air lingered in the tenement-lined streets, or along the banks of the canal, or around the bonded warehouses of the whisky firms. And here and there, as further reminder of the nature of the place, the faded façade of an old shop, the letters just visible, as in a palimpsest, recalled

Leith's maritime heritage: a chandlery, perhaps, or a rope firm; or tarnished brass signs stubbornly marking the position of the sometime offices of ship brokers, firms rejoicing under Scottish names such as Forbes or Meldrum that long ago matched merchants to mariners, and brought lumbering cargo vessels nosing into the nearby docks.

It was true that Fat Bob and his friend did not appear to have noticed his followers, but this was not so of such other citizens of Leith who were out on the streets at the time. These included various grubby-faced small boys, socks hanging about their ankles, knees grazed, and teeth missing – perfect specimens for a casting agency wishing to populate a street scene circa 1934 – but who had somehow survived encroaching modernity. These boys, four or five in number, started to follow Angus and Roger, calling out various remarks and suggestions.

"Hey, mister," shouted the leader of this small mob, "you lost your way doon here? Morningside's that way, ken!"

This remark brought howls of laughter from the others, emboldening its author to follow up with, "Those are fantoosh breeks you've got, mister. Dinnae get any grease on them if you visit the chippie, mind."

Angus grinned. "The keelies o' the toon," he muttered. "Stand by."

Turning round sharply, he roared at the boys, "Youses got naething better to dae than bother respectable fowk wi' yer stupid havering and snashes? You – I ken fine who youse wee mince-heids are. I'll gi' you a right skelping, so I will . . ."

The boys stood still, shocked by the onslaught. Then, as one, they turned and fled.

"An old-fashioned approach is often most effective," said Angus. "And I must say it's encouraging to see that nothing much has changed down here."

Sister Maria-Fiore dei Fiori di Montagna had not been

paying attention to this altercation, but she now stopped and pointed to the street ahead.

"They're going into that bar," she said. "Look, there they go."

Angus read the sign above the door. The Flenser. "There's a bit of history," he said. "Flensers worked on the whaling fleet. Salvesen's of Leith. They were down here, of course."

"What shall we do?" asked Roger.

"We go in," said Sister Maria-Fiore dei Fiori di Montagna, adding, "Discreetly, so as not to call attention to ourselves."

Angus was past pointing out that the sight of a nun entering a maritime bar in Leith might not go unnoticed by the denizens of such an establishment – and therefore by Fat Bob himself – but he refrained from giving voice to his concerns. There was no point, he had decided, in drawing Sister Maria-Fiore's attention to anything, as she appeared to have made up her mind on all matters, more or less.

So he said, "All right, let's go in."

From within there came the sound of singing.

"Listen," said Angus. "'The Shoals of Herring'. Do you know that song, Roger? That's a favourite of mine. It's about going off on the herring boats. A young man remembers. He was a cabin boy on a sailing lugger. He learned to swear like the rest of the men. He was so tired he slept on his feet. It was hard."

They stood for a moment and listened before they entered the bar from which the song emanated.

44

Very Uxorious

"The Shoals of Herring" came to an end, and there was applause throughout the bar. The instrumentalists in the band, a local folk group of three bearded musicians, laid down their fiddle, accordion, and small pipes, while the singer wiped at his brow and took a swig of the dark beer he had been nursing. They were regulars in the bar, which had a reputation for its folk evenings, and they were amongst an audience of friends. Now, with a break in the music, a hubbub of chatter rose to the ceiling as people surged to the bar to refresh their glasses.

"This is busy for lunchtime," observed Angus.

"It's Saturday, of course," Roger pointed out. "There was a sign outside saying that there was lunchtime music on a Saturday."

Angus looked around him. Sister Maria-Fiore dei Fiori di Montagna had moved away from them; she had recognised a young woman at one of the tables and had drawn up a chair to engage her and her companions in conversation.

"Sister Maria-Fiore," observed Roger, "seems to know everybody – everywhere. Look at that."

Angus suggested that he should buy the two of them a drink and that they might leave any watching of Fat Bob to Sister Maria-Fiore. He was increasingly uncomfortable about following Bob, which seemed to him to be an increasingly pointless exercise. They had already confirmed beyond any doubt that Bob was seeing another woman, and that they were spending at least part of their Saturday together. That, surely, was all Sister Maria-Fiore needed to know if she was intending to raise the matter with Big Lou or – and this was a possibility, he supposed – if she were thinking of tackling Fat Bob over it. Either way, Angus wanted no further part in the affair. He would give Big Lou whatever support he could, but he did not think it was in any way appropriate for him to act as an unofficial enquiry agent. Sister Maria-Fiore obviously delighted in poking her nose into the business of others, and he suspected that she was, in that respect, largely incorrigible. He would not try to dissuade her from unwanted interventions: sooner or later, people like that simply moved on to pastures new. She might even return to Italy, having conquered at least the foothills of Scottish society, if not its highest peaks. Presumably there was plenty for her to do in Italy with its elaborate and at times arcane social and political reaches.

Angus returned with a glass of low-alcohol beer for both of them, and they toasted one another and, in her absence, Sister Maria-Fiore dei Fiori di Montagna.

"What were we talking about before we were interrupted?" Angus asked.

"National sagas," said Roger.

"Ah yes," said Angus. "I was burdening you with my quest for a great theme."

"I'm sure it will come," said Roger. "But in the meantime . . ."

A man sitting on a bench seat next to their table leaned across and introduced himself. "You here for the singing?" he asked.

Angus nodded. He could hardly explain that they were there in the course of a tawdry exercise in shadowing an errant Highland Games strongman.

"We get a lot of people coming down to listen to these boys," he said, nodding in the direction of the band. "They're local, you see, but they're building up a great reputation. They were singing up in Ullapool last week and next week they'll be over in Antrim for some sort of festival. They're well on their way now."

Angus said that he particularly liked "The Shoals of Herring".

"Aye, me too," said the man, who now introduced himself as Will. "Anything to do with the sea."

"You were at sea?" asked Roger.

Will nodded. "Ben Line," he said. "And then I spent fifteen years down in New Zealand. The Cook Islands. A couple of years in Singapore. I was on the engineering side."

"You've seen it all," said Angus. "I've been nowhere, really. Italy, I suppose, and one or two other places, but I've hardly seen the world."

Will grinned. "I'm not sure how much you've missed," he said. "People are people wherever you go. The scenery changes a bit, of course, but there are the same old problems wherever you go."

Angus said, "I know what you mean. I used to be an idealist – I'm not sure if I still am." He paused. "Although I hope I'm not becoming cynical."

"You can be a realist without being cynical," Will said. "But look, the boys are going to play again."

The bearded musicians picked up their instruments again. There was a quick consultation between them, and then a nod of the head from their leader. "'Mist-Covered Mountains'," he announced to the audience.

Will smiled. "That tune gets to me right here," he said, placing his hand over his heart. "That tune . . ." He shook his head. "I love this country, you know. I've been all over the world, as I was telling you, but it's always Scotland that . . ."

He did not finish – nor did he need to, as Angus knew what he meant.

The band began to play. Will turned to Angus. "You know anybody here?" he asked.

Angus was about to say no, when he stopped himself. "Just one or two," he said. "Fat Bob over there, for instance." Will's gaze crossed the room. "Oh yes, I've known him for a long time. And his missus over there." Angus caught his breath. "Her?" "Aye," said Will. "That's Bob's wife, Betty. They married about six years ago." Angus felt his heart thudding within him. The outrage; the outrage. "A good marriage?" he asked. "Well, he's still with her," said Will. "I suppose that says something."

Roger had been listening to the music and had not heard this conversation. Now Angus leaned over and, still in a state of shock, whispered to him, "Fat Bob is *very* uxorious. More so than average, if you get what I mean."

Of course Roger did. He gasped. Angus closed his eyes. This was far messier than he had imagined – so much so that even "Mist-Covered Mountains" failed to distract him from the blanket of gloom – and distaste – that descended on him: a melody of longing can so easily become a lament: only a few notes, here and there, can make the difference. Will's casual disclosure had changed everything: this was no longer a private matter between Big Lou and her husband – if you could still call him that, which, legally, Angus thought, you probably could not.

45

The Road to Carlops

Irene and Stuart drove Bertie to his camp near Carlops. Stuart was doing his best to spend time with Irene for the sake of the children, but in the event had found it far easier than he had imagined it would be. Since Irene had moved in with Antonia Collie and Sister Maria-Fiore dei Fiori di Montagna, her general attitude appeared to have softened and there was very little rancour.

Nicola, too, had noticed this change, after that initial encounter in Scotland Street when Irene had unexpectedly struck a conciliatory, even apologetic note. That had led to an immediate and equally unanticipated change of heart in Nicola. It was as if a glacier had suddenly melted, to reveal a gentle landscape below – a carpet of spring flowers, perhaps. Had the train journey from Aberdeen been routed through Damascus?

"We must give her the benefit of the doubt," said Stuart.

Nicola, with a very slight trace of reluctance, agreed. "I must admit I feel a bit better about her – and about myself too. Dislike of others is corrosive, I think: it eats away at the soul."

Stuart nodded. "You're right, Mother."

Nicola had smiled at her son. My son is a good man, she thought. He is not a strong man – I have to accept that – but at heart he is good and kind. And even Irene, for all her unbearable behaviour in the past, had a notion of the good and wanted to do the best for her family. Unfortunately, she had been so wrong about everything, had been so opinionated and stubborn, so desperately keen to be in what she thought was the vanguard of progressive thought that she seemed to lose all sense of proportion. There was nothing wrong with progressive values – in so far as they championed justice and kindness and consideration – but at times they could slip into intolerance and extremism, the very evils they sought to address. That had happened with Irene: her vision of the good was not a bad or insupportable one, it was just that she pursued it in a way that distorted its underlying values.

Now, as Stuart and Irene travelled the short distance to Carlops, the Lammermuirs to the east were blue in the warm light of summer; the sky virtually cloudless. Alongside the road, rising to the north and west, the Pentland Hills were bathed in mid-morning sun, dotted here and there with grazing sheep, small bundles of untidy wool moving amongst the patches of gorse.

At Nine Mile Burn they passed the end of the road that led to Matthew and Elspeth's house, just visible beyond a small forest of Scots pine.

"How are their triplets?" asked Irene.

"Shooting up," said Stuart. "And extremely noisy. They lead a fairly outdoor life, I think."

"Good," said Irene. "Boys need that sort of thing."

The car swerved slightly as Stuart, at the wheel, took in this remark. This was not the sort of thing he had ever heard Irene say. Had he heard it correctly? Had she really said: *Boys need that sort of thing*?

"Elspeth had an accident, I hear," he said. "She hit a lamppost."

Irene shook her head. "Or the lamppost hit her," she said.

Stuart glanced at her. "No, she went off the road . . ."

Irene laughed. "I know, I know. I was just pointing out that people are very ready to blame drivers for things that are not their fault."

Stuart thought about this. It was true. Accidents happened to even the most careful of drivers.

"We mustn't lose sight of the true meaning of *accident*," he said.

"Are you talking as a statistician?" asked Irene.

"Yes, I suppose I am," he said. "We're careful about these things. And it seems to me that we need to ring-fence the idea of things happening without anybody being at fault. In the same way as we need to make sure that we don't change the meaning of the word *mistake*."

And he thought, for a disconcertingly poignant moment: *was my marriage a mistake?* It probably was. But it was not a mistake for which he felt he would attribute any blame.

"Oh, yes?"

"Yes," said Stuart. "A mistake usually doesn't involve culpability. It depresses me when I hear politicians talking about having made mistakes when what they're talking about is deliberate wrongdoing. To label telling a lie as a mistake is a dangerous distortion of language. Yet that's what we've been hearing in certain quarters, isn't it?"

In the back of the car, Bertie was quiet, and they travelled on in silence until they reached the turn off for the camp – a bumpy, untarred track leading up into the hills.

"Are you sure this is a road, Daddy?" Bertie suddenly asked from the back.

Stuart smiled. "It is, Bertie," he answered. "Don't worry."

Bertie looked doubtful. "It'll be hard for ambulances to come along here," he said. "They'll get stuck."

Irene caught Stuart's eye and grinned. "I don't think many ambulances would try to come along here, Bertie."

"But when people fall off the hills," Bertie said, "what will they do then? Or get food poisoning?"

Irene intervened. "Nothing like that will happen in this camp, Bertie. You have nothing to worry about."

Bertie hesitated. "Olive says . . ." He did not complete the sentence.

"What does Olive say?" prompted Irene "Not that I'd pay much attention."

"She says that last year thirty people went to this camp, but only twenty came back."

"But that's complete nonsense," exploded Irene. "Olive's making that up, Bertie. That's completely untrue."

"She's a real little fabricator," muttered Irene to Stuart.

"She said that there are old mineshafts near here," Bertie continued. "She says that two boys from South Morningside School climbed down them and were never seen again. She said that somebody else was washed away in a burn and another got food poisoning from rotten sausages. She said . . ."

Irene brought this litany of disasters to an end. "Bertie," she admonished, "what Olive has been telling you is pure invention. She's trying to frighten you. That is what she's doing. You should just laugh at her when she says this sort of thing."

Stuart slowed down. A vehicle was coming down from the other direction. It was barely visible at this point, but a thinning out of the trees now revealed it. It was an ambulance. He pulled over to one side to allow it to pass. Inside the car, nobody spoke.

They resumed their journey in silence until Irene cleared her throat. "I don't think that was an emergency," she said. "If it had been, its siren would have been turned on."

Stuart seized the opportunity to agree. "Absolutely," he said. "I suspect that they lost their way and were heading back to the main road. That's all there is to it, I think."

46

Olive Takes Command

The following morning, Bertie and Ranald Braveheart Macpherson were amongst the first to be up and about at the campsite. They were sharing a tent with two other boys, both from Lanark, and by the time breakfast was ready in the mess tent, they had already explored a nearby burn together and made a small dam out of stones. There was no sign yet of Olive and Pansy, and Ranald had expressed the hope that perhaps their reservations had been cancelled. Bertie, though, was less sanguine. He felt that there was some cosmic plan that meant that he would never be completely free of Olive's influence. Perhaps she was right when she said that he would, in due course, have to marry her; perhaps that was his unavoidable destiny, decreed by some indifferent Fate somewhere, perhaps even by the planets in their unchangeable rotations. If that was the case, his only hope, he had decided, was to make good his escape to Glasgow. He should talk to Ranald about that, he felt, as his friend claimed to have known of several instances where Edinburgh people had managed to get to Glasgow and had never looked back.

"They have a really good time over there," Ranald said. "You can do what you like in Glasgow, you know, Bertie."

"I know that," said Bertie. He thought for a moment. "But how old do you have to be before you can go there, Ranald?"

Ranald pondered this. "Probably about ten," he said at last. "Yes, I think it's ten. That's if you want to go and live there permanently."

Bertie nodded, slightly despondently. He was seven and it would be three years before he would be ten. But it seemed to be taking an awfully long time.

"You can get a job in Glasgow when you're ten," Ranald continued. "That's the law, Bertie."

Bertie cheered up. "You know that pie factory that my granny has? You remember that place, Ranald? It's called Inclusive Pies."

Ranald nodded. "Would they give us a job, Bertie? Do you think they would?"

"Definitely," said Bertie.

The conversation had gone no further, and no concrete plans were laid to escape. But the idea of Glasgow was still there – a luminous, golden prospect – a city upon a hill to which the eyes of all Scotland might turn.

Now, though, the reality of the situation was that there was a good chance that the morning, which had started so promisingly with the construction of the dam on the burn, would take a rather different turn with the arrival of Olive and Pansy. And so it proved, as Olive and Pansy arrived in the mess tent shortly after Bertie, Ranald, and the two boys from Lanark had sat down to eggs and bacon at a trestle table.

"Oh, there you are, Bertie Pollock," Olive had called out on entering their tent. "And you, too, Ranald Braveheart Macpherson."

Olive strode across to the boys' table, followed by Pansy. "Who's this, then?" she asked, pointing at the two boys from Lanark.

"He's called Hamish," answered Bertie, "And he's called Rab."

Hamish and Rab stared at Olive, who was giving them a look of cool appraisal. "Where are you from?" she asked.

"Lanark," replied Hamish.

"Never heard of it," snapped Olive. And turning to Pansy,

she asked, "Have you ever heard of a place called Lanark, Pansy?"

Pansy shook her head. "Never," she replied.

"Oh well," continued Olive, "we're from Edinburgh, you see. And so is Bertie."

"I told them that," muttered Bertie.

"And did you tell them that you're my fiancé?" asked Olive.

Bertie blushed deep red.

"You engaged, Bertie?" asked Hamish.

Bertie shook his head.

"Don't you shake your head like that, Bertie Pollock," said Olive, her voice rising in indignation.

"Yes, don't you act all innocent," Pansy joined in. And to Hamish she said, "Bertie and Olive have been engaged for ages. They're very happy."

This conversation was interrupted by one of the staff, a young woman wearing a khaki top and green fatigue trousers. "I'm glad you've all met," she said. "Because you boys are going to be in Olive's section this morning. You're going on a hike."

Olive smiled. "I'm going to be expedition leader, aren't I, Miss Summers?"

The instructor nodded. "Yes, Olive will be leader today, everybody. Pansy will be her deputy. And you boys will be the troop. Is everybody happy with that?"

"Yes," said Olive quickly. "Everybody's really happy, Miss Summers."

Miss Summers gave a benevolent smile. "That's really nice, Olive. So, this is the plan: your group is going to go up a hill, and then come down again."

Bertie looked out towards the hill behind the camp. It was, he thought, very high, and already there were mists swirling about its summit. Was that almost as high as Everest? Would they have to set up a base camp? He looked at Miss Summers. "By ourselves, Miss Summers?" he asked, trying not to sound nervous.

Miss Summers laughed. "No, Bertie. I wouldn't dream of sending anybody up there by themselves. I'll be coming with you."

"With an ice axe?" asked Ranald Braveheart Macpherson. Miss Summers seemed to find this most amusing. "No, Ranald. That won't be necessary. I think that hill is probably barely a thousand feet high. There's no ice up there. But don't worry, I shall be with you every step of the way. Olive will be leader, but I'll be with you just to make sure that everything is all right."

They were all told to go off to their tents to collect their sweaters and the water bottles with which they had been issued the previous evening. "Then we'll all meet at the gate in ten minutes," instructed Miss Summers. "Does everybody understand?"

There were nods all round, and ten minutes later Bertie, Ranald Braveheart Macpherson, Olive, Pansy, and the two boys from Lanark were all waiting by the gate that marked the beginning of the hill track.

Miss Summers, though, was not there. She had received a telephone call from her frail aunt in St Andrews and was busy making domestic arrangements. This took longer than anticipated, and after the children had been waiting for fifteen minutes, Olive clapped her hands and made an announcement.

"We're going to start all by ourselves," she said. "I've got a map and I'm the leader. So, we're going to start."

Bertie looked doubtful. "Do you think we should, Olive?" he asked.

"Yes," said Olive. "I've made an executive decision, Bertie, and so you can just shut up. We're going."

47

Vigils

Bruce had awoken shortly after four, when the first rays of the sun had penetrated the shutter-boards of his window. In those latitudes there is little darkness in the small hours of the morning, and claims that one might read the *Inverness Courier* outside at two in the morning are by no means apocryphal. The question of whether one might *wish* to read a newspaper at that time and in those conditions is another matter, but it is certainly possible. For Bruce, though, any thought of reading a newspaper, even in the cold light of day, seemed unattractive – even pointless. He had come to Pluscarden not to immerse himself in the world and its problems, but to abstract himself from them in order to find something that, until that point – or, to be precise, until the point that he was struck by lightning on Dundas Street – was lacking. His life, he realised, had been empty. He had tried to fill it with a social whirl – one in which young women vied with one another to be with him at the parties at Prestonfield House, in the fashionable bars of the Edinburgh New Town, on the three-day breaks to Reykjavik or Berlin – and he had succeeded in that project, in so far as what was really a complete failure can be regarded as a success. And it *was* all failure, he now felt – every moment of it was dust in his mouth, because it meant nothing. He had been diverted by it – yes, that was so – but he now knew that he had been chasing after an *ignis fatuus* – no more than that.

As a guest in the abbey, he was under no obligation to attend the services that punctuated the monastic day – guests could, if they wished, sleep in while the monks began their devotions

– but Bruce was there in the chapel for Vigils, technically a Night Office notwithstanding the first appearance of the sun. There was one other guest, another early riser, a young man from Aberdeen, a fisherman, whom Bruce had met the day before and with whom he had had a brief conversation. This young man was wearing a grey garment, a hoodie, that he had pulled up over his head, a street garment that here, in this particular setting, seemed like a monastic cowl. He had greeted Bruce with a nod of the head, but neither had spoken, as it had been impressed on them that silence was expected in most of the monastic areas of the abbey.

The monks entered the chapel, white-clad figures taking their seats in the rows of stalls set aside for them. There was a calm timelessness about their movement: this was something that happened at the same fixed points of every day, no matter the season; something that required no practice, no choreography. It was like a tide that one might see on the shore: eternal, fixed.

And then they began to chant, guided by a chord played on the organ. The psalmody followed its appointed musical intervals, rising and falling within a narrow compass, the sound of something that had been performed in such settings for centuries, unaltered by fashion, surviving all the uncertainties of human life: wars, oppression, and times when love and kindness had been threatened by the busy doings of Hate.

Nobody who sat in that place could be unmoved, and Bruce now closed his eyes and let the Gregorian chant embrace him. He thought: how can I have been so wrong about everything? How can I have been so selfish, so absorbed in myself, so vain? How can I have believed that material things would make me, or anybody else for that matter, any happier?

It was a moment of conversion, as radical and as complete as when an item of clothing is dipped into a vat of dye and comes out a completely different colour. He did not believe in anything that he had not believed in half an hour before this moment: Bruce wanted to be seized by faith, even if he was still unconvinced of the literal truth of what was on offer in this place – that story still seemed inherently unlikely to him – but he *felt* entirely different.

He sat quite still throughout the saying of the Office. When the last notes of the chanting had died away and the monks had retreated from the chapel, he rose from his seat, nodded in the direction of the young fisherman, and made his way out into the field on the other side of the abbey. This was a paddock in which sheep were grazing – ewes with their growing lambs – and they now looked at him with the balefulness of animals disturbed at forage, before returning to their grazing. One or two bleated to reassure their offspring. "Don't worry," said Bruce. "I'm not going to harm you."

He walked across the grass, heading for the far side of the field, and then turned round to make his way back to the abbey. Just outside the purlieu of the main building, separated from the abbey by a line of trees, was a vegetable garden, at the end of which several lengthy growing tunnels marked the edge of the cultivated land.

Bruce decided to explore the garden. Brother Gregory had spoken to him about the possibility of his working on the land, and Bruce had quickly accepted. He liked digging, and he thought that here, at last, he could put to use all those hours he had spent in the gym in Edinburgh. It had been vanity that had driven him to those long sessions with the weights and on the running machine, but now he would use the muscle built up to do something useful.

He walked past neatly ordered beds of salad vegetables. Lettuces of various shapes and sizes stretched out in long lines, the soil around them weeded and finely raked. Then there were rows of peas and beans, supported by a scaffolding of canes; and cabbages, nibbled at by caterpillars but still generous in their profusion; and bed upon bed of herbs: rosemary, thyme, parsley, sage, chives in purple flower; and there were Jerusalem artichokes, too, proliferating like weeds.

And then a long bed of what he thought were onions. He bent down to examine the legend on the stake that had been driven into the ground at the edge of the first bed of this crop. *Garlic.*

48

Rust on Garlic

Bruce surveyed the garlic plants. He had never seen it growing before: garlic, in his experience, came wrapped in cellophane or worked into neatly-plaited strings. But of course it had to grow somehow, and this was it, these rather unexpected tall shoots that, had he not seen the label, he would have probably taken for large onions. The shoots were, for the most part, green, but here and there they had browned. One or two of the plants, those on the edge of the first bed, had yellowed, as if starved of water, even if the plants around them were still green.

He had been unaware of the presence of anybody else in the garden, but now he heard a voice, and he turned round, startled. It was a man in a set of brown overalls, ripped at the knees. He was carrying a gardening fork.

"I'm worried about that," the man said, nodding in the direction of the garlic plants. "Some of them seem to have rust."

Bruce followed the man's gaze. It was the yellowed plants that concerned him.

"Rust?"

The man nodded. "There's not much you can do – other than to cut off the affected parts. Then you hope that you've nipped it in the bud. Otherwise . . ."

Bruce waited.

"Otherwise, it takes over, and the whole plant gets it. It's not a complete disaster, of course. You still get a good enough crop, and the garlic will taste just as good. But the bulbs won't be as large."

"I see."

The man stepped forward. "Let me show you." He bent down to uproot one of the yellowed plants. It came away easily, the bulb surrounded by earth that he brushed away with his bare hands. "See?"

He twisted the exposed bulb away from the shoots and showed it to Bruce. "Not bad," he said. "But it would have been almost twice the size if it weren't for the rust. Such a shame. The abbot likes his garlic. I don't like giving him these smaller bulbs – not that he ever complains. They don't, you know. These monks don't complain about anything."

Bruce smiled. "I imagine that's true."

The man gave him a quizzical look. "You're on retreat?" he asked. "Or just visiting?"

Bruce hesitated. He was not sure of his exact status, and so he said, "Visitor. Maybe more."

The man's stare became more intense. "Maybe more? Thinking longer term, then?"

Bruce did not want to presume. "Perhaps," he said. "I wanted to experience it."

The man nodded. "I'm Jimmy, by the way."

Bruce introduced himself, and then asked, "You're not one of the brothers, then?"

Jimmy laughed. "Heavens, no. I have a wife down there." He tossed his head in the direction of Elgin. "They don't take you if you have a wife in the background. But they do let you help, which is what I do. I've been helping them in this garden for twelve years now – ever since I left the RAF."

Bruce raised an eyebrow. "You were a pilot?"

Jimmy shook his head. "Military police. The RAF has people like me to look after their planes and keep order about the place. That's what I did." He paused. "And then I developed a bit of arthritis and they offered me ill-health retirement. I took it and decided to stay in the area – I was at

Lossiemouth, you see – just up the road. There's a base there."

"So now you help the brothers?"

"Yes." Jimmy smiled. "Are you a Catholic, Bruce?"

Bruce shook his head. "No. But they don't seem to mind. In fact, they didn't ask me."

"They don't," said Jimmy. "They're very . . . what's the word? Ecumenical, I think. They're very open. They have all sorts of people coming to stay here. People who don't believe in anything. Everyone."

"It's all the same, I suppose," said Bruce. "It's all about the same feeling, don't you think? Even those who don't believe in anything may still feel that there's something . . . not to believe in."

Jimmy smiled. "I'll have to think about that, but maybe you're right. In my case, I just came round here one day – to see the place – and I found myself talking to one of the monks. He was a very nice man – he went down to England a few years ago, to a house they have there – and he showed me the gardens and said that they found it a bit hard to keep them going in the state they'd like them to be in, and one thing led to another. I offered to come and give them a hand, and I've been doing it since then. These are good men, Bruce, and I was glad that I was able to help them. They don't ask for much."

"I don't imagine they do," agreed Bruce. He thought of the breakfast he was yet to have. It would be light, they said.

Jimmy dusted the last traces of soil from the garlic bulb. He held it up and began to peel off the outer skin. "You'll see that it's healthy inside. Look. See? Beautiful."

He prised out a single clove, removing the papery skin surrounding it. "There. Inside. Isn't it miraculous?"

Bruce looked at the small bulb of ivory.

"I never get over the miracle," said Jimmy. "Each time I pick something. Beans. Apples. Chard. Garlic. Anything that grows is a miracle in its way. Or a mystery, perhaps."

"Plant genetics," said Bruce.

Jimmy shook his head. "Oh yes, plant genetics. But if you look at plant genetics, you're only taking it back one level. And then can't you find yourself saying exactly the same thing? Saying that it's a miracle?"

"I don't know if that helps," said Bruce.

"Perhaps not," said Jimmy. "But that's what I still think. I look up at night – on a clear night – and I see stars that go on and on. And I think of how we're a tiny, insignificant little dot in a universe that's only one of millions of universes. And then I look down at the earth we stand upon and think how small it is, and how . . . how beautiful. And I think: how can we possibly be fighting one another, when we're just so small and insignificant, and I can find no answer to that, and so I come back here and plant things and make them grow because . . . because that's what you have to do if you don't know any of the answers to the big questions." He paused. "You ever read Albert Camus? He said something like that, you know. He put it better than I do, of course . . ." Jimmy laughed. "But then he was French, you see." He paused again. "*Il faut cultiver son jardin.*"

He looked at Bruce. "Of course, that was Voltaire."

Then he stopped, and looked at Bruce with sudden concern. "You're crying."

Bruce wiped at his eyes. "I'm sorry."

"It's onions that make you cry, you know, not garlic."

"I know. I know."

49

Lion-tamers, Change, Truth

That morning, as Bruce stood in the vegetable garden at Pluscarden talking to Jimmy about garlic and growth and French philosophers, in the house at Nine Mile Burn Matthew was struggling to dress Tobermory, Rognvald and Fergus. It was an almost impossible task, as no sooner did he get one garment onto one of the boys and turn to clothe the next, than the first one would wander off, half-clad, to do something else, and would have to be hauled back for the donning of further clothes. And even when shirts and shorts had been located and put on, there would be the question of shoes, which were never in the right place, or were unevenly matched, with the result that three left shoes would be found with one right shoe, or vice versa. On the average day, preparing the triplets for any outing took at least twenty minutes, which was quite long enough for even the most patient of parents to lose his or her temper and end up shouting at a recalcitrant small boy.

Fortunately, James was due to come on duty, and when he did, the whole business became much more efficient. Now he took over, and succeeded in getting the boys to co-operate without so much as raising his voice. Matthew watched in complete admiration.

"I don't know how on earth you do it," he complimented James. "I imagine that lion-taming would be easier than getting these three to stand still for two minutes."

James laughed. "I went to a circus in France once," he said. "I was just thirteen. They had two lions. You could have wild animals in French circuses until very recently. Now they're illegal."

"And a good thing too," said Matthew. "I don't like the idea of forcing animals to perform for people. It's humiliating. Cruel."

"I agree," said James. "But at thirteen or whatever I didn't think that. I just remember being thrilled by the sight of the lions. I remember the lion-tamer quite vividly. He had a superb French moustache – you know the sort – twirled up at the end. And one eye."

"And a whip?"

"Yes. A whip. Top hat. The works."

"And the lions?"

"They were very moth-eaten. They roared when he cracked his whip at them, but they seemed really bored with proceedings. And I noticed a really odd thing: one of the lions also only had one eye. I didn't spot it at first, but then he jumped off a stool that he was being made to sit on and ran round the edge of the bars around the ring. I had a good view of him and I saw that on one side there was just an empty socket."

"What a poignant image," said Matthew. "This lion-tamer . . ."

James interrupted him. "He looked so sad. I noticed it and I felt so sorry for him. I remember thinking – even though, as I say, I was only thirteen – that he looked totally discouraged. At that age you think that most adults are happy with what they do, but I remember thinking *this man is unhappy*."

"Perhaps he knew that it was all coming to an end," said Matthew. "Perhaps he knew that the writing was on the wall for lion-tamers and that his career was almost over. What do you do if you've trained as a lion-tamer and then, suddenly, thanks to—"

"It was President Macron," said James, "He was the one who brought about the ban."

"All right, so you think, *Thanks to President Macron, it's all coming to an end.* You might be expected to feel sad."

Matthew thought about this. "Conditions change. There must be lots of people who find their jobs disappear because there's a change in the law – or in technology. The people who made vinyl records must have thought that way when CDs first came in. They must have said to themselves, *We never saw this coming.*"

"Of course, they're back, aren't they? Vinyl has returned."

"To an extent," said Matthew. "But what about coal miners? They saw their livelihood come to an end when they closed the pits."

"I suppose so," said James. "And I read somewhere that some of the miners spent their redundancy money on buying video rental shops. And then . . ."

Matthew sighed. "That was very bad luck. Whole communities disappeared. Families that had been doing the same thing for generations saw their whole world dismantled. I can understand how bitter they must have felt." He paused. "But does it make sense to encourage people to do things that we no longer need?"

James shook his head. "Probably not. And yet . . ."

"Would you send fishermen out to sea after fish that are no longer there?"

"No," said James. "But that doesn't mean I wouldn't feel for the fishermen."

"And so you should," said Matthew.

Now, he watched James taking the rumbustious triplets in hand while he went into the kitchen to prepare a breakfast tray for Elspeth. She had slept in, and he had not disturbed her though it was almost eleven. He had promised her breakfast in bed, as she was still feeling some discomfort from her injured rib, even though the worst of the pain seemed to be over.

He took the tray in and balanced it on her bedside table. "Here we are," he said. "Two boiled eggs. Toast. Marmite, of course. And a bowl of that disgusting sweetened muesli you like so much."

She looked at him fondly. "You spoil me," she said.

And he noticed that as she said this a strange look crossed her face. He hesitated for a moment before he said, "You look unhappy."

She stared at the tray. She was avoiding looking at him. Then she said, "I'm unhappy about not having told you the truth."

He stood quite still. Outside, somewhere in the distance, somebody was cutting wood with a chainsaw. Trees were always falling down, he thought – incongruously; branches came down; whole trees came down. And then his neighbour, a man who liked to fly microlight aircraft at East Fortune airfield, would go out with his chainsaw and salvage the timber as firewood. And there he was at it, right now, as Elspeth confessed that she had kept from Matthew the truth of what she had been doing immediately before her accident on Colinton Road.

He simply said, "I knew. I knew all along that you weren't telling me something."

She gave a start; a stab of pain from her fractured rib made her cry out.

He said, "Darling, darling. Don't. Don't make it worse. Your rib. Don't."

50

Waterfalls, Scotland, Everything

Elspeth's confession was over very quickly. She expected it to be followed by silence and reproach, which was Matthew's normal reaction when he felt wronged, but, in the event, there was neither of these. Instead, he blamed himself: he had not given her time to tell him what had happened; he had no right to tell her not to ask her cousin about what she knew, and he was sorry; he had himself been suspicious of her – with no justification, of course; she was completely blameless – and so on, until Elspeth, having had enough, simply raised a hand and said, "Let's draw a line right there. There's no more to be said." And then, before Matthew could protest that his apology had hardly begun, she went on, "My rib is getting better, but the last thing I need – the very last thing – is a long-drawn-out discussion of who said what or who thought what – or anything like that."

He did not press the matter. "So . . ." he began.

"So, I should get out of bed. I was told that I needed to get back on my feet." She gestured towards her breakfast tray. "I can have that later on."

He looked concerned. "Are you up to getting out of bed?"

She answered by throwing off the sheet under which she had been sleeping and swung her legs over the side of the mattress. She gave the slightest of winces, and then rose to her feet. "You see," she said. "I'm ready."

"For what?" asked Matthew.

"A picnic," she said. "The boys are with James?"

"At the activity centre – until three this afternoon."

"Then we're free."

"Yes," he said. "We are."

She looked out of the window. The sky over the Borders was empty, except in the far distance, over Biggar, where a few wispy clouds were being chased away by a warm wind from the west. "Let's go up to that place on the burn. It's not a long walk. I'll manage that."

"Are you sure? They told you to take things easy."

"I'll be fine."

He told her that he would make the picnic; that she shouldn't feel she had to do anything yet – not until her rib had disappeared. She laughed at the expression and found, to her surprise, that she had laughed without pain. "So it is disappearing," she said.

He had olives and sun-dried tomatoes and some San Daniele ham that Olivia Contini had sliced for him in Elm Row. He had a tub of couscous mixed with diced artichoke hearts and slices of roasted pepper. He had a crusty Puglian loaf. He had apricots and two flat peaches. "What more does one need for a picnic?" he asked.

She laughed again. "You do realise how New Town-ish that sounds? How Mediterranean diet-ish?"

He shrugged. "I've never tried to be something I'm not. I've never been particularly ashamed of being a bit . . ."

"Edinburgh?"

It was his turn to laugh. "We are, aren't we?"

On impulse, she kissed him.

"What was that for?" he asked.

"For being you," she said.

They left the house on foot. The burn was not far from the house – twenty minutes' walk in normal circumstances – but now, with Elspeth making her way carefully, not tempting Providence to remind her of her recent injury, it took almost fifty minutes for them to reach the spot they had in mind.

Matthew had packed the picnic in a rucksack, which he carried, leaving his hands free to help Elspeth over the rougher ground.

Their route took them over a field belonging to their neighbour, the man who liked to fly microlight aircraft at East Fortune, the man with the noisy chainsaw. And there he was in the distance, dealing with a branch that had split from one of his trees. Seeing them, the neighbour waved, and then resumed his work.

"It would be better to leave some of those branches," Matthew remarked to Elspeth. "They provide a home for things that are good for the soil."

"You should tell him that," she suggested. "Perhaps he doesn't know."

Matthew shook his head. "You can't tell anybody anything. Especially your neighbours."

They arrived at their place beside the burn – *their* place, because once they had come here with the boys on a particularly hot day and they had all swum in a pool that the burn made when it encountered an outcrop of rock. There they ate their picnic. Elspeth was hungry, having left her breakfast tray untouched. Then they sat, saying nothing until Matthew suddenly reached into his pocket and took out a piece of paper.

"What's that?" she asked.

"It's something Angus gave me. One of his poems. I asked him to write something that I might say to you. He said he would, and he did. He said they were his words, but they were meant to be me talking to you."

She was immediately intrigued. "Read it to me, then."

He began:

I can't help but love you, you see,
I know I should be doing

Something else – anything would do,
There is a list somewhere,
Scribbled on an envelope;
I know I should be doing that,
But, instead, I am spending my time
Loving you, thinking about you.
And about what I might say to you,
If only you would listen to me,
Which you do, sometimes.

I know I should be doing something
More constructive, I know that;
I know that time is not infinite,
And passes rather quickly,
Cannot be put in reverse,
Cannot be made larger
Than it is; you cannot stretch
An hour into a day, a week
Into a month, much as you
Might have ambitions to do just that;
Nor can you love more suitable people
Than the ones you find yourself
Loving; love, you see, is not
A matter of choice, it happens to you
Just as you happened to me.
I know it would be better to forget about you,
But I cannot, I cannot do things that
A reasonable person would do,
Because it is not reason nor common sense
That makes me feel this about you,
But love, which is something quite different.

And so, dearest one, irreplaceable other
In my tiny bit of this universe,

Source of meaning in a world
Which I, like so many,
Occasionally find opaque
And hard to make sense of,
Does it really matter that I continue
Obstinately and ill-advisedly
To think about you? It does not,
Because private meaning
Rarely matters to others;
These flowers are for you, these lines,
These thoughts, as is the morning sun
And evening light, the clear sky,
The beating of the heart, the silent wishes,
The shared joke, the moment of feeling,
The winds that blow, the healing rain,
The waterfalls, Scotland, everything.

51

Vitamin D: A National Issue

Angus made lists for himself only on those occasions when there were things to be done that he did not want to do. Those tasks to which he looked forward never required to be listed, and were always tackled promptly; they were never shelved. That, he decided, required no complicated psychological explanation: by and large, unless we were exceptional – and he readily admitted that he was not – we did what we wanted to do, and we looked for, and frequently found, reasons why we should not do what we did not want to do. Or we simply forgot to do those things, which pointed to another truth of psychology: human memory is quite capable of operating on a selective basis, enabling us to forget that which we want to forget and to remember, often with striking clarity, that which we want to remember.

That is what Angus thought of the matter, although, being a modest man and having a strong distaste for the doctrinaire, he was prepared to accept that he might be wrong and that things might be the exact opposite of the way he imagined them to be. It was possible then, he admitted, that he was wrong even about contemporary conceptual art, and that, far from being a celebration of banality, awards in that field were a recognition of real, even if very successfully hidden, talent in painting or sculpture. Perhaps those who were considered for such attention really could paint, but had simply not got round to it, or had forgotten to do so, and had simply engaged in the rearrangement of objects out of absent-mindedness. That was possible, Angus admitted, although he thought it unlikely.

But that morning, as he lingered over a cup of coffee in the flat at 44 Scotland Street, with Cyril at his feet, half-asleep in the shaft of warm sunlight that bathed this particular section of floor, Angus was making a list on the back of a small scrap of paper – a receipt that Domenica had obtained from the local pharmacy when she had purchased – he noticed – a supply of vitamin D tablets and a shower cap. Angus was indifferent to shower caps – men so frequently are – although Angus had a friend, a resolutely *new man*, who wore a shower cap, he had told him, out of a sense of solidarity. Patriarchy, he had explained, would be undermined if more men wore shower caps and Angus thought that was probably true. He himself did not like patriarchal attitudes, the defeat of which he had always welcomed – if anybody ran their household and made the decisions, it was Domenica, and Angus was grateful that she did this, as she did it so much better than he would.

His thoughts turned to vitamin D. Domenica had said something about it the other day, and he was trying to remember what it was. It was something she had read about in the newspaper, although he could not recall exactly what she had said. Was it that everybody in Scotland had a vitamin D deficiency? That rang a vague bell, and he himself had heard somebody talking about that over lunch one day in the Scottish Arts Club. Or had they said that everybody in the Scottish Arts Club was deficient in vitamin D, rather than everybody in Scotland? There was a difference, of course. It had something to do with exposure to sunlight, he seemed to remember. And there you could see that Scotland had a problem.

Some people, it had to be said, got all the vitamin D, or rather more than their fair share. Because of the fact that the earth was tilted in a particular way, people in the south of Italy enjoyed rather more sunlight than those in the central belt of Scotland and, *a fortiori*, those who lived north of Inverness.

Of course, you only had to look at southern Italians to see that they were not vitamin D deficient. There was something about them – a sort of glow – that was suggestive of adequate vitamin D: and the same went for their music, too, which had that infectious, vitamin D gaiety to it. Listen to a Neapolitan song and you *knew* that you were in strong vitamin D territory; whereas, a lament on the pipes, "Lochaber No More", for example, left you in no doubt at all on the inadequacy of vitamin D levels in the Western Highlands.

He thought about lunch at the Scottish Arts Club, and remembered that he had seen something on the table that he assumed was a salt cellar but that did not appear to produce salt when shaken over the roast potatoes accompanying his lamb chop. Angus had examined the fine white powder this shaker produced, and had tasted it on the tip of his tongue. He had been puzzled because it did not taste salty, and he had drawn the attention of his lunch companions to the issue. They had been only slightly interested, one of them suggesting that the shaker contained salt-free salt, the latest thing to be proposed as an aid to a healthy diet. That was possible, Angus agreed, although another member had raised the possibility that it could be fluoride, which was important for strong teeth. But would the catering committee of the Scottish Arts Club have taken upon itself to dose the members with fluoride without first asking their permission? There were issues there, Angus thought.

Now it occurred to him that the white powder could well have been vitamin D, which the committee, quite rightly, might want to make available to the members on an optional basis. Nobody was suggesting that anybody should be obliged to take vitamin D supplements; putting the vitamin in a shaker on the table was, of course, only an invitation and involved no personal liberty issues.

He looked at the receipt on which he was about to write

his list. What had Domenica done with the vitamin D she had purchased from the pharmacy? Was she proposing to use it all herself, to a sort of vitamin D advantage or *edge*, or was it for him too? Had she put it in the bowl of porridge he had enjoyed for his breakfast?

She was there in the kitchen with him, and he asked her. She looked at him blankly. "Vitamin D?" And then she remembered. "Oh yes, I bought a vitamin D supplement. I think we should take it. I was reading the other day that everybody in Scotland should be taking a vitamin D supplement."

"Don't feel too much pressure to conform," said Angus, and then laughed. "No, I think it's a good idea – if, indeed, we need it."

"We do," said Domenica. "And we shall start this morning."

"After my coffee," said Angus.

52

Angus Makes a List

As it turned out, the list that Angus made was a short one: containing only one item – that of a proposed visit to Sister Maria-Fiore dei Fiori di Montagna in the Drummond Place flat she shared with Antonia Collie and now, on a temporary basis, with Irene. Angus was not looking forward to this visit – hence the need for its inclusion on a list – and yet he felt that he could not leave things where they were. As it was, he and Roger had extracted themselves from The Flenser in Leith, leaving Sister Maria-Fiore there in deep conversation with a small group of the bar's habitués. These locals had been delighted to welcome the unlikely visitor to their company, and had formed a tight and attentive ring about her, listening to her account of a trip she had made a few years earlier to Palermo and the ancient sites of Sicily. She would make her own way home, she said to Angus.

And he believed that she had done that safely enough, as he had seen her the following day walking through Drummond Place when he was exercising Cyril in the garden. She had waved cheerily, but had not stopped to converse, and he had consequently remained in the dark as to whether she had managed to elicit any further information about Fat Bob and his woman friend.

Not that there was much more to find out, Angus imagined. The whole story had a tawdry familiarity: a selfish man had persuaded a good woman to marry him but had been unwilling to divest himself of an existing lover – or, in his case – and this made all the moral difference – an existing wife. It was just so sad that this had happened to Big Lou, who so deserved to find the happiness that came with a stable relationship. But life was unfair; it was monstrously unfair, and although we might rail against such things, we would never be able to change them. The ancient Greeks, Angus thought, understood that well enough. They never expected the gods to behave in anything but a petulant way, handing out undeserved punishment with little thought as to just deserts. People should pay more attention to classical antiquity, Angus felt; they should try to understand that there are still echoes of that ancient order in our modern world; after all, the Greek ideal, or one understanding of it, was there in Edinburgh, in the very buildings. Where else was there an unfinished Parthenon on a hill, a monument to unfinished projects everywhere – a tribute to people who started something and then ran out of money, or ideas, or energy?

He sighed. He would have to go to see Sister Maria-Fiore dei Fiori di Montagna and discuss with her what they should do with the information they had obtained. Any approach to Big Lou would need to be made with tact, a quality with which he was not sure Sister Mari-Fiore was over-endowed. He could well imagine her bursting in with a vivid description of Fat Bob's blatant consorting in public with another woman. He could picture her saying to Big Lou that she should immediately expel him from their flat. He could even imagine the nun confronting Fat Bob himself and giving him a piece of her mind, unfiltered by considerations of what might be done to salvage the relationship.

He discussed the matter with Domenica, who agreed that he should seek out Sister Maria-Fiore before deciding what to say to Big Lou.

"I agree with you about that woman," she said. "She has her good points, but I'm sorry to have to say this: she is such an . . . an interferer."

"Yes," said Angus. "Do you know there's an old Scots expression for somebody who interferes in another's business? It's a Scots law term – a *vitious intromitter.* My uncle was a solicitor in Aberfeldy and he told me about it. A vitious intromitter is somebody who deals with the goods in a deceased estate without authority. Isn't that a lovely expression? So useful when dealing with people like Sister Maria-Fiore dei Fiori di Montagna."

"Perhaps she's changed," said Domenica. "I mean, people might be vitious intromitters and then suddenly they realise the error of their ways."

Angus looked doubtful. "I'm not sure if people change all that much."

Domenica frowned. "Do you really think that?"

Angus nodded.

"What about Irene?" asked Domenica. "I heard from Nicola that Irene has changed considerably. And that young surveyor, Bruce . . . You know, the one with the face."

Angus smiled at the expression. Domenica had a few endearing verbal quirks, one of which was to describe any good-looking person as "the one with the face". "Bruce Anderson? Yes, but he was struck by lightning."

"And Irene?"

Angus shrugged. "Are you sure she's changed?"

Domenica hesitated. "No, I'm not sure, I suppose. But I think there's a certain amount of evidence in that direction."

"But the jury's still out?"

"Possibly."

Angus left the flat. When he emerged on Scotland Street, he looked up the hill towards Drummond Place at the end of the street. We are so lucky, he thought. We live on a cobbled street in a city so beautiful it breaks the heart. And there are trees in the distance and all about us are buildings that look as if they are part of an opera set. We are so lucky.

He looked up. A window had been opened on the top floor of the neighbouring tenement. A head poked out and suddenly a tenor voice could be heard. It was an aria from *Pagliacci*, or was it *Cavalleria Rusticana*? Did it matter? Angus drew in his breath.

He walked up the street and, at the top, turned into Drummond Place. Antonia's flat was only a few doors away. Now he stood before her front door. A small brass plate by the bell announced *Collie*. A further plate, placed slightly underneath, bore the name *Fiori di Montagna*. Did Sister Maria-Fiore consider that to be her surname? Nuns tended not to use family names, but the postman had to have something to go on.

He rang the bell, and waited. After a couple of minutes, the door was opened and Antonia stood before him. She looked slightly peevish.

"Oh," she said. "It's only you." And then, with a glance over his shoulder, added, "How disappointing."

Angus could not help but show his surprise. "You're so kind," he said.

"Oh, I'm sorry," said Antonia. "I was hoping for a delivery. I didn't mean to sound unwelcoming."

Angus enquired whether Sister Maria-Fiore was in.

"She is," said Antonia. "And I think she'll be pleased to see you. She has something that she wants to tell you." She paused. "Not that the dear botanical one ever tells me anything."

Angus tried to look sympathetic. It was a mystery to him how Antonia put up with Sister Maria-Fiore dei Fiori di Montagna. He wouldn't. Not for ten minutes. But then, he thought, people looked for different things in life, and perhaps Antonia had, at some deep level, a need for constant exposure to aphorism.

53

In the Pentlands

Olive surveyed the group over which she had been given command.

"Now, I want you all to keep together," she said. "I shall be in the front, because I'm the leader. Miss Summers said so – remember?"

Olive's lieutenant, Pansy, nodded enthusiastically. "Everybody knows that, Olive. You're the leader." She paused, giving the four boys a challenging look. "And I'm the deputy leader. Miss Summers also said that. Even if you didn't hear her, she did. Deputy leader . . . which means that if Olive dies, then I take over. That's true, isn't it, Olive?"

Olive smiled tolerantly. "Yes, that's true, Pansy. But I'm not going to die, so you shouldn't worry too much. But it's good to know about that – just in case."

She reached into her rucksack and withdrew a folded map. "This is the map," she said. "Miss Summers gave it to me."

Rab, one of the two boys sharing with Bertie and Ranald Braveheart Macpherson, put out a hand. "Could I take a look at it, Olive?" Then he added, "Please, Olive."

Olive pursed her lips before replying. "No, you can't," she said. "I need it. I'm going to be using it to see where we're going."

"I just wanted to look," Rab complained. "You can't have everything, you know. Just because you're the leader doesn't mean you can do everything and the rest of us can do nothing."

This was dangerous, Bolshevist talk, and Olive acted swiftly. "You'd better be careful about what you say, Rab. I'm going to be putting in a report to Miss Summers . . ."

"A report," interjected Pansy. "See? Like those reports you get at school – only this one will be from Olive."

"That's right," said Olive. "I shall have to put in a report, and so you'd better be jolly careful what you do or you'll be sorry."

"Big time," said Pansy.

"So, now we're going to set off," Olive continued. "I'll be at the front and Pansy will come after me. Then you can come, Bertie, because you're sort of third in charge . . ."

"After me," Pansy put in quickly.

"Yes, after Pansy."

They began to make their way along the path that led off alongside a small burn before branching off up the hillside. The ground was rough, and the path was overgrown in several places, overwhelmed by clumps of heather and bog myrtle. The ubiquitous bracken was making its presence felt too, its fronds obscuring the more reticent vegetation and needing to be brushed aside by the walker.

"Are you sure this is the right way, Olive?" Bertie called out, as he steadied Ranald Braveheart Macpherson. Ranald had put a foot down what looked like a rabbit hole, had stumbled, and been saved from falling by Bertie.

"Of course it is," Olive replied from the head of the small column. "I've looked at the map, Bertie. Do you think I can't read?"

"I didn't say you can't read, Olive. All I asked was whether this was the right way."

"I can't see much of a path," said Ranald Braveheart Macpherson. "When my dad and I went walking in the Pentlands, there was a proper path. There was a sign that pointed the way to Bonaly. You couldn't go wrong."

"Do you want to be the leader, Ranald Braveheart Macpherson?" asked Pansy.

"I didn't say that," protested Ranald. "I was only asking."

"This is definitely the right way," said Olive. "And stop complaining, Ranald. I'm not going to warn you again."

Ranald was silenced, but, some twenty minutes later, as they found themselves surrounded by large clumps of gorse on a sharply rising section of hillside, he whispered to Bertie, "I think we're lost, Bertie. I can't see any path here, can you?"

Bertie shook his head.

"Olive says she knows where we are," Ranald continued. "But I don't think she does."

"She's really stupid," muttered Rab. "I've met some stupid people in my life, but she's one of the stupidest."

"I want to go home," said Hamish, the other boy from Lanark. He sounded miserable. "I dinnae want to be here. I dinnae. If there's mist, then we could walk off the edge of a cliff. That happens, you know. There are loads of people who walk off cliffs in the mist."

"We shouldn't have come by ourselves," said Ranald Braveheart Macpherson. "Miss Summers was meant to be with us. Now we haven't got an adult. You can't climb mountains without an adult. We should go back."

Olive overheard this. "Go back, Ranald Braveheart Macpherson? Is that all you can say? Go back?"

"Yes," said Pansy. "Go back? Who said anything about going back?"

They stood for a moment. Earlier mentions of mist now seemed prescient, as a low bank of white seemed to be rolling towards them, already obscuring the low ground to the east. Bertie glanced at this nervously, and nudged Ranald to draw his attention to it. Seeing it, Hamish began to cry, ignoring the withering looks this sign of distress elicited from Olive and Pansy.

"Is that what you do in Lanark?" asked Olive. "Cry? Is that what you do there?"

"Wherever Lanark is," added Pansy scornfully.

"Please don't be mean to Hamish," Bertie asked mildly. "Maybe he's frightened because we don't know where we are."

"Because you can't read that stupid map," said Ranald Braveheart Macpherson, suddenly emboldened.

Olive opened her mouth to deal with this latest insurrection, when a shout merged from the hillside below. This was followed by another shout, and then the shrill blast of a whistle. Then, suddenly coming into sight, Miss Summers and two young men could be seen running towards them.

"Thank heavens!" exclaimed Miss Summers as she reached the party of youthful hikers. Then, in a more scolding tone, "Why did you set off by yourselves? Whose idea was that?"

Swiftly, and in such a way as to be undetected by others, Olive slipped the folded map into Bertie's hands. "Please, Miss Summers," she said. "It was Bertie's – wasn't it, Pansy?"

Pansy hesitated only for a second or two. Then she said, "Yes, it was."

Miss Summers turned to Bertie. "You should never do that sort of thing, Bertie. The hills can be dangerous. Never forget that."

Bertie said nothing. There was no point. He found himself carrying the map, and there were occasions on which it would be futile to protest. Besides, Bertie was composed of goodness, and sometimes goodness means that you take the blame for things you haven't done. You accept it. You bear it. And he had borne so much in his brief seven years that a little more would not make much difference.

54

Swallows and House Martins

After he said goodbye to Jimmy and left the vegetable garden, Bruce returned to the guest wing of the abbey and to a simple breakfast – the *pittance* – as the monks called it. He now had a few hours at his disposal – a time that he could, if he wished, devote to reading or to quiet contemplation. He chose to think, going over in his mind the decision he had made to come to Pluscarden. By any standards, it had been an impetuous one, but he did not regret it. It was obvious to him now that life in this place, for all the tranquillity and sense of purpose it brought, would not suit everyone. And it was clear to him, too, even after a very short time there, that he was unworthy of the life on offer. He realised that he had been changed by the lightning bolt that had struck him in Dundas Street, and he was sure that he now looked upon the world in an entirely different manner, but there would be other ways of putting to use the energy that seemed to have been transmitted to him by the lightning. He would return to Edinburgh, perhaps after a few more days here in the company of these kind men, and he would find some sort of work that would enable him to feel positive about the world. He had read about a food bank in Dalkeith that needed delivery drivers. He could do something like that.

Shortly after eleven, Brother Gregory came to tell him that there was to be a talk in the refectory and that he was welcome to join the monks and a small, invited audience of abbey supporters. It was to be given by a visiting member of the Order, Brother Gregory said, one Brother Barnabas, a Trinidadian, who had worked for years as a professor of English at the University of the West Indies before he took his vows. He was also a poet – highly regarded in the Caribbean. He might talk about that, or he might talk about something quite different. "You never know with these talks," Brother Gregory said, with a smile. "Somebody starts talking about one thing, and then gets on to something else. You never know."

Bruce sat in the back of the chapel. The young fisherman from Aberdeen was there, too, and now, without his hood, Bruce could see that he had a small whale delicately tattooed on the side of his neck. It was beautiful.

Brother Barnabas stood up. "Dear brethren," he began, "as I rose this morning in this quiet place, I looked out of my window and saw a bird soaring in the sky. It was not a large bird. I am no ornithologist, but I think it might, from its darting flight, have been a swallow or a house martin. There is a way of telling those two apart, but I am not sure what it is. Of course, it does not matter to the bird: these are our labels, and mean nothing to them or indeed to any of the other creatures that we feel it necessary to classify and name. When God created swallows he did not think it necessary to give them a name: He felt, I am sure, that swallows would *announce* themselves through their very being.

"Seeing this bird from my window, seeing it dipping and soaring with such ease in its medium, the air, made me think of how all of us, at some time or another, yearn for the freedom of flight. I am told that many people dream that they can fly, and then are disappointed when morning brings the realisation that it was no more than a dream. It is natural to think of that sort of freedom, because that is something for which we all yearn, some of us desperately, with every fibre of our being; for others the yearning may be no more than the occasional ache. But it is something that most of us feel at one time or another.

"We tell ourselves, wrongly, that freedom comes with the absence of quotidian obligations. We think that we shall be free when we no longer have to think of the needs of others; when we no longer have to perform certain chores and duties that we may find onerous; when we no longer have to work every day to obtain the means of life. Oh, false belief piled upon false belief! That is not any sort of recognisable freedom, because it is only in the acceptance of the claims of others that we find true freedom.

"What I am saying, I suppose, is that engagement in the world is the way in which we achieve the sort of freedom that will really mean something. When we fix our gaze on the world and see the things that need to be done – when we do that, and then begin to start doing them – we shall find that we are free. Only then. And how does that work? I shall tell you: engagement brings love, and it is love that is the enemy of the servitude of selfishness and hatred into which we can so easily lock ourselves. Love. Look at the faces of those men, those public figures who preach antagonism towards others. Do you see freedom there? I do not. Look into the faces of those who espouse the cause of peace and co-operation and kindness to others. Do you see freedom there? I do."

At the end of the talk, Bruce left by the door at the back. For a few minutes, he stood outside, feeling the late morning sun warm upon his face. He became aware that the young fisherman was standing beside him, and he turned to greet him. He was called Lewis.

"What did you think of that?" asked Bruce.

Lewis inclined his head. "I thought that what he said was true."

"Brother Gregory said you're a fisherman."

Lewis looked up. He smiled. "Yes. But I don't think I'm going to go back to it."

Bruce asked why.

"We snagged out nets," Lewis said. "It almost capsized the trawler. I decided that it was not for me." He paused. "I'm a bit scared of the sea, I suppose."

"I understand," said Bruce. "It's dangerous. So, what are you going to do now?"

"I'm hoping to go to Australia. My brother went. He has a small business installing lightning conductors."

Bruce stared at him. Then he said, "Perth's great, and there are lots of Scottish people there. But . . . well, why are you here at Pluscarden?"

"I was doing a long bike ride," said Lewis. "I wanted to cycle all the way across Scotland – from Aberdeen to Stornoway. I was riding past the road-end there and my front wheel buckled. I pushed the bike up the drive and I found myself here. Brother Gregory took the wheel into Elgin to see if they could get a replacement. I didn't ask him – he just did it. They said I could stay until the wheel they ordered turned up."

"Just like that?" asked Bruce.

"Yes," said Lewis. "These are good people."

"They are," said Bruce.

"I wish there were more good people in the world," said Lewis.

Bruce did not hesitate. "But there are. There are far more than most of us think."

"Are you sure?"

"Yes," said Bruce. "Pretty sure."

55

The Talented Mr Borthwick

Bruce travelled back to Edinburgh three days later, catching a bus from Elgin that swept him swiftly down the Forth Crossing and then on into Edinburgh. His farewell to Brother Gregory was an emotional one, as Bruce found it difficult to contain the gratitude he felt for the vision of peace and purpose that he had glimpsed during his few short days at the abbey.

"It doesn't take long, does it, to see where we've been going wrong with our lives," said Brother Gregory. "Sometimes it comes very quickly indeed, as it has in your case. It's like a tropical dawn – the sun comes up very quickly." He paused. "Not that I have ever been in the tropics, although Brother Barnabas told me about that. He said dawn and dusk are very quick in those latitudes. They fall like curtains."

Bruce struggled for words. "I don't know what to say," he began. "I think . . ."

Brother Gregory rested his hand on Bruce's forearm. "We don't always need to say anything, you know. Far too much of our time is spent saying things we really don't need to say."

Bruce nodded. "Then I won't say anything."

Brother Gregory smiled. "Although I think I know what you might say – were you to say anything. And for that, all I would say – were I to say anything – which I won't necessarily do – is thank you."

And now Bruce's bus rolled into St Andrew Square bus station, where the hissing doors opened to allow the passengers to alight. Having given away his possessions at Pluscarden in that initial spurt of generosity, Bruce had only a small linen tote-bag with him. He remembered, as he walked down Broughton Street, that he no longer had a computer. He had not felt the need for it at Pluscarden – now he would have to see whether he could survive in Edinburgh without being online. I can, he thought. I must. Do I really need email? Do I really need to spend my time scrolling through social media posts about nothing? The answer he gave to both of these – a clear no – made him feel lighter. It was as if a burden had been removed from his shoulders – the burden of worrying about what other people were thinking.

He reached the shared outer door of his flat. He had no key, and he realised that he had left that in the suitcase that he had given away at Pluscarden. That did not matter. If you did not need emails and social media, then you didn't necessarily need a key.

He pressed the bell – the bell that bore his name – and after a few moments a woman's voice responded.

"It's me," said Bruce.

There was a brief silence. Then the woman said, "Who's me?"

"Bruce. Bruce Anderson. I live here."

"Here?"

"Yes. That's my flat."

There was a further silence, and then the buzzer that released the door sounded. "Just come right up," said the disembodied female voice.

The door of the flat was open by the time Bruce reached the landing. Standing there was a young woman wearing dark jeans and a white linen top. She was nervously fingering a necklace of wooden beads.

"Hi, Bruce," she said. "Borthy said he wasn't expecting you. He wondered if you could come back maybe tomorrow morning . . ."

Bruce frowned. "But this is my place," he said.

"So, you're Borthy's flatmate: he said something about you, come to think of it."

Bruce took a step forward. She did not seek to impede him. "Borthy?" he called out.

"He's in the kitchen," the young woman said.

Bruce strode down the corridor that led to the kitchen. He went in and stopped short.

"Bruce!" exclaimed Borthy. "Great to see you. I didn't know . . ."

Bruce took in his old friend's appearance. He recognised the jeans; he recognised the shirt – a green linen one he had bought a couple of years ago. He recognised the wristwatch.

"I see you've made yourself at home," said Bruce.

Borthy hesitated. Then he said, "You asked me to, you know."

Bruce turned away, and went into the living room next door.

"Where's my turntable, Borthy? You know the one – the special hi-fi." It had cost three thousand pounds. It had a very well-balanced arm.

"Ah," said Borthy. "Well, actually . . ."

"You've nicked it?" asked Bruce.

"Nicked? Of course not. I'd never nick your gear, Bruce – you know that."

"Then where is it?"

"I lent it to a guy who likes these things."

"Which guy?"

"Oh, a guy called Vince. He lives down in Trinity. You don't know him. He's got a lot of vinyl."

The young woman now came into the living room. "You met Clare?" asked Borthy.

Bruce nodded.

"Borthy tells me you guys have been sharing since he bought the flat," Clare said.

Bruce glanced at Borthy, who looked away. Clare stared at Bruce, briefly, and then at Borthy.

"Yes," said Bruce. "Quite some time."

Borthy looked back at Bruce.

Bruce said, "And you guys? How did you meet?"

"Online," said Borthy. "Like everybody does these days."

Bruce nodded. Then, to Borthy, he said, "I thought I might come back here and stay – if that's all right with you, Borthy."

Borthy's relief was obvious. "Oh, that would be fine, Bruce. Just fine. Clare's got her own place, you see, down near Canonmills."

"Nice," said Bruce.

"Very," said Clare.

Clare went back into the kitchen. Bruce turned to Borthy. "I don't mind your staying on for a while," he said quietly. "If you need to."

"Jeez, Bruce," said Borthy. "You're a real pal."

Bruce gestured towards the kitchen. "You're lucky, Borthy. She's quite a looker, isn't she?"

Borthy seemed to inflate with pride. "Worth waiting for," he said. "I never had much luck with girls, you know, Bruce. Not until now."

Bruce smiled. "The right setting can help, can't it?"

He turned away, to stare out of the window, down onto the street below. It was better to forgive – much better. One of the books he had read at Pluscarden had said something about that. And it was right. He forgave Borthy, and he was pleased that Borthy had found a girlfriend – at long last. He felt better – so much so that he laughed, quietly, and to himself. It was very funny. He had been struck by lightning; he had drifted off to a monastery of all places; he had met a man in the garden and had discussed garlic; he had listened to a man from Trinidad talk about how we needed to engage with the world. All of this had happened to him. He had dreamed none of it. It was real.

56

At The Chaumer

It was while Bertie was off at his camp near Carlops that Nicola eventually prevailed upon Stuart to allow her to activate his online dating persona.

"It's all set up, Stuart," she said. "I've filled in all the details for you. You don't have to do a thing."

Stuart groaned. "What did you put, Mother?"

"I told the truth," Nicola replied. "And no need to varnish the truth in your case. You're very eligible, Stuart."

"Tell me," said Stuart. He was not sure that he wanted to hear, but he felt that he probably had to.

Nicola brought up the page on the computer. "You see," she said. "Here you are. And isn't that a flattering photograph?"

Stuart peered at the screen. "I don't think that's me," he said.

"Well, it looks close enough," said Nicola.

Stuart gave her a reproachful stare. "Where did you get it from?" he asked.

She shrugged. "Oh, somewhere online. I didn't have a recent photo of you and so I found one that I thought would do the trick. And I think that one does it."

Stuart sighed. "But, Mother," he said, "that's mistake number one in online dating. You *never* ever put a misleading photograph on one of these services. People get really cross. They see somebody aged thirty or whatever, and then they find that the person in question is closer to fifty-five. They don't like it. Dates like that don't even pass Go."

"Well," said Nicola. "We shall see. And would you like to

hear what I wrote about you?"

Stuart closed his eyes. "You read. I can't face it."

"Successful man; late thirties; solvent—"

Stuart interrupted her. "Mother, I've had my fortieth birthday."

She shrugged again. "These things are approximate, darling. Now let me continue. Successful man; late thirties; solvent; own flat; good sense of humour; considered highly attractive . . ."

"Oh, Mother," he protested.

"Well, you are."

"By you, perhaps, but then you're my mother."

Undaunted, Nicola continued. "Artistic interests. Likes classical music and statistics."

Stuart stopped her. "Likes statistics? What sort of woman is going to respond to that? A man who says that he likes statistics on an online dating site is going to be considered seriously – no, *deeply* – geeky."

"I don't agree," said Nicola. "I imagine: *oh, I'm sure he's got some interesting statistics to discuss.* People like that sort of thing. Haven't you heard that programme on the radio where they talk about that sort of thing? Lots of people listen to that.

"And then, I've given you a name. You don't want to use your real name on these things, and so I've called you Paul."

Stuart shook his head. "I want you to take me off, Mother."

She looked at him reproachfully. "Too late, darling. I activated you – and there are already a couple of replies."

Stuart took a deep breath. He was irritated by his mother's interference, but at the same time he was intrigued at the thought that there were already a couple of women who were sufficiently interested in him to reply. Perhaps they were types who could see beyond a professed interest in statistics.

"They've both sent emails," said Nicola. "And I've taken the liberty of reading them." Stuart let this pass.

"And there's one of whom I like the look," Nicola went on. "She's called Francesca and she's interested in the Renaissance and in motor racing."

Stuart laughed. "An odd combination."

"I think she sounds a real possibility. She suggests a meeting in The Chaumer on Queen Street. You know the place, don't you?"

Stuart did. "I'm only going because you've jumped the gun and it would be rude to stand this woman up," he said. "My heart isn't in this, Mother."

The proposed meeting was for the following day. Francesca would be there at midday, she said. "I look forward to seeing more of you if we think we have something in common. Who knows?"

He wrote back to confirm the arrangement. "Here's hoping," he wrote at the end of his message, but decided against that, and took it out in favour of "All very best".

He was there well in advance – shortly after eleven-thirty – and he spent an anxious half hour trying to read a copy of *The Economist*, but not concentrating sufficiently to take anything in. He found himself reading an article on Japanese banks three times, before he realised he was as ignorant of the problems facing Japanese banks as he had been before – possibly even more so.

And then the door opened, and from the street Irene appeared. She did not see him at first, and sat down at a table before she looked about and saw Stuart sitting at the opposite end of the room. They stared at one another blankly.

Stuart thought: *Just my luck. I go on a date and who do I bump into but my ex. That's luck for you.*

Irene thought: *This is ridiculous. How can I possibly sit and talk to Paul when he turns up if Stuart is there, well within earshot? This isn't going to work.*

Then, more or less at the same time, Stuart realised that Irene was Francesca, and she came to the conclusion that Stuart was Paul. They both gasped, and blushed.

Stuart got up from his chair and joined Irene at her table. "Should I call you Francesca?" he asked.

For a few moments, she looked down at the floor, before looking back up at him. He noticed her eyes. There was something about her eyes that he had always liked. There had been a light to them when he first met her – now that light seemed to have returned. And she thought: I've yet to find a man who has a dimple like that on his cheek. It was irresistible back in the day, and it's still there – it's still there!

Stuart broke the silence. "Why did you do it?"

"Do what?"

"Go online – to meet somebody."

She hesitated. Then she said, "Because I'm lonely, Stuart. It's as simple as that. Hugo Fairbairn and I have drifted apart, I'm afraid." She paused. "And you?"

He toyed with telling her that it was all his mother's idea, but he thought that might be ungallant. A man should not blame his mother, no matter what the late Professor Freud had to say on the subject. So, he said, instead, "Ditto. Lonely."

She was looking at him as if weighing something up. "We could try again."

He should have hesitated, but he did not. He still loved her. In spite of everything, he loved her; because love was like that – stubborn, persistent, at times irrational. "I think we could."

"It would make Bertie very happy," she said.

"Which is the most important consideration of all," said Stuart.

"I've changed," said Irene. "You may not believe it, but I've changed."

"I do believe it," said Stuart quietly. And thought, but did not say, *Should I be doing this?*

57

Sumptuary Laws

"Ah!" said Domenica's friend, Dilly Emslie, holding up a small jar filled with artichoke hearts. "People love these."

"And these too," said Domenica, pointing to a jar of sun-dried tomatoes. "We can put these on small oatcakes, along with a slice of salami. And there's hummus that people can ladle out with celery sticks."

"Then drop on the carpet," added Dilly.

Domenica smiled. "If you invite people round, you have to expect a certain amount of wear and tear. And a buffet supper is inherently risky. James Holloway told me that he was at a dinner in India Street – it was a buffet – and somebody sat on a plate of food left on a chair by somebody else." She paused, remembering another detail of the story. "The house in question was up at the top of India Street, on the corner with Heriot Row. But because it was on the corner, it had a couple of windows that actually faced onto Heriot Row. So, they put a letterbox in one of the windows so that they could use the Heriot Row address – it being a whole lot grander than India Street. The Heriot Row people didn't like that one little bit. They said you had to have a *door* on Heriot Row in order to say you lived there."

Dilly laughed. "Oh well, these things are important to some people. It's ridiculous, really."

"Addresses are an odd thing," Domenica mused. "They confer status on people, don't they? As do buildings themselves. Yet status should have nothing to do with geography."

"Do you mean status, or worth?" asked Dilly.

"I probably mean worth," said Domenica. "It's all the same to me – I take the view that what matters is character . . ." She thought of Robert Burns, and that great egalitarian hymn, "A Man's a Man For a' That". That was a fundamental text as far as Scotland was concerned. If there was one thing that distinguished Scotland from her neighbour, it was that. Scots believed that it did not matter what bed you were born in; Domenica was not so sure that the same could yet be said of England, where there was a more entrenched tradition of deference being shown to those higher up the pecking order. It was harder to change where you were in England, because of the rigidity and the insidious effect of an antiquated class structure. And yet that was changing, she thought; everything was changing, everything was fluid, and people were breaking free of the grasp of old institutions and prejudices. And not before time, she felt.

This line of thought led her, unexpectedly, to Rome – not in a theological sense, of course – but in a sartorial one.

"Do you think," she asked her friend, "that people still use clothing to signal things?"

Dilly looked thoughtful. "Possibly."

"I was just thinking," Domenica continued, "if you went out into Scotland Street right now and walked up the hill, do you think that you'd be able to *place* the first, say, dozen people you encountered? And by place, I mean be able to say something about what they did, what their likely tastes were, what they believed in? I ask that because I was just thinking of Rome and how your clothing revealed your lineage, or membership, very precisely. If you were a member of the equestrian order, your toga had a thin purple stripe. If you were of senatorial rank, then it was broader."

"As in a naval uniform? Three rings of gold braid, slightly separated, if you're a commander. Put those three rings together, leave a tiny space, and then add a fourth ring, and you're a . . ."

She looked for guidance.

"Angus might know," said Domenica. "A captain? Or even higher? A rear-admiral perhaps. In Rome, of course, the toga could show how much you actually had – in money terms. To be a senator, and have the appropriate stripe on your toga, you needed to be worth four hundred thousand sesterces – later it was more, I believe. Very precise. Ordinary people wore plain or dark togas. Brown and so on. Of course, there have been many other societies where what you might wear depends on rank and was legally controlled by sumptuary laws."

"Conspicuous consumption is never very attractive," mused Dilly. She looked at the jar of sun-dried tomatoes – a look that was intercepted by Domenica.

"Sun-dried tomatoes are okay," Domenica said, with a smile. "I very much doubt whether they've ever been caught by sumptuary laws. But those laws did affect some sorts of food. You had to eat according to your station. Montaigne railed against that in one of his essays, I seem to recall. He said that legislating that only princes could eat turbot was surely an invitation to make everybody else long to eat it. So, a sumptuary law could have the opposite effect from that intended."

She reached for a salami and started to slice it, while Dilly buttered oatcakes.

"We had sumptuary laws in Scotland, you know," Domenica said. "Under James I, I think – not the English James I, of course – the real one – James the McCoy, so to speak. Anyway, there were laws about how commoners were not allowed by law to wear coloured outfits that went lower than the knee. And even in America – pre-Tea Party – the Boston one, that is – in the Massachusetts Bay Colony you had to be worth at least two hundred pounds to be allowed legally to wear things like lace or buckles."

"That's somewhat prescriptive, don't you think?" said Dilly.

"I don't think people obeyed it much," Domenica said. "Of course, sumptuary laws were really about power. Those at the top of the tree – those in power – did not want people beneath them outdoing them in signs of wealth. So the aristocracy didn't want the bourgeoisie to look smarter and richer than them, although of course they often were. And the bourgeoisie didn't want artisans and so on looking better off than they were in case they might get ideas." She paused. "Of course, the Scottish Parliament could turn all this on its head and introduce sumptuary provisions that punished people who pay themselves too much, who cream money off the top. Hedge fund managers, for instance. They should be made to wear clothes of hodden grey. Then we'd be able to identify them. Hah! Would they like that? I don't think they would. And we'd take away their Porsche Cayennes and so on and make them drive small Fiats. Or reconditioned Trabis! Hah! Pass the sun-dried tomatoes, Dilly."

58

Glasgow Is Our Only Hope

They had prepared the canapés for the guests who were coming to Angus and Domenica's buffet dinner. Now, everyone had arrived, and the flat was a hubbub of conversation. Nobody turned down an invitation to these dinners in Scotland Street, where the conversation could go off in the most unexpected and engaging directions, and where the hosts' generosity with food and wine was unsurpassed. People looked forward to Angus's recital of a new poem – a fixed feature of these gatherings, even if the poet himself had to be prompted into recitation. They enjoyed, too, the telling of the same stories by the same guests, as we all do, for none of us, if we are being honest, wants to hear anything new from our friends. Friendship, after all, is founded on recognition and the comfort of familiarity.

The first to arrive had been Sister Maria-Fiore dei Fiori di Montagna and her friend and confidante, Antonia Collie. They always arrived early, in order, Domenica once said, to ensure that they had more than their fair share of canapés and, indeed, of anything else that was going.

"You must have lived well in that convent of yours in Tuscany," Domenica observed to Sister Maria-Fiore, as the socialite nun piled her plate high with oatcakes, cheese straws, and small pieces of Parma ham skewered on cocktail sticks.

"Not really," said Sister Maria-Fiore. "We cured our own ham, though. Sister Gabriella-Stellata was a very good shot. She used to stalk wild boars in the woods on the hill above the convent. The man who drove our tractor would go up and pull the carcases down on a sort of wooden sled he made. They were very large, those wild boars. Then Sister Gabriella-Stellata would cut them up and start curing the hams." She paused. "There's much that I miss about the religious life, but I have my work to do here in Scotland, and I must be strong."

"Your work . . ." Domenica began. She changed her mind, and rather than try to elicit information about what Sister Maria-Fiore dei Fiori di Montagna actually *did*, she asked after Big Lou. Angus had told her that Sister Maria-Fiore had gone to see Big Lou in her coffee bar.

"I saw Big Lou a couple of days ago," said Sister Maria-Fiore. "I was able to tell her that her concerns over her new husband were entirely without foundation. She thought he was seeing another woman. And we ourselves thought for a while that this other woman was actually his wife. Happily, that proved not to be true – as further enquiries on my part revealed. I spoke to some of her neighbours down there."

Domenica waited for the explanation to be continued.

"They told me," Sister Maria-Fiore went on, "that this woman *was* his wife, but she was his ex-wife – they divorced, amicably, a couple of years ago. She drank, apparently, although she's got that under control now. Bob was seeing her, but only out of decency towards one to whom he had once been married. She – the ex-wife – I'm happy to say, has found a new partner, but he's gone off to work in Nigeria for three months – he's one of these oil men – and Bob's ex-wife had gone down with depression. She's been a bit fragile, and so Bob very decently has been seeing a bit of her to cheer her up – helping her out. He's a good man, you see."

"I'm delighted to hear that," said Domenica. "I do like to hear of people doing generous things. I know that sounds, well, a bit sentimental, because I know that the world is a vale of tears etc., but . . ."

"You shouldn't be ashamed of thinking that," said Sister Maria-Fiore. "And you've heard, I take it, about Irene. She's staying with us at the moment, but I imagine she'll be moving back into Scotland Street."

Domenica nodded. Irene and Stuart had been invited, but had not yet arrived. "I did hear something to that effect."

"He went on a date with her," Sister Maria-Fiore dei Fiori di Montagna continued. "It was a mistake, but apparently it worked out rather well."

"I hope so," said Domenica. "I still have some doubts when it comes to Irene. And I gather that Nicola is also a bit cautious about it. I suppose it's a question of whether leopards can change their spots. Can they?"

"We shall see," said Sister Maria-Fiore dei Fiori di Montagna. "We should, in general, give leopards every opportunity. Besides, I feel we shall see what there is to be seen, even if we do not see what is not."

"True," said Domenica, frowning slightly, and then added, "Very true, I suppose."

More guests arrived. Roger Collins and Judith McClure arrived with a large bunch of flowers for Domenica and a tub of olives for Angus. They quickly became involved in conversation with James Holloway, who showed them a copy of a book he had written about his collection of paintings. Angus's friend, Colin Mumford, arrived with a picture of a motorbike he was hoping to buy from its owner, who had tired of biking and had bought a three-wheeled Morgan sports car with a wooden frame. Several members of the Scottish Arts Club had been invited too, and all came, including the dentist who all those years ago had given Cyril his gold tooth. Outside, away from the crowd, seated on the stone stair, Bertie talked to his friend, Ranald Braveheart Macpherson.

"We're lucky to be alive, Ranald," he said. "Olive and Pansy could have killed us all."

"You were really kind to take the blame, Bertie," said Ranald. "I think that's why I like you, you know – because you're really kind."

"That's good of you to say that, Ranald," replied Bertie, and then changed the subject, as he was modest and did not want to talk about himself. He said, "Do you think we could go to Glasgow again one day, Ranald?"

"I'm sure we can," said Ranald. "Glasgow is our only hope, Bertie."

Inside, Angus had risen to recite his poem, having been asked to do so by James, and others.

"This is a short poem," he said. "But sometimes what you want to say is best said in a few words. Shall I read it?"

"You must," said James and Roger, almost simultaneously. Angus began:

Our life is a short one, or so we're told:
Youth, middle-age, and then we're old,
The world we occupy is so small,
A fragile planet is our all;
But I raise my eyes to survey a sky
That goes on for ever, blue and high,
Beside that immensity, what are we?
Two people in love, my dear, you and me,
Two people in love, my dear, you and me.

He stopped. Nobody spoke. Angus looked at Domenica. She looked back at him, and smiled.

THE END